NIGHT AT THE FIESTAS

W. W. NORTON & COMPANY • NEW YORK LONDON

NIGHT *at the* FIESTAS

Stories

. . . .

KIRSTIN VALDEZ QUADE

The following stories have appeared, in slightly different form, elsewhere: "The Five Wounds" and "Ordinary Sins" in *The New Yorker*; "The Manzanos" and "Nemecia" in *Narrative Magazine*, "Jubilee" in *Guernica*, and "Night at the Fiestas" in *The Southern Review*. "Nemecia" was included in *The Best American Short Stories 2013* and *The O. Henry Prize Stories 2014*, and "The Five Wounds" was included in *The Best of the West 2010: New Stories from the Wide Side of the Missouri*.

For information about permission to reproduce selections from this book, write to Permissions, W. W. Norton & Company, Inc., 500 Fifth Avenue, New York, NY 10110

For information about special discounts for bulk purchases, please contact W. W. Norton Special Sales at specialsales@wwnorton.com or 800-233-4830

Manufacturing by Courier Westford
Book design by Barbara M. Bachman
Production managers: Devon Zahn and Ruth Toda

Library of Congress Cataloging-in-Publication Data
Quade, Kirstin Valdez.
[Short stories. Selections]
Night at the Fiestas : stories / Kirstin Valdez Quade. – First Edition.
pages cm
ISBN 978-0-393-24298-0 (hardcover)
I. Title.
PS3617.U25N54 2015
813'.6—dc23
                        2014038352

W. W. Norton & Company, Inc.
500 Fifth Avenue, New York, N.Y. 10110
www.wwnorton.com

W. W. Norton & Company Ltd.
Castle House, 75/76 Wells Street, London W1T 3QT

1 2 3 4 5 6 7 8 9 0

For my grandparents,
LORENZO EPIFANIO VALDEZ
and JENNY ZAMORA VALDEZ,
and my great-aunt,
LEILA VALDEZ HALLUMS,
with love and gratitude

CONTENTS

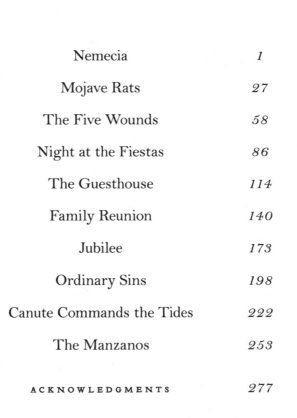

N E M E C I A

IN MY EARLIEST MEMORY OF MY COUSIN NEMECIA, WE ARE walking together in the bean field. I've been crying, and my breath is still juddering and wrecked. She holds tight to my hand and says cheerfully, "Just wait, Maria, wait 'til you see." I don't recall why I was upset or what my cousin showed me that day. I remember only that my sadness receded like a tide, replaced by a new quiet fizz of anticipation, and that Nemecia's shoes had heels. She had to walk tipped forward on her toes to prevent them from sinking into the dirt.

Nemecia was the daughter of my mother's sister. She came to live with my parents before I was born because my aunt Benigna couldn't care for her. Later, when Aunt Benigna recovered and moved to Los Angeles, Nemecia had already lived with us for so long that she stayed. This wasn't unusual in our New Mexico town in those years between the wars; if someone died, or came upon hard times, or simply had too many children, there were always aunts or sisters or grandmothers with room for an extra child.

The day after I was born, my great-aunt Paulita led seven-year-old Nemecia into my mother's bedroom to meet me. Nemecia was carrying the porcelain baby doll that had once belonged to her own mother. When they moved the blanket from my face so that she could see me, she smashed her doll against the plank floor. The pieces were all found; my father glued them together, wiping the surface with his handkerchief to remove what oozed between the cracks. The glue dried brown, or maybe it dried white and only turned brown with age. The doll sat on the bureau in our bedroom, its face round and placidly smiling behind its net of cracks, hands folded primly across white lace, a strange and terrifying mix of young and old.

Nemecia had an air of tragedy and glamour about her, which she cultivated. She blackened her eyes with a kohl pencil, and wore glass beads and silk stockings, gifts from her mother in California. She spent her allowance on magazines and pinned the photographs of actors from silent films around the mirror on our dresser. I don't think she ever saw a film—not, at least, until after she left us, since the nearest theater was all the way in Albuquerque, and my parents would not in any case have thought movies suitable for a young girl. Still, Nemecia modeled the upward glances and pouts of Mary Pickford and Greta Garbo in our small bedroom mirror.

When I think of Nemecia as she was then, I think of her eating. My cousin was ravenous. She needed things, and she needed food. She took small bites, swallowed everything as neatly as a cat. She was never full and the food never showed on her figure.

She told jokes as she served herself helping after helping, so that we were distracted and didn't notice how many tortillas or how many bowls of green chili stew she had eaten. If my father or little brothers teased her for her appetite, she burned red. My mother would shush my father and say she was a growing girl.

At night she stole food from the pantry, handfuls of prunes, beef jerky, pieces of ham. Her stealth was unnecessary; my mother would gladly have fed her until she was full. Still, in the mornings everything was in its place, the waxed paper folded neatly around the cheese, the lids tight on the jars. She was adept at slicing and spooning so her thefts weren't noticeable. I'd wake to her kneeling on my bed, a tortilla spread with honey against my lips. "Here," she'd whisper, and even if I was still full from dinner and not awake, I'd take a bite, because she needed me to participate in her crime.

Watching her eat made me hate food. The quick efficient bites, the movement of her jaw, the way the food slid down her throat—it sickened me to think of her body permitting such quantities. Her exquisite manners and the ladylike dip of her head as she accepted each mouthful somehow made it worse. But if I was a small eater, if I resented my dependence on food, no matter, because Nemecia would eat my portion, and nothing was ever wasted.

I WAS AFRAID OF NEMECIA because I knew her greatest secret: when she was five, she put her mother in a coma and killed our grandfather.

I knew this because she told me late one Sunday as we lay awake in our beds. The whole family had eaten together at our house, as we did every week, and I could hear the adults in the front room, still talking.

"I killed them," Nemecia said into the darkness. She spoke as if reciting, and I didn't at first know if she was talking to me. "My mother was dead. Almost a month she was dead, killed by me. Then she came back, like Christ, except it was a bigger miracle because she was dead longer, not just three days." Her voice was matter-of-fact.

"Why did you kill our grandpa?" I whispered.

"I don't remember," she said. "I must have been angry."

I stared hard at the darkness, then blinked. Eyes open or shut, the darkness was the same. Unsettling. I couldn't hear Nemecia breathe, just the distant voices of the adults. I had the feeling I was alone in the room.

Then Nemecia spoke. "I can't remember how I did it, though."

"Did you kill your father too?" I asked. For the first time I became aware of a mantle of safety around me that I'd never noticed before, and it was dissolving.

"Oh, no," Nemecia told me. Her voice was decided again. "I didn't need to, because he ran away on his own."

Her only mistake, she said, is that she didn't kill the miracle child. The miracle child was her brother, my cousin Patrick, two years older than me. He was a miracle because even as Aunt Benigna slept, dead to the world for those weeks, his cells multiplied and his features emerged. I thought of him growing strong on sugar water and my aunt's wasting body, his soul glowing steadily inside her. I thought of him turning flips in the liquid quiet.

"I was so close," Nemecia said, almost wistfully.

A photograph of Patrick as a toddler stood in a frame

on the piano. He was seated between Aunt Benigna, whom I had never met, and her new husband, all of them living in California. The Patrick in the photograph was fat-cheeked and unsmiling. He seemed content there, between a mother and a father. He did not seem aware of the sister who lived with us in another house nine hundred miles away. Certainly he didn't miss her.

"You better not tell anyone," my cousin said.

"I won't," I said, fear and loyalty swelling in me. I reached my hand into the dark space between our beds.

THE NEXT DAY, THE WORLD looked different; every adult I encountered was diminished now, made frail by Nemecia's secret.

That afternoon I went to the store and stood quietly at my mother's side as she worked at the messy rolltop desk behind the counter. She was balancing the accounts, tapping her lower lip with the end of her pencil. As always by the end of the day, a halo of frizz had sprung around her face.

My heart pounded and my throat was tight. "What happened to Aunt Benigna? What happened to your dad?"

My mother turned to look at me. She put down the pencil, was still for a moment, and then shook her head and made a gesture like she was pushing it all away from her.

"The important thing is we got our miracle. Miracles. Benigna lived, and that baby lived." Her voice was hard. "God at least granted us that. I'll always thank him for that." She didn't look thankful.

"But what happened?" My question was less forceful now.

"My poor, poor sister." My mother's eyes welled and she shook her head again. "It's best forgotten. It hurts me to think about it."

I believed that what Nemecia told me was true. What confused me was that no one ever treated Nemecia like a murderer. If anything, they were especially nice to her. I wondered if they knew what she'd done. I wondered if they were afraid of what she might do to them. My mother afraid of a child—the idea was outrageous, but it explained, perhaps, the little extra attentions she gave my cousin that so stung me: the brush of her fingertips on Nemecia's cheek, the way, when kissing us goodnight, her lips lingered against Nemecia's hair.

Perhaps the whole town was terrified, watching my cousin, and I watched Nemecia, too, as she talked with her teacher on the school steps, as she helped my mother before dinner. But my cousin never slipped, and though sometimes I thought I caught glimmers of caution in the faces of the adults, I couldn't be sure.

The whole town seemed to have agreed to keep me in the dark, but I thought if anyone would be vocal about her disapproval—and surely she disapproved of murder—it would be my great-aunt Paulita. I asked her about it one afternoon at her house as we made tortillas, careful not to betray Nemecia's secret. "What happened to my grand-father?" I pinched off a ball of dough and handed it to her.

"It was beyond imagining," Paulita said. She rolled the dough in fierce, sharp thrusts. I thought she'd go on, but she only said again, "Beyond imagining."

Except that I *could* imagine Nemecia killing someone.

Hell, demons, flames—these were the horrors I couldn't picture. Nemecia's fury, though—that was completely plausible.

"But what *happened?*"

Paulita flipped the disk of dough, rolled it again, slapped it on the hot iron top of the stove, where it blistered. She pointed at me with the rolling pin. "You're lucky, Maria, to have been born after that day. You're untouched. The rest of us will never forget it, but you, mi hijita, and the twins, are untouched." She opened the front door of her stove with an iron hook and jabbed at the fire inside.

No one would talk about what had happened when Nemecia was five. And soon I stopped asking. Each night I thought Nemecia might say something more about her crime, but she never mentioned it again.

And each night, I stayed awake as long as I could, waiting for Nemecia to come after me in the dark.

ANY NEW THING I GOT, Nemecia ruined, not enough that it was unusable, or even very noticeable, but just a little: a scrape with her fingernail in the wood of a pencil, a tear on the inside hem of a dress, a crease in the page of a book. I complained once, when Nemecia knocked my new windup jumping frog against the stone step. I thrust the frog at my mother, demanding she look at the scratch in the tin. My mother folded the toy back into my palm and shook her head, disappointed. "Think of other children," she said. She meant children I knew, children from Cuipas. "So many children don't have such beautiful new things."

I was often put in my cousin's care. My mother was glad of Nemecia's help; she was busy with the store and with my three-year-old brothers. I don't think she ever imagined that my cousin wished me harm. My mother was hawkish about her children's safety—later, when I was fifteen, she refused to serve a neighbor's aging farmhand in the store for a year because he'd whistled at me—but she trusted Nemecia. Nemecia, almost an orphan, the daughter of my mother's beloved older sister. Nemecia was my mother's first and—I knew it even then—favorite child.

My cousin was fierce with her love and with her hate, and sometimes I couldn't tell the difference. I seemed to provoke her without meaning to. At her angriest, she would lash out with slaps and pinches that turned my skin red and blue. Her anger would sometimes last weeks, aggression that would fade into long silences. I knew I was forgiven when she would begin to tell me stories, ghost stories about La Llorona, who haunted arroyos and wailed like the wind at approaching death, stories about bandits and the terrible things they would do to young girls, and, worse, stories about our family. Then she would hold and kiss me and tell me that though it was all true, every word, and though I was bad and didn't deserve it, she loved me still.

Not all her stories scared me. Some were wonderful—elaborate sagas that unfurled over weeks, adventures of girls like us who ran away. And every one of her stories belonged to us alone. She braided my hair at night, snapped back if a boy teased me, showed me how to walk so that I looked taller. "I'm here to take care of you," she told me. "That's why I'm here."

—

WHEN SHE TURNED FOURTEEN, Nemecia's skin turned red and oily and swollen with pustules. It looked tender. She began to laugh at me for my thick eyebrows and crooked teeth, things I hadn't noticed until then.

One night she came into our bedroom and looked at herself in the mirror for a long time. When she moved away, she crossed to where I sat on the bed and dug her nail into my right cheek. I yelped, jerked my head. "Shh," she said kindly. With one hand she smoothed my hair, and I felt myself soften under her touch as she worked her nail through my skin. It hurt only a little, and what did I, at seven years old, care about beauty? As I sat snug between Nemecia's knees, my face in her hands, her attention swept over me the way I imagined a wave would, warm and slow and salty.

Night after night I sat between her knees while she opened and reopened the wound. One day she'd make a game of it, tell me that I looked like a pirate; another day she'd say it was her duty to mark me, because I had sinned. Daily she and my mother worked against each other, my mother spreading salve on the scab each morning, Nemecia easing it open each night with her nails. "Why don't you heal, Maria?" my mother wondered as she fed me cloves of raw garlic. Why didn't I tell her? I don't know exactly, but I suppose I needed to be drawn into Nemecia's story.

By the time Nemecia finally lost interest and let my cheek heal, the scar reached from the side of my nose to my lip. It made me look dissatisfied, and it turned purple in the winter.

—

AFTER HER SIXTEENTH BIRTHDAY, Nemecia left me alone. It was normal, my mother said, for her to spend more time by herself or with friends. At dinner my cousin was still funny with my parents, chatty with the aunts and uncles. But those strange secret fits of rage and adoration—all the attention she'd once focused on me—ended completely. She had turned away from me, but instead of relief, I felt emptiness.

I tried to force Nemecia back into our old closeness. I bought her caramels, nudged her in church as though we shared some secret joke. Once at school I ran up to where she stood with some older girls. "Nemecia!" I exclaimed, as though I'd been looking everywhere for her, and grabbed her hand. She didn't push me away or snap at me, just smiled distantly and turned back to her friends.

We still shared our room, but she went to bed late. She no longer told stories, no longer brushed my hair, no longer walked with me to school. Nemecia stopped seeing me, and without her gaze I became indistinct to myself. I'd lie in bed waiting for her, holding myself still until I could no longer feel the sheets on my skin, until I was bodiless in the dark. Eventually, Nemecia would come in, and when she did, I'd be unable to speak.

My skin lost its color, my body its mass, until one morning in May when, as I gazed out the classroom window, I saw old Mrs. Romero walking down the street, her shawl billowing around her like wings. My teacher called my name sharply, and I was surprised to find myself in my body, sitting solid in my desk. I decided right then: I would lead the Corpus Christi procession. I would wear the wings and everyone would see me.

CORPUS CHRISTI HAD BEEN my mother's favorite feast day since she was a child, when each summer she walked with the other girls through the dirt streets flinging rose petals. Every year my mother made Nemecia and me new white dresses and wound our braids with ribbons in coronets around our heads. I'd always loved the ceremony: the solemnity of the procession, the blessed sacrament in its gold box held high by the priest under the gold-tasseled canopy, the prayers at the altars along the way. Now I could think only of leading that procession.

My mother's altar was her pride. Each year she set up the card table on the street in front of the house. The Sacred Heart stood in the center of the crocheted lace cloth, flanked by candles and flowers in mason jars.

Everyone took part in the procession, and the girls of the town led it all with baskets of petals to cast before the Body of Christ. On that day we were transformed from dusty, scraggle-haired children into angels. But it was the girl at the head of the procession who really was an angel, because she wore the wings that were stored between sheets of tissue paper in a box on top of my mother's wardrobe. Those wings were beautiful, gauze and wire, and tied with white ribbon on the upper arms.

A girl had to have been confirmed to lead the procession, and was chosen based on her recitation of a psalm. I was ten now, and this was the first year I qualified. In the days leading up to the recitation, I surveyed the competition. Most of the girls were from ranches outside town. Even if they had a sister or parent who could read well enough to help them with their memorization, I knew they wouldn't pronounce the words right. Only my cousin Antonia was a real threat; she had led the procession the year before and was always beautifully behaved, but she would recite an easy psalm. Nemecia was too old and had never shown interest anyway.

I settled on Psalm 38, which I chose from my mother's cardboard-covered *Manna* for its impressive length and difficult words.

I practiced fervently, in the bathtub, walking to school, in bed at night. The way I imagined it, I would give my recitation in front of the entire town. Father Chavez would hold up his hand at the end of Mass, before people could shift and cough and gather their hats, and he would say, "Wait. There is one thing more you need to hear." One or two girls would go before me, stumble through their psalms (short ones, unremarkable ones). Then I would stand, walk with grace to the front of the church, and there, before the altar, I'd speak with eloquence that people afterward would describe as *unearthly*. I'd offer my psalm as a gift to my mother. I'd watch her watch me from the pew, her eyes full of tears and pride meant only for me.

Instead, of course, our recitations took place in Sunday school before Mass. One by one we stood before our classmates as our teacher, Mrs. Reyes, followed our words from her Bible. Antonia recited the same psalm she had recited the year before. When it was my turn, I stumbled over the phrase, "For my iniquities are gone over my head: and as a heavy burden are become heavy upon me." When I sat down with the other children, tears gathered behind my eyes and I told myself that none of it mattered.

A week before the procession, my mother met me outside school. During the day she rarely left the store or my little brothers, so I knew it was important.

"Mrs. Reyes came by the store today," my mother said. I couldn't tell from her face if the news had been good or bad, or about me at all. She put her hand on my shoulder and led me home.

I walked stiffly under her hand, waiting, eyes on the dusty toes of my shoes.

Finally my mother turned and hugged me. "You did it, Maria."

That night we celebrated. My mother brought bottles of ginger ale from the store, and we shared them, passing them around the table. My father raised his and drank to me. Nemecia grabbed my hand and squeezed it.

Before we had finished dinner, my mother stood and beckoned me to follow her down the hall. In her bedroom she took down the box from her wardrobe and lifted out the wings. "Here," she said, "let's try them on." She tied the ribbons around my arms over my checked dress and led me back to where my family sat waiting.

The wings were light, and they scraped against the doorway. They moved ever so slightly as I walked, the way I imagined real angel wings might.

"Turn around," my father said. My brothers slid off their chairs and came at me. My mother caught them by the wrists. "Don't go get your greasy hands on those wings." I twirled and spun for my family, and my brothers clapped. Nemecia smiled and served herself seconds.

That night Nemecia went up to bed when I did. As we pulled on our nightgowns, she said, "They had to pick you, you know."

I turned to her, surprised. "That's not true."

"It is," she said simply. "Think about it. Antonia was last year, Christina Moya the year before. It's always the daughters of the Altar Society."

It hadn't occurred to me before, but of course she was right. I would have liked to argue, but instead I began to cry. I hated myself for crying in front of her, and I hated Nemecia. I got into bed, turned away, and fell asleep.

Sometime later I woke to darkness. Nemecia was beside me in bed, her breath hot on my face. She patted my head and whispered, "I'm sorry, I'm sorry, I'm sorry." Her strokes became harder. Her breath was hot and hissing. "I am the miracle child. They never knew. *I* am the miracle because *I* lived."

I lay still. Her arms were tight around my head, my face pressed against her hard sternum. I couldn't hear some of the things she said to me, and the air I breathed tasted like Nemecia. It was only from the shudders that passed through her thin chest into my skull that I finally realized she was crying. After a while she released me and set me back on my pillow like a doll. "There now," she said, arranging my arms over the covers. "Go to sleep." I shut my eyes and tried to obey.

I spent the afternoon before Corpus Christi watching my brothers play in the garden while my mother worked on her altar. They were digging a hole. Any other time I would have helped them, but tomorrow was Corpus

Christi. It was hot and windy and my eyes were dry. I hoped the wind would settle overnight. I didn't want dust on my wings.

I saw Nemecia step out onto the porch. She shaded her eyes and stood still for a moment. When she caught sight of us crouched in the corner of the garden, she came over, her strides long and adult.

"Maria. I'm going to walk with you tomorrow in the procession. I'm going to help you."

"I don't need any help," I said.

Nemecia smiled as though it was out of her hands. "Well." She shrugged.

"But I'm leading it," I said. "Mrs. Reyes chose me."

"Your mother told me I had to help you, and that maybe I would get to wear the wings."

I stood. Even standing, I came only to her shoulder. I heard the screen door slam, and my mother was on the porch. She came over to us, steps quick, face worried.

"Mama, I don't *need* help. Tell her Mrs. Reyes chose *me*."

"I only thought that there will be other years for you." My mother's tone was imploring. "Nemecia will be too old next year."

"But I may never memorize anything so well ever!" My voice rose. "This may be my only chance."

My mother brightened. "Maria, of course you'll memorize something. It's only a year. You'll get picked again, I promise."

I couldn't say anything. I saw what had happened: Nemecia had decided she would wear the wings, and my mother had decided to let her. Nemecia would lead the town, tall in her white dress, the wings framing her. And following would be me, small and angry and ugly. I wouldn't want it next year, after Nemecia. I wouldn't want it ever again.

Nemecia put her hand on my shoulder. "It's about the blessed sacrament, Maria. It's not about you." She spoke gently. "Besides, you'll still be leading it. I'll just be there with you. To help."

"Hijita, listen—"

"I don't want your help," I said. I was as dark and savage as an animal.

"Maria—"

Nemecia shook her head and smiled sadly. "That's why I am here," she said. "I lived so I could help you." Her face was calm, and a kind of holiness settled into it.

Hate flooded me. "I wish you hadn't," I said. "I wish you hadn't lived. This isn't your home. You're a killer." I turned to my mother. My words were choked and furious. "She's trying to kill us all. Don't you know? Everyone around her ends up dead. Why don't you ever punish her?"

My mother paled, and suddenly I was afraid. Nemecia was still for a moment, and then her face clenched and she ran into the house.

AFTER THAT, EVERYTHING HAPPENED very quickly. My mother didn't shout, didn't say a word. She came into my room carrying the carpetbag she used when she had to stay at the home of a sick relative. I made my face more sullen than I felt. Her silence was frightening. She opened my bureau and began to pack things into the bag: three dresses, all my drawers and undershirts. She put my Sunday shoes in too, my hairbrush, the book that lay beside my bed, enough things for a very long absence.

My father came in and sat beside me on the bed. He was in his work clothes, pants dusty from the field.

"You're just going to stay with Paulita for a while," he said.

I knew what I'd said was terrible, but I never guessed that they would get rid of me. I didn't cry, though, not even when my mother folded up the small quilt that had been mine since I was born and set it into the top of the carpetbag. She buckled it all shut.

My mother's head was bent over the bag, and for a moment I thought I'd made her cry, but when I ventured to look at her face, I couldn't tell.

"It won't be long," my father said. "It's just to Paulita's. So close it's almost the same house." He examined his hands for a long time, and I too looked at the crescents of soil under his nails. "Your cousin has had a hard life," he said finally. "You have to understand."

"Come on, Maria," my mother said gently.

Nemecia was sitting in the parlor, her hands folded and still on her lap. I wished she would stick out her tongue or glare, but she only watched me pass. My mother held open the door and then closed it behind us. She took my hand, and we walked together down the street to Paulita's house with its garden of dusty hollyhocks.

My mother knocked on the door and then went in, telling me to run along to the kitchen. I heard her whispering. Paulita came in for a moment to pour me milk and set out some cookies, and then she left again.

I didn't eat. I tried to listen, but couldn't make out any

words. I heard Paulita click her tongue, the way she clicked it when someone had behaved shamefully, like when it was discovered that Charlie Padilla had been stealing from his grandmother.

My mother came into the kitchen. She patted my wrist. "It's not for long, Maria." She kissed the top of my head.

I heard Paulita's front door shut, heard her slow steps come toward the kitchen. She sat opposite me and took a cookie.

"It's good you came for a visit. I never see enough of you."

The next day I didn't go to Mass. I said I was sick, and Paulita touched my forehead but didn't contradict me. I stayed in bed, my eyes closed and dry. I could hear the bells and the intonations as the town passed outside the house. Antonia led the procession, and Nemecia walked with the adults; I know this because I asked Paulita days later. I wondered if Nemecia had chosen not to lead or if she had not been allowed, but I couldn't bring myself to ask.

I stayed with Paulita for three months. She spoiled me, fed me sweets, kept me up late with her. Each night she put her feet on the arm of the couch to stop the swelling, balanced her jigger of whiskey on her stomach, and stroked the stiff gray hair on her chin while she told stories: about Cuipas when she was a girl, about the time she snuck out to the fiestas after she was supposed to be asleep. I loved Paulita and enjoyed her attention, but my anger at my parents simmered even when I was laughing.

My mother stopped by, tried to talk to me, but in her presence the easy atmosphere of Paulita's house became stale. Over and over she urged me to visit her in the store, and I did once, but I was silent, wanting so much to be drawn out, disdaining her attempts.

"Hijita," she said, pushing candy at me across the counter.

I stood stiff in her embrace and left the candy. My mother had sent me away, and my father had done nothing to stop her. They'd picked Nemecia, picked Nemecia over their real daughter.

Nemecia and I saw each other at school, but we didn't speak. The teachers seemed aware of the changes in our household and kept us apart. People were kind to me during this time, a strange, pitying kindness. I thought they knew how angry I was, knew there was no hope left for me. I too would be kind, I thought, if I met myself on the road.

The family gathered on Sundays, as always, at my mother's house for dinner. That was how I had begun to think of it during those months: my mother's house. My mother hugged me, and my father kissed me, and I sat in my old place, but at the end of dinner, I always left with Paulita. Nemecia seemed more at home than ever. She laughed and told stories and swallowed bite after neat bite. She seemed to have grown older, more graceful. She neither spoke to nor looked at me. Everyone talked and laughed, and it seemed only I remembered that we were eating with a murderer.

"Nemecia looks well," Paulita said one night as we walked home.

I didn't answer, and she didn't speak again until she had shut the door behind us.

"One day you'll be friends again, Maria. You two are sisters." Her hand trembled as she lit the lamp.

I couldn't stand it anymore. "No," I said. "We won't.

We'll never be friends. We aren't sisters. She's the killer, and *I'm* the one who was sent away. Do you even know who killed your brother?" I demanded. "Nemecia. And she tried to kill her own mother too. Why doesn't anyone *know* this?"

"Sit down," Paulita said to me sternly. She'd never spoken to me in this tone. "First of all, you were not sent away. You could shout to your mother from this house. And, my God, Nemecia is not a killer. I don't know where you picked up such lies."

Paulita lowered herself into a chair. When she spoke again, her voice was even, her old eyes pale brown and watery. "Your grandfather decided he would give your mother and Benigna each fifty acres." Paulita put her hand to her forehead and exhaled slowly. "My God. So your grandfather stopped by one morning to see Benigna about the deed. He was still on the road, he hadn't even made it to the door, when he heard the shouting. Benigna's cries were that loud. Her husband was beating her." Paulita paused. She pressed the pads of her fingers against the table.

I thought of the sound of fist on flesh. I could almost hear it. The flame of the lamp wavered and the light wobbled along the wide planks of Paulita's kitchen floor.

"This wasn't the first time it had happened, just the first time your grandfather walked in on it. So he pushed open the door, angry, ready to kill the man. There was a fight, but Benigna's husband was drunk and your grandfather wasn't young anymore. Benigna's husband must have been closer to the stove and to the iron poker. When they were discovered—" Paulita's voice remained flat. "When they were discovered, your grandfather was already dead. Benigna was unconscious on the floor. And they found Nemecia behind the wood box. She'd seen the whole thing. She was five."

I wondered who had walked in first on that brutality? Surely someone I knew, someone I passed at church or outside the post office. Maybe someone in my family. Maybe Paulita. "What about Nemecia's father?"

"He was there on his knees, crying over Benigna. 'I love you, I love you, I love you,' he kept saying."

How had it never occurred to me that, at five years old, Nemecia would have been too small to attack a grown man and woman all at once? How could I have been so stupid?

"It was terrible for your mother, you know. That day she lost her father, and she lost her sister, too. Oh, how those girls loved each other." Paulita laughed without mirth. "But Benigna won't be back. She barely even writes."

If my mother didn't fear Nemecia, then the love she showed my cousin was just that: love. Love for her sister, love for her father, love for a child terrified and abandoned, love for an entire life lost to my mother forever. It was even possible that amid all that loss, caring for Nemecia was what had saved my mother. And there was absolutely nothing—no recitation, no feat of strength—I could do to shift that.

At school I watched from across the yard for signs of what Paulita had told me, but Nemecia was the same: graceful, laughing, distant. I felt humiliated for believing her, and I resented the demands she made on my sympathy. Pity and hatred and guilt nearly choked me. If anything, I hated my cousin more, she who had once been a terrified child, she who could call that tragedy her own. Nemecia would always have the best of everything.

———

Nemecia left for California three months after Corpus Christi. In Los Angeles, Aunt Benigna bought secondhand furniture and turned the small sewing room into a bedroom. She introduced Nemecia to her husband and to the miracle child. There was a palm tree in the front yard and a pink-painted gravel walkway. I know this from a letter my cousin sent my mother, signed with a flourish, *Norma*.

I moved back to my mother's house and to the room that was all mine. My mother stood in the middle of the floor as I unpacked my things into the now-empty bureau. She looked lost.

"We missed you," she said, looking out the window. And then, "It's not right for a child to be away from her parents. It's not right that you left us."

I wanted to tell her that *I* had not left, that I had *been* left, led away and dropped at Paulita's door.

"Listen." Then she stopped and shook her head. "Ah, well," she said, with an intake of breath.

I placed my camisoles in the drawer, one on top of the other. I didn't look at my mother. The reconciliation and tears and embraces that I'd dreamt about didn't come, so I hardened myself against her.

Our family quickly grew over the space Nemecia left, so quickly that I often wondered if she'd meant anything to us at all.

Nemecia's life became glamorous in my mind—beautiful, tragic, the story of an orphan. I imagined that I could take that life for myself. Night after night I told myself the story: a prettier me, swept away to California, and the boy who would find me and save me from my unhappiness. Cuipas slept among the vast, whispering grasses, coyotes called in the distance, and Nemecia's story set my body alight.

We attended Nemecia's wedding, my family and I. We took the long trip across New Mexico and Arizona to Los Angeles, me in the backseat between my brothers. For years I'd pictured Nemecia living a magazine shoot, running on the beach, stretched on a chaise longue beside a flat, blue pool. As we crossed the Mojave Desert, though, I began to get nervous—that I wouldn't recognize her, that she'd have forgotten me. I found myself hoping that her life wasn't as beautiful as I'd imagined it, that she'd finally been punished.

When we drove up to the little house, Nemecia ran outside in bare feet and hugged each of us as we unfolded ourselves from the car.

"Maria!" she cried, smiling, and kissed both my cheeks, and I fell into a shyness I couldn't shake all that week.

"Nemecia, hijita," my mother said. She stepped back and looked at my cousin happily.

"Norma," my cousin said. "My name is Norma."

It was remarkable how completely she'd changed. Her hair was blond now, her skin tanned dark and even.

My mother nodded slowly and repeated, "Norma."

The wedding was the most beautiful thing I'd ever seen, and I was wrung with jealousy. I must have understood then that I wouldn't have a wedding of my own. Like everything else in Los Angeles, the church was large and modern. The pews were pale and sleek, and the empty crucifix shone. Nemecia confessed to me that she didn't know the priest here, that she rarely even went to church anymore. In a few years, I too would stop going, but it shocked me then to hear my cousin say it.

They didn't speak Spanish in my aunt's house. When my mother or father said something in Spanish, my aunt or cousin answered resolutely in English. I was embarrassed by my parents that week, the way their awkward English made them seem confused and childish.

The day before the wedding, Nemecia invited me to the beach with her girlfriend. I said I couldn't go—I was fifteen, younger than they were, and I didn't have a swimming suit.

"Of course you'll come. You're my little sister." Nemecia opened a messy drawer and tossed me a tangled blue suit. I remember I changed in her bedroom, turned in the full-length mirror, stretched across her pink satin bed and posed like a pinup. I felt older, sensual. There, in Nemecia's bedroom, I liked the image of myself in that swimming suit, but on the beach my courage left me. Someone took our picture, standing with a tanned, smiling man. I still have the picture. Nemecia and her friend look easy in their suits, arms draped around the man's neck. The man—who is he? How did he come to be in the photograph?—has his arm around Nemecia's small waist. I am beside her, hand on her shoulder, but standing as though I'm afraid to touch her. She leans into the man and away from me, her smile broad and white. I smile with my lips closed, and my other arm is folded in front of my chest. My scar shows as a gray smear on my cheek.

———

WHEN SHE LEFT FOR LOS ANGELES, Nemecia didn't take the doll that sat on the bureau. The doll came with us when we moved to Albuquerque; we saved it, I suppose, for Nemecia's children, though we never said so out loud. Later, after my mother died in 1981, I brought it from her house, where for years my mother had kept it on her own bureau. For five days it lay on the table in my apartment before I called Nemecia and asked if she wanted it back.

"I don't know what you're talking about," she said. "I never had a doll."

"The cracked one, remember?" My voice went high with disbelief. It seemed impossible that she could have forgotten. It had sat in our room for years, facing us in our beds each night as we fell asleep. A flare of anger ignited—she was lying, she had to be lying—then died.

I touched the yellowed hem of the doll's dress, while Nemecia told me about the cruise she and her husband were taking through the Panama Canal. "Ten days," she said, "and then we're going to stay for three days in Puerto Rico. It's a new boat, with casinos and pools and ballrooms. I hear they treat you royally." While she talked, I ran my finger along the ridge of the cracks in the doll's head. From the sound of her voice, I could almost imagine she'd never aged, and it seemed to me I'd spent my whole life listening to Nemecia's stories.

"So what about the doll?" I asked when it was almost time to hang up. "Do you want me to send it?"

"I can't even picture it," she said and laughed. "Do whatever you want. I don't need old things lying around the house."

I was tempted to take offense, to think it was me she was rejecting, our whole shared past in Cuipas. I was tempted to slip back into that same old envy for how easily Nemecia had let those years drop away from her, leaving me to remember her stories. But by then I was old enough to know that she wasn't thinking about me at all.

Nemecia spent the rest of her life in Los Angeles. I visited her once when I had some vacation time saved, in her long, low house surrounded by bougainvillea. She collected Dolls of the World and Waterford Crystal, which she displayed in glass cases. She sat me at the dining room table and took the dolls out one by one. "Holland," she said and set it before me. "Italy. Greece." I tried to see some evidence in her face of what she had witnessed as a child, but there was nothing.

Nemecia held a wineglass up to the window and turned it. "See how clear?" Shards of light moved across her face.

M O J A V E   R A T S

L<small>AST NIGHT</small> M<small>ONICA</small> V<small>IGIL</small>-R<small>IOS HAD LAIN AWAKE, LIS</small>-
tening to the wind whip across the salt flats and buffet
the trailer, imagining intruders with dark intentions outside. They were living in a piece of aluminum foil, Monica
thought. That paltry lock wouldn't withstand a can opener.

And so, as if in retaliation for her ingratitude, the trailer's heater stopped working. Monica awoke at dawn to
seven-year-old Cordelia whimpering from the loft above
the dinette. "Mama," Cordelia said, still half-asleep. "It's
cold."

"Goddamn it," said Monica. It was like a scene out of
Dickens, she thought: her very own Little Dorrit, failed
once again by her feckless parent. An unpleasant rush of
guilt came over her, followed by a prickling irritation at
Cordelia for causing this guilt, followed, predictably, by a
fresh surge of remorse.

It *was* cold, a dry hopeless cold that made Monica gasp
when she slid out of her sleeping bag on the foldout sofa.

"Come on, sweet pea." She helped the shivering Cordelia down from the loft and tucked her into her own warm bed beside the baby, who was still blissfully asleep, cheeks chilled and pink, the skin at her nose and mouth raw and crusted. "You snuggle close to Beatrice. She'll be your own personal heater." Monica slipped on her jacket, wincing at the icy lining, and pushed out into the wind to see what could be done about the furnace.

If only the heat had held on just one more day. Elliot was due back tonight. He'd been away for a week with the car and his rock pick, collecting soil samples, his thoughts locked on some million-year-old landscape only he could see. God, she hoped he'd found what he was looking for.

"I'll be afraid here all alone," she'd told him before he left, meaning, "I'll miss you."

"Of course you won't," he'd said kindly, and they'd all waved as he pulled away, Cordelia shouting to her stepfather, "Goodbye, Elliot! Goodbye!" until the dust settled. As the week progressed, Monica had found herself increasingly lonely, and though she'd read endless stories and done cooking projects and kept chipper for the girls, she'd never felt so stuck or at such loose ends.

Now Monica was furious with Elliot for leaving her stranded, furious with him for not finishing his fieldwork months ago, when he was supposed to. "I was out there for hours," she imagined telling him, though she never would. "I had to leave the girls unattended."

When she finally located the furnace on the rear of the trailer, the panel, of course, had to be screwed off, so Monica went back inside to rummage through Elliot's tools in the greasy storage space under the bench seat. After rejecting several Phillips-head screwdrivers, she finally found a too-small flathead she would have to make work.

Monica went through these motions knowing all the while that once she finally managed to remove the panel, she would have no idea how to begin to repair the furnace. Still, she felt compelled to stay outside as the wind slashed at her face and hair, the screwdriver almost too frigid to hold, stabbing away at the edge of the aluminum panel (which had, it seemed, rusted itself stubbornly in place), as if locating the problem were somehow the same as fixing it.

The sun peered weakly over the Spring Mountains and the salt flats glowed a faint orange. From where she stood, huddled against the trailer, Monica could hear the sign out on the highway, which had come loose from one of its posts and flapped in the wind, a violent, incessant popping. Years from now, Monica thought bitterly, when she looked back on this time in her life, the sign with its faded palm tree is what she'd remember. WELCOME TO FABULOUS GYPSUM!

Fabulous Gypsum! was all exposure and dust, wind and bleak, pale sky, and, at least until Elliot finished the fieldwork that would form the basis of his dissertation on the Death Valley fault system, it was home. The Shady Lanes RV Park was three miles from the town, which was comprised of a school, a post office operating out of a sun-bleached single-wide, and a grocery store with its wall of clanging slot machines. The Lucky Token, the store was called, as if gambling were the necessity and food an afterthought. Faint mountains ringed the horizon, and the cracked flats stretched into the distance, punctuated only by creosote and desert needle.

Finally, Monica gave up on the furnace. Inside, she

rejoined the girls in bed, trying to get warm, then fell into a deep sleep until Cordelia stirred beside her. "Shit," said Monica, glancing at her watch. "Shit, shit, shit." They were late; already the schoolbus, half-filled with shaggy-headed blond children from the outlying ranches, had passed them by.

"We can run," Cordelia said encouragingly.

"Honey, the bus is miles away now."

Cordelia slumped and flung her head back in despair. "But it's art day!"

Monica sighed. Cordelia would not be spared the cold, and Monica would not be spared Cordelia.

Monica zipped Cordelia into her jacket, tucked Elliot's old down parka around Beatrice, and turned the stroller on its stiff wheels. "We're going on an adventure!" called Monica, and the three of them leaned into the blowing grit and made their bumpy way across the dirt expanse toward the bathrooms and the pay phone.

The park could accommodate forty trailers, each with electric and water hookups, but since they'd arrived eight months ago, there had never been more than ten vehicles scattered at any given time. Today there were six. Across the way, the NASA engineer bent, as usual, over the open hood of his truck. He looked up as she passed, and Monica gave a tight smile, acutely aware that she was a woman encumbered with children, carless and alone in the middle of nowhere.

Cordelia, trotting along with her hand on the stroller, waved. The NASA engineer grunted and ducked his head, though when Monica glanced back, he was watching her.

His truck hadn't run for years, the park manager

had told Elliot. When he wasn't tinkering with the dead engine, the NASA engineer lived beneath the camper shell, the plastic windows murky with things piled against them. Once, when the tailgate was down, Monica had glimpsed the crammed nest of blankets and electronics and engine parts among which, apparently, the man burrowed like a rodent.

According to the park manager, the man had once been brilliant, working on high-tech heat-resistant compounds. This didn't surprise Monica. He could have been anything: child molester, gambling addict, harmless kook. Why not a NASA engineer? She wondered if Gypsum had been his destination, or if this was simply where his truck had sputtered to a stop.

If only they had the car, she'd drive into town, spend the day in the heated grocery store wandering up and down the three short aisles. After school, she'd buy Cordelia a treat, let her stand at a safe distance and watch the old men at the slot machines. Maybe they'd skip Gypsum altogether and drive all the way to Las Vegas.

"It's not fair that Elliot gets the car and not us." Cordelia kicked the dirt.

"You're right," said Monica. "It's not fair."

"You maybe don't know this about me, but I'm a kid who loves school."

Monica catalogued her neighbors, but there was no one she could envision asking for a ride to town. The torpid, obese family in the RV across the way; the desiccated couple with their nylon shorts and extreme low-calorie diet, running endlessly along the highway; the ubiquitous single men as filthy and bearded as miners. When she encountered them, returning a word or a wave in the icy cinder-block bathroom or passing on her walks with Beatrice, Monica couldn't help imagining sordid stories for them: mental illness, violent crime, shattering personal tragedy. The place caught people like trash in a wire fence, damaged, discarded people blown out of the bright tree-lined towns of America, held here until the wind came up.

Mojave rats, Elliot called them, these denizens of the dust. The Manson Family had camped out here, he informed Monica, had squatted in various ghost towns, lurking in falling wood-framed buildings, carving their names in porch posts and crumbling plaster, before moving on to prepare for Helter Skelter. To Elliot these facts were secondary to the facts about the area's geology, interesting in their way, but having nothing to do with him.

So Monica held herself aloof, determined that people understand she wasn't like them. On her walks, she recited poetry to Beatrice. She carried her paperback of *Middlemarch* with its cover facing out, displaying the nineteenth-century painting. Monica wasn't proud of her pretentions. But it was so easy to feel disdain for these people, so vital that she not be mistaken for one of them. "My husband is doing research here," she told the few people she spoke to, and just saying the words comforted her. *Research. Husband.* These words were her talismans, all that prevented her from sliding into their grim lives. She told herself again and again that her time at Shady Lanes was only prelude to her real life: she would live in a little house filled with books, attend dinner parties with well-traveled intellectuals. She would finish college, the first in her family, maybe even get her master's. She would be a professor's wife. Occasionally,

Monica even allowed herself to imagine teaching a literature class in a seminar room overlooking a grassy quad. "Come over, have a coffee," a retired woman from Calgary had invited in the fall, but Monica had declined and afterward had been forced to avoid her. It had been a relief when the woman and her husband fired up their RV and drove east to Arizona.

At the edge of the highway, Monica parked the stroller outside the pay phone, the plexiglass walls of which had been sandblasted into opacity. The phone book covered all of Nye County, but every listing under Heaters, Furnaces, and RVs was located in either Beatty or Tonopah. As Monica leafed through the dusty pages, they flapped and tore. The phone number for the Gypsum hardware store was apparently no longer in service. Just as well, thought Monica dismally; fixing the furnace would cost money they didn't have.

When Monica looked up, an oncoming semi was growing steadily larger, and Cordelia had drifted away and was inspecting rocks dangerously close to the shoulder of the road.

"Get back!" yelled Monica.

Cordelia looked up, her hands crammed with rocks. "I am back," she protested.

Just then the eighteen-wheeler passed in a shuddering rush, stirring loose curls of dust along the road. Monica dropped the phone, sending it clanging against the booth, and yanked Cordelia by the arm.

"Don't you *ever*—" she started, not caring how much she hurt Cordelia—glad to hurt her, even—but Beatrice, strapped into her stroller as the dust storm blew over her, clutched at her eyes and began to wail.

"Mama!" called Cordelia urgently over the baby's squalls. "Beatrice has dirt in her eyes."

"I *know*," snapped Monica, and now Cordelia's face crumpled, her feelings, as always, wounded.

It was pointless to look at Beatrice's eyes here; each time Monica managed to pull the little fist away and pry one open, a new gust assaulted them. Beatrice arched her back and screamed in outraged pain. "We're going home," said Monica, defeated.

"I'm going to be in deep trouble for missing school," said Cordelia. She stomped along behind, her thick black hair tangled, lips shading violet.

"You won't be in trouble. It's my fault."

"I know," said Cordelia.

As Monica collapsed the stroller, she glanced at the RV across the way, where the overweight family lived, and for a brief alarming moment thought she saw a pale face in the dim window, watching her. She blinked and looked again: nothing.

Cordelia hauled herself up the metal steps. "So?" she accused. "What about the heater?"

There was nothing frightening about a face in a window, Monica thought, jiggling Beatrice in her arms. Didn't Monica look out her own windows? Still, Monica missed Elliot, with his electrical know-how, his logic and warm, male bulk.

"Well?" asked Cordelia.

"Today we're going to be pioneers." Monica held open the door for her, and the grit gusted through, chattering on the linoleum.

———

IMAGINING THEIR LIFE in a trailer from the comfort of their rental in Santa Fe (a ten-minute walk from her mother's house and where she'd grown up), Monica had thought of Mr. Toad with his gypsy caravan. Before Elliot and Monica had married last year, Elliot's mother had bought Cordelia a beautiful illustrated copy of *The Wind in the Willows*. Monica had never read it as a child, and she, with Cordelia, loved the picture of Toad's caravan, the bright paint ("canary yellow picked out in green"), snug curtained bed, patterned dishes lined up on shelves. The promise of both comfort and adventure.

Their eighteen-foot aluminum Travel Lite, however, delivered neither. Brown stripes outside, dingy brick-patterned linoleum inside, hideous orange plaid curtains that snapped shut. The trailer smelled of particleboard and dust.

Monica turned the oven on high and bundled herself and the girls into the sleeping loft. This might have been a nice way to spend the morning, cozy and giggling in the nest of sleeping bags with their books. When she wanted to be, Cordelia was excellent company, a watchful performer, making droll observations for her mother's benefit. Instead, they were all sluggish and irritable. Beatrice whimpered with discomfort while Monica and Cordelia took turns wiping her chapped nose.

"*Toad* has a heater," Cordelia observed pointedly. She clawed through the book and indicated the cozy potbellied woodstove on their favorite page.

"Yes," Monica agreed and sighed, exhausted by the relentless optimism motherhood demanded. "But Toad didn't have lots of things we have. Radio. Indoor plumbing."

"Not here. Not here we don't have indoor plumbing." Her tone was injured. "Look at Beatrice," she demanded, pointing to the baby's unsightly muzzle. "You should take her to a doctor. She isn't even cute anymore."

Monica dabbed at the baby's nose, which certainly did look worse than it was. "It's dry skin. We live in a very dry place. The doctor will just tell us to put Vaseline on her, Cordelia. Which I'm doing."

Monica was no fool: she could read the signs of a child in survival mode. Even as a baby, Cordelia had known to fall silent when her parents fought; to this day, if Elliot was curt, she stiffened, wary. Cordelia's watchfulness made Monica uneasy. Now, with the arrival of Beatrice, her personality had developed into something sterner still. She guarded her sister vigilantly, turned a fierce eye on her mother and stepfather, evaluating their every move. "Too *rough*," she'd scold Elliot when he swung the gleeful baby. "Her arms could fall off."

Beatrice showed no such complexity. The baby laughed often and loudly, and when she was tired or hungry, she wailed with the entire force of her strong little being. The world revolved around Beatrice, and Beatrice was appropriately ungrateful.

Likely, Monica thought, Cordelia would grow to resent this trait in her sister, this assumption that her needs would be met, that the world had a place for her. But for now, Cordelia nestled around Beatrice, her body curved protectively. To keep her from the cold, or from Monica? If Monica wasn't careful, the two of them would grow ever closer, in league against her.

After lunch—tomato soup that chilled almost as soon as it touched the bowls—Beatrice fell into a fierce sleep: fists balled up tight, brow pinched, her red cheeks splotched and tear-streaked.

"I hope she doesn't freeze," said Cordelia.

"Just a few more hours, then Elliot will fix the heater."

"What if he doesn't know how?"

"He probably will. And if not we'll drive to buy a new one."

Bleakly, Cordelia said, "You love him more than you love us."

Monica put her arm around the girl, gave a gentle shake. They'd been down this road before. "That's silly. I love you differently. You two are my precious daughters."

Cordelia was stiff and muffled under her arm. She was looking at her sleeping sister. "But you love him more than you love me."

"Want me to read to you?" Monica tapped her *Riverside Shakespeare*, which she had planned to study cover to cover months ago and still hadn't touched, except to read aloud, at Cordelia's insistence, scenes featuring her namesake. Now Cordelia just shook her head.

"I have an idea," Monica said. "We can play dress-up!" Actually, it was an idiotic idea—it was far too cold to be changing in and out of clothes.

"Fine," said Cordelia, listless.

Monica dropped down from the loft and began rummaging in the tiny particleboard closet, while Cordelia peered over the bunk. There wasn't much worth dressing up in. Some scarves: heavy, knitted, utilitarian. A cotton skirt. Elliot's felt Indiana Jones hat, brim stained with dirt and sweat. Monica didn't even like to touch it.

She reached for her dress. It was in its dry-cleaning plastic, hadn't been worn in years, not since Monica had left Cordelia with her mother and gone with her first husband to one of his parents' gallery openings in Los Angeles. Black, elegant, heavy with beadwork. Silk embroidery ringed the hem and climbed the length of the dress to the deep neckline. She remembered her mother-in-law handing her the box, the shock of being given a gift so absolutely perfect, as though the woman had been a fairy godmother, able to gauge her aspirations along with her size. And the attention: that night, the gallery lights glinting off the beads, Monica had felt as though she were as essential to this evening as the artist, and it seemed the dress itself had had the power to transform her.

"Do you like it?" Monica held it against her body, rocked her hips so the skirt swung.

Cordelia shrugged.

Monica was surprised at her disappointment. She'd imagined Cordelia reaching out to touch the hem with a single reverent finger.

"Your dad's parents bought this for me when you were a baby."

Cordelia's face was shuttered, as it always was when her father was mentioned, as if, knowing how little interest he had in her, she'd decided to show none in him. "It's ugly," she said finally.

"Oh, come on. It's not ugly. It cost over three hundred dollars."

The dress was the most expensive item Monica owned—except for her car, which had been her father's before he died. God knows why she'd brought the dress when the rest of her belongings went to her mother's basement. Did Monica think there would be any place within three hundred miles where a dress like this would be appropriate? Did she think Elliot was that kind of man?

"Want to try it on?" She slipped it off the hanger. "We can pin the straps."

"No," said Cordelia, her cheek pressed into her forearm. "You put it on."

Monica slid out of her down vest, peeled off the two sweaters and her jeans and her long underwear. She unhooked the heavy white nursing bra and slid the thick straps off her shoulders, pulled off her wool socks. She stood naked before the narrow mirror that hung on the closet door. The skin at her belly was still loose and puckered from Beatrice, her legs purplish and hairy. Her swollen breasts hung heavy, and despite the temperature, her nipples barely tightened.

"Well?" said Cordelia. "What are you waiting for?"

"Yes, yes." Monica slipped the dress over her head. The silk was so cold against her skin that she gasped, laughing, and her goosebumps rippled through the light fabric. "Last time I wore this it was ninety degrees in L.A.!" Monica's smile faded as she caught her reflection—the ridges of belly and hip under the fabric, her face, broad and splotchy hovering above—and she couldn't help feeling as though she'd done some violence to the dress by letting herself get like this.

"What did I wear that day?"

"It was just me and your dad."

Cordelia rolled away. "You look ugly."

Hurt flashed through Monica, then fury. This child, seven years old, wanted to wound her and knew exactly how. In a minute Cordelia was paging sulkily through a book.

Monica was beautiful—men were always telling her so—and at one time it had seemed only right that she should wear clothes like this. After all, Monica had at seventeen been proposed to in the waiting room of her dentist's office by a wealthy Frenchman who was visiting Santa Fe. "You are the most beautiful woman I have ever saw," he told her, and Monica had believed him. He'd waited for her to have her teeth cleaned, and she'd allowed him to take her to dinner at a restaurant on Canyon Road, a restaurant so expensive there were no prices on the menu. Her whole life in Santa Fe, and she'd never even known this restaurant existed. "This is French," he explained, and ordered escargot and old wine, pâté de lapin and roast duck avec sauce Roquefort, gratinée de Coquille St. Jacques. He insisted she try it all, kept passing his full fork across the table to her. "Beautiful women should eat beautiful food," he said, and she'd agreed. At the end of the night he drove her back to her mother's house and seemed resigned when she told him she couldn't marry him because she had to finish high school. She'd thought then that's what her future was: opportunity after opportunity unspooling around her.

Monica had therefore been ready two years later when

she began dating the man who would be her first husband, ready to exchange college and literature for proximity to wealth, ready to stand smiling with a glass of wine in his parents' galleries and to be kissed by old men who were influential in the art world. How embarrassed she'd been by her mother, with her faulty grammar and fake Anglicized name, her eagerness around his family, her transparent admiration of their money.

But Peter had liked her mother's accent, had liked explaining things to Monica. "My little conquistador," he called her. "My little Mexican." Peter felt he'd discovered Monica, plucked her out of a provincial existence, just as he'd begun to discover and show outsider artists: an autistic man who built intricate scale models of his neighborhood out of toothpicks and plaster, an elderly woman who made elaborate cut-paper crowd scenes with an X-ACTO knife, a soybean farmer who painted large canvases of sloppy, expressive horses. Always seeking in people overlooked value that he could commodify.

Monica hadn't, however, anticipated the pleasure he got in humiliating her—laughing at her in public for working her way through the classics or for not knowing framed Monet prints were tacky or for pretending to taste the difference in wine. Once, passing her as she read *War and Peace*, Peter yanked the book from her hands and snapped it shut. "You think reading Tolstoy means you're smart. But it just means you're literate." She hadn't been prepared for her own screaming rage, or an existence, which, even in the house his parents bought them with real art on the walls, still seemed cramped and insignificant. And above all she hadn't been prepared for pregnancy: Cordelia, a curled exacting weight in her womb, anchoring her in the life she'd chosen.

Monica looked up at the back of her daughter's dark, disapproving head on the crumpled pillow.

Well, hadn't Monica done her best to undo all that? It hadn't been easy to leave Peter, and it certainly hadn't been easy dating with a child. Regardless of how pretty you might be, add a kid to the mix and your value plunged. Surely she deserved some credit. She was lucky: Elliot Rios was brilliant, attractive, a good person. And most important, he was good to Cordelia. He'd bought her a globe for her birthday, let her wear his hand lens around her neck so she could inspect rocks and dirt. He'd made her a geology kit in a canvas sample bag with her name on the label. It contained sample bags, a Sharpie, a bottle of weak acid to test for calcite, and a roll of pH paper. Before she or anyone else drank anything, Cordelia determined its pH: Folgers coffee, milk, apple juice. "Really yellow," she'd announce before quaffing her juice with gusto. "Pure acid." Cordelia might take Elliot's kindness to her for granted, but Monica didn't have that luxury.

They'd had idyllic evenings together, evenings Monica could never have imagined when she was seventeen: the four of them clustered around the hissing Coleman lantern with its glowing green mantle, Beatrice nursing, Cordelia absorbed in her workbooks, filling in boxes and pasting stickers. Elliot would tell Monica about the things he'd found in the desert: a concrete Jesus in a gulch fifty miles from the nearest settlement, a fossilized camel jaw, pieces of a crashed World War II fighter plane. And she would tell him about the old man at the Lucky Token who'd called

her a sight for sore eyes, or how Cordelia had made a name
for herself at school for knowing to use a hyphen when she
could not fit the word into the end of the line.

Certainly these were pleasures her mother would never
understand with her cheap ideas about success and her
determined pursuit of gaiety. Monica's mother: hell-bent on
having the things that were unimaginable in the ranching
town where she'd grown up, liquor cabinets and televisions
and shag carpeting. Monica couldn't leave that desperation
behind fast enough.

Tonight, Monica decided, they'd all sleep in the foldout
bed together, the whole family, warm and close. She longed
for Elliot so deeply her throat ached.

"When you grow out of it, can I have your dress?" Cordelia's voice was gruff, her head still turned away.

"Sure," said Monica, feeling as though she'd won an
argument. "But I don't intend to grow out of it."

At first Monica thought the knocking was the wind, and
then with a surge of fear, the NASA engineer, come to get
her. She felt naked in the dress and pulled on her vest.

"Who could it be?" she asked Cordelia theatrically,
heart pounding. She glanced at the knife drawer.

On the step stood a little girl. She was wearing a purple
coat fringed with dingy fake fur on the hood; the hood was
down and the coat unzipped, and in her hand she carried
a smudged pink backpack. This was Amanda, from across
the way, and Monica smiled with relief, remembering the
pale watching face and her own absurd fear.

Monica knew Amanda from the schoolbus stop, where

(while Cordelia fussed over Beatrice, sneaking looks at the older kids) Amanda's big brother whipped at the ground—and Amanda—with a dangerous length of rope. She lived crammed in with her enormous relatives: parents, grandmother, uncle, brother. Amanda alone was thin, skinny, really. She reminded Monica of the baby orangutan at the Albuquerque zoo, startled-looking and wiry, bounding over her parents, who sat slumped and shapeless on the bare concrete floor.

"Amanda. Hi. What can I do for you?"

Amanda looked past Monica, as if waiting for the person she really wanted. Or maybe she was simply curious about how they lived. Wouldn't Monica like a peek into Amanda's trailer?—provided, of course, she wouldn't have to interact with anyone. But to walk around, inspect their things, judge—of course she'd like that.

Monica stepped aside to let the girl in from the wind, and, when Amanda entered without hesitation, reminded herself to warn Cordelia never to set foot in anyone's home alone, ever.

Amanda surveyed the trailer: the *Riverside Shakespeare*, Beatrice's wipes and diapers on the table, Beatrice herself, who'd wakened and stopped mawing her fist to greet Amanda with a pleasured gurgle.

Amanda looked Monica over. "Why are you wearing that?"

"It's my mom's best dress," Cordelia said, clambering down from the loft. "It cost over three hundred dollars."

Amanda frowned. "What's *she* doing here?" she asked Monica.

"I missed the bus," said Cordelia. She had brightened at

the arrival of the older girl. "And Elliot took our car. Are you here to play?"

Amanda didn't answer, just looked with discontent at her backpack.

"Is everything okay, Amanda?" Monica asked. "Why aren't you in school?"

Amanda straightened her shirt carefully under her coat, shrugged her skinny shoulders. "Why isn't *she* in school?"

Though Amanda was only nine, there was something teenagerish about her, something disturbing and sexual. She wore her sleek dark hair parted on the side, and it slipped off her shoulders and down her back. The white tips of her rather large ears poked though the silky curtain. In October, when it was still hot during the day, Monica had seen her in a bikini, spreading a towel on the hard-packed dirt to sunbathe. Another day, Amanda tucked the hem of her shirt into the neck and pulled it down so that it resembled a bra. Monica had watched over the edge of her book as the girl walked the length of the park, sashaying past the adults. Who knew what went on in that trailer?

Now Amanda bit her lip, looked around critically, then set her backpack on the bench seat and scooted in. She folded her hands on the table.

"Are you sick, honey? If you're sick, you should probably be home in bed."

When Amanda didn't answer, Monica abandoned the role of concerned, motherly neighbor. She sat at the table opposite her, pulled Beatrice to her lap, and waited. Cordelia sat beside Monica and folded her own hands, mirroring the older girl.

Amanda frowned at the baby. "She's got boogers all over

her face," she said, then seemed to lose interest. "Where's all your stuff? Don't you even got a TV?"

"No," said Monica, the same hint of pride in her voice she always had when asked this. "We don't watch TV." Stupid, showing off to a nine-year-old.

"You don't got heat either?"

"Well," Monica laughed. "Usually we have heat."

"It's *broken*." Cordelia shot an accusing glance at Monica. "And anyway," she told Amanda, placing a protective hand on Beatrice's forearm, "that's not boogers. She's just chapped."

Amanda pointed to the cardboard box that held Elliot's soil samples, each tied and carefully labeled. "What's that stuff?"

"My husband's samples. He's a geologist, which means he studies rocks. *Geo* means *rock* in Greek."

To that teachable moment, Amanda made no reply.

Several times over the months, they'd heard Amanda's mother yelling at her children from across the lot. "You get back here this minute or I don't want to see your face 'til you're twenty-one!" She'd shout breathlessly, bracing herself with a hand in the doorway, as if even standing were an enormous effort, and Monica and Elliot would laugh. Elliot did a strangely accurate impression of Amanda's mother, but made her seem both crazier and shriller than she was.

Funny, only now did Monica feel ashamed, mocking the woman's impotence, mocking the despair and futility that would lead to such a pointless threat.

"Can I get you anything?" She would have liked to offer the girl cookies and milk, but they'd just used the last of the milk and never had cookies.

Amanda scratched the back of her hand with a dirty nail, leaving dry tracks in the skin. "I thought maybe you'd want to buy something from me," she said finally.

"Buy something?"

"Is it expensive?" asked Cordelia.

Beatrice patted Monica's chest, ready to nurse.

Amanda indicated her backpack, distracted by the sight of Monica's breast as Monica maneuvered it out from the neck of the dress and into Beatrice's waiting mouth.

"What are you selling? Cookies? Magazines?" Amanda was still looking at her, and Monica suddenly felt very aware of the sensation of Beatrice's mouth pulling on her nipple. "So," she said. "Let's see what you have."

Amanda pulled her gaze away and unzipped her backpack. She arranged her wares on the table: a porcelain figurine of a milkmaid with a pail in her one remaining hand, a slack-needled odometer with loose wires, a worn pornographic magazine without a cover, a quarter-full bottle of shampoo. She turned the odometer slightly, to better display its virtues. "A dollar each. Except this"—she indicated the magazine—"is three dollars."

"Let me see that," said Cordelia, reaching for the magazine with its confusing fleshy close-ups.

Monica pushed it away. "It's inappropriate," she said, and Cordelia slumped, glowering.

Beatrice released Monica's nipple with a pop and strained toward the objects.

"Amanda, where did you get these things? Do they belong to you?"

Amanda scowled. "Yes," she said defensively, then added, "Duh."

Monica pictured the scenario: Amanda picking them from the park's dumpster, or, more likely, selecting them from the objects in her own home, turning them in her hands, evaluating them, stepping around calves and over-stuffed shoes, while her family sat oblivious, watching television. "Why are you selling them?"

"Why are you here?" Amanda countered. "At Shady Lanes."

"For my husband's work." Monica gestured again at the box of samples. The real question, Monica thought, was what Amanda needed the money for. Candy? Cigarettes? Maybe she was saving up for her escape. Maybe she simply wanted to have the money, to know she could make choices.

"Elliot's getting his Ph.D.," said Cordelia self-importantly. "In Santa Fe I lived one block from a swimming pool. We're going back there." She turned to Monica. "Aren't we going back there?"

"I'm not sure where we'll end up," said Monica.

"Elliot got in a fight with his advisor," Cordelia told Amanda, shaking her head with regret.

"Where did you hear that?" asked Monica. "It wasn't a real fight."

"It was," said Cordelia. "That's why it's taking so long for him to get his Ph.D."

For the first time Amanda looked mildly interested. "Did he punch him?"

"No," Cordelia said with scorn.

"It's not true, Cordelia," Monica said.

"It *is* true," Cordelia insisted. "You said. I heard you."

Monica was having trouble breathing. It wasn't Elliot's fault he'd had to switch topics and start all over, just because of some unfounded insinuations. No one ever said the words *falsified data*, but Elliot had insisted on starting all over, insisted it was the only way to clear his name. He'd made the decision on his own, swiftly, had refused to consider rethinking it. And now, a year later, his funding had run out, and he seemed further and further from completion. What if he never finished?

What if they stayed out here—or if not here, in some equally godforsaken place—and this was her whole life? What if there was no tenure-track job on the horizon? No trim green quad, no book-lined living room? Monica thought of their bank balance, dangerously low, no infusions in sight, thought about how there was nothing left to cut from their budget, how she didn't even know anymore if Elliot *was* brilliant. For all his flaws, Peter would never have found himself in Elliot's position, chipping away stubbornly at some theory without guarantee of success. Peter was too savvy and self-interested. Monica glimpsed a future as barren as the salt flats, and as she did, the enormity of her disloyalty to Elliot made her catch her breath.

"Well? Are you going to buy something or not?" Amanda asked. Her hand was on the milkmaid.

"I'm sorry, no," Monica said. Amanda was already packing the objects into her backpack.

What choice had Monica had, really? A lifetime of impossible hours at menial jobs, single-motherhood, her looks straining and distorting—that was no choice, not for her.

"Can you zip me?" Amanda waited, gazing over Monica's head while Monica fumbled with her coat, then she swung her backpack over her shoulder. Her lips were blue. Monica shivered.

Monica held the door open for the girl, and the wind yanked it back and forth in her hands. "Goodbye, Amanda." If Monica's voice was taut, the child didn't seem to notice. She jumped down the steps and into the wind. A dust devil whirled across the lot.

When Monica turned from the door, Cordelia had Beatrice on her lap, her skinny arms tight around the fat, smiling baby. She glared at Monica. Her brows were straight and thick, her father's brows. "You lied. I don't care what you do, but you shouldn't lie in front of a baby." Under those brows, Cordelia's eyes blazed.

"You don't know the first thing about it, Cordelia." Monica turned her back on her daughter, the blood hot in her face. From the window she watched as Amanda trudged across the dirt to the bathrooms. The child's shoulders were straight; she didn't seem defeated.

In a rush Monica pushed open the door, stuck her head into the wind. "Wait!" Amanda stopped, then after the briefest pause, turned. "Wait a minute. You may be able to do something with this." Monica was already sliding the straps off her shoulder.

"No!" cried Cordelia. "What are you doing?"

It was the right gesture, Monica saw now, to slough off everything that had come before, to give herself entirely to this life with Elliot. Monica imagined the dress tossed and wrinkled among Cordelia's clothes, the straps knotted, the hem dragging on the floor, beads cascading every time it was touched. She imagined her daughter wearing the dress, reminding her. No, Monica couldn't have borne it.

"How much is it?" Amanda eyed her from the doorway. "I have to save my money."

Arm across her breasts, Monica hunched to cover herself and stepped out of the dress. She pulled on her sweater and jeans, hurrying, suddenly afraid Amanda might leave without it. "It's a gift."

"You can't give it to her!" Cordelia cried. "You said it could be *mine!*"

Monica folded the dress into a square, the cold silk slipping against itself, handed it to Amanda.

Amanda shoved it into her backpack.

Cordelia's eyes filled with angry tears. "I don't really think it's ugly."

"We'll talk about this later, Cordelia."

This time Monica did not watch to see where Amanda went; she shut the door on the child with a profound sense of relief. Monica pulled Beatrice from Cordelia's arms—too hard—and bounced the baby on her hip, covered the warm scalp with kisses. She did not look at Cordelia.

Monica knew what she'd tell her daughter later: that Amanda didn't have nice things, that it was important to be kind to people who didn't have the same opportunities. And when Cordelia made a fuss, as she was sure to, then Monica would remind her sharply that the dress was hers, Monica's, to do with as she liked.

ELLIOT ARRIVED HOME that night after they'd all fallen asleep.

"Jesus," he said and rezipped his coat. "It's colder in here than outside."

Monica swung herself into his arms. The night air clung to him, and she shivered.

"You've been sitting in here like this? God, you're tough."

Monica smiled, pleased, as he kissed her hair. "How was it?" She took Elliot's jacket zipper in her fingers, pulled it down again and folded herself against his chest, breathing the cold, sour smell of wool and his week-old sweat, the dry scent of blowing dirt and sagebrush. "We missed you," she said happily into his sweater. "We missed you so much."

For nearly an hour, they stood outside—Monica stood, Elliot crouched—by the heating panel. Monica, lips and nose numb, held the flashlight while Elliot fiddled with the heater with gloved fingers.

"Did you find what you needed?"

One by one the stubborn screws loosened under Elliot's screwdriver. "I checked out a bunch of deposits that looked promising. Lots of gravel, lots of sediment, but in the end, nothing datable."

The relief she'd felt at his arrival drained, and now all the uneasiness of the day was upon her again. "You didn't find *anything* you could use?"

"Monica, honey, it's very complicated." He paused in his work, looked at her over his shoulder. "You have to find the right cross-cutting relationships, the right exposure. If it were *easy*, we'd already have this figured out." He spoke with forbearance, but she could see the irritation in his face. Hadn't he just wanted to come home to his snug family? And now here he was in the cold while his wife judged, harassed, blamed.

Elliot turned back to the heating panel. "Shine it here."

The wind had died down, and the desert was oddly quiet. Out on the dark highway, the sign was motionless on its post.

"I'm sorry," she said. She concentrated on holding the light steady. "It's just been an awful day."

At bedtime, Cordelia had asked, "Can I sleep with you and Beatrice tonight?"

"No," Monica had said. "You have your own bed. And Elliot will be home." She'd patted the mattress in the loft, and Cordelia, clumsy in her layers of sweaters and sweatpants, hauled herself up the ladder.

Monica kissed her daughter goodnight over the edge of the loft, descended, then stepped back up the ladder and placed her hand on Cordelia's back. "Listen. Tomorrow will be better, sweet pea."

Cordelia burrowed deeper into her sleeping bag, teeth chattering. "Okay," she said, then fell asleep with her usual ease.

Now Monica said, "I did something stupid today." She told Elliot about Amanda's visit. "And then after her sales pitch, I gave her my dress." Elliot's hands cast outsized shadows against the side of the trailer. He frowned into the panel. "My best dress. Out of the blue. I don't know what I was thinking."

Elliot held the screwdriver in his teeth and peered. "Hold on." He seemed to be counting wires. Elliot pinched a wire in his fingers and looked up at her, his face lit by the edge of the flashlight beam. "Your judgment was impaired, maybe. Onset of hypothermia. I'm amazed you didn't start a fire in the sink."

"I shouldn't have given it away. Or I should have given it to Cordelia. If anything, it belongs to Cordelia."

Elliot shrugged. "You felt bad for the kid. It's a just dress. You don't even wear dresses."

Once, when they were hiking, Monica had picked up a beautiful rock, worn smooth by some ancient creek and intricately marked, as if with a fine-nibbed pen. She'd handed it to Elliot, expecting him, the geologist, to see what made it beautiful. "Hm," he'd said, glancing at it absently. "Limestone." And with that both she and the rock were dismissed, while he returned to his thoughts about contact formations and pre-Cambrian flood plains. Monica's feelings had been hurt, but she hadn't shown it. His thoughts were simply on a grander scale than hers, concerned not just with the minutia of a single life, or even of their species; he was concerned with the life of the planet itself.

Elliot was right. What, really, had Monica given away? An old dress. A relic of difficult times. So why, then, was she angry?

"I should have given it to Cordelia," Monica insisted, and she felt her voice rise. If she wasn't careful, she might cry.

"She won't remember," said Elliot. "Kids don't."

Maybe Cordelia wouldn't remember. It was possible. But despite being a child, Cordelia knew more about Monica's first marriage than anyone else, knew how bad it had gotten and how long Monica had stayed. Cordelia never talked about those days or about what she'd seen, never discussed what it was like to hear her mother yelling and sobbing and smashing plates; a mother could almost fool herself into believing a child could forget these things.

It occurred to Monica that now Cordelia herself was

the only thing left from that old life. When she'd taken off the dress today, Monica hadn't even felt cold, so filled was she with the dark exhilaration of punishing Cordelia. In giving away Cordelia's lovely, meaningless inheritance, she'd made an adversary of her seven-year-old daughter, and now even that she held against her.

The park was dark, the trailers asleep, except for Amanda's, where the blue light of a TV glowed, shifting and desolate.

"I should go over there. I should go explain to Amanda's mother that I made a mistake. Right now. Before they go to bed."

"Monica." Elliot laughed. "You can't do that."

"Of course I can." Of course she could. She'd knock at the door, wait while Amanda's mother pulled herself to her feet, switched on a lamp, and made her way across the carpet. Monica would step into the warm trailer, introduce herself, explain, and Amanda's mother would fetch the dress. The interaction would be awkward, perhaps, but nothing Monica couldn't smooth over, and it wouldn't matter because Monica had the chance to make things right. "I'm so glad to finally meet you," Monica would say. "Amanda's always welcome at our place. And you, too. We should have coffee."

"I'm going." She pushed the flashlight at Elliot, but he wouldn't take it. The beam danced across the dirt. "*Here*," she said.

"Come on, Monica. Think about it. You're going to go over there and snatch back something you gave to a little kid? That mother of hers is going to drop dead of a coronary any minute, and you're going to go fight with her about an old dress in the middle of the night?"

"It doesn't mean anything to Amanda," Monica said, and as she said it she knew she wouldn't go. "It doesn't even fit her."

"It doesn't fit Cordelia, honey." He put a hand on her leg, patted her briefly. "You're not thinking."

"What do you know?" Monica said with bitterness she hadn't realized she felt. "You don't even know Cordelia. You're not her father. You've just met her."

Elliot's hands stilled on the wire. He turned, face wide open and hurt. "That's not fair, Monica. I care about her very much."

He wouldn't be able to see her beyond the flashlight's beam. Monica bit her lip, glad for the dark.

"That's not fair," he repeated.

Elliot returned his attention to the heater, and they stood in silence. Out on the highway a car passed. After a time he clipped a wire.

"Fixed." He dangled a twisted length of wire in his gloved fingers. His voice was stiff. "The lead to the thermostat had corroded. The heat should kick in now."

They'd make it up, she and Elliot, find each other under the covers as the chill ebbed around them. Outside, the wind would pick up again, and in Amanda's trailer the television would flicker all night. In the morning, Cordelia would awaken early. She would look down from the loft at her family: her mother, her stepfather, and between them, arms flung wide, her little sister. Cordelia would forever feel on the outside, Monica saw, and Monica herself had put her there, because a person couldn't live with that kind of reproach. It would only get harder between them, Monica saw that, too; Cordelia's judgments would become more pointed, Monica would rankle ever more under her sharp eye. But Cordelia wouldn't know any of this, not yet. Tomorrow, while her family slept below her in the gray dawn light, she would place her cheek back on the pillow and watch them, waiting for them to stir, and she wouldn't even notice that she was finally warm.

T H E

F I V E   W O U N D S

⭐

THIS YEAR AMADEO PADILLA IS JESUS. THE HERMANOS HAVE been practicing in the dirt yard behind the morada, which used to be a filling station. People are saying that Amadeo is the best Jesus they've had in years, maybe the best since Manuel Garcia.

Here it is, just Holy Tuesday, and even those who would rather spend the evening at home watching their satellite TVs are lined up in the alley, leaning in, fingers curled around the chain-link, because they can see that Amadeo is bringing something special to the role.

This is no silky-haired, rosy-cheeked, honey-eyed Jesus, no Jesus-of-the-children, Jesus-with-the-lambs. Amadeo is pockmarked and bad-toothed, hair shaved close to a scalp scarred from fights, roll of skin where skull meets thick neck. You name the sin, he's done it: gluttony, sloth, fucked a second cousin on the dark bleachers at the high school.

Amadeo builds the cross out of heavy rough oak instead of pine. He's barefoot like the rest of the hermanos, who have rolled up the cuffs of their pants and now drag the arches of their feet over sharp rocks behind him. The Hermano Mayor—Amadeo's grand-tío Tíve, who owns the electronics store, and who surprised them all when he chose his niece's lazy son (because, he told Yolanda, Amadeo could use a lesson in sacrifice)—plays the pito, and the thin piping notes rise in a whine. A few hermanos swat their backs with disciplinas. Unlike the others, though, Amadeo does not groan, and he is shirtless, his tattooed back broad under the still-hot sun.

Today, he woke with the idea of studding the cross with nails to give it extra weight, and this is what people watch: he holds the hammer with both hands high above his head, brings it down with a crack. The boards bounce; the sound strikes sharply off the outside wall of the morada.

Amadeo has broken out in a sweat, and they all take note. Amadeo sweats, but not usually from work. He sweats when he eats, he sweats when he drinks too much. Thirty-three years old, the same as Our Lord, but Amadeo is not a man with ambition. Even his mother will tell you that. Yolanda still cooks for him, pushes one plate across the table at him and another at whatever man she's got with her.

And now here comes old Manuel Garcia, dragging his bad foot up the alley, his wounded hands curled at his sides.

He must have heard about the show Amadeo is putting on, because when else does he exert himself, except to buy liquor at the Peerless? As he nears the morada, the people part to give him a spot against the chain-link, right there in the middle. Now, instead of watching Amadeo, they watch Manuel. He coughs wetly between strikes of the hammer.

Manuel Garcia is old, but still a legend: in 1962 he begged the hermanos to use nails, and he hasn't been able to open or close his hands since. It's true the legend has soured a little, now that he hasn't been able to work for forty-five years and has been kept alive by the combined generosity of the hermandad, the parish, and the state, and shows no sign of dying. Some people have stopped paying their tithes for this very reason. Some have even gone so far as to say that maybe the man was suicidal, and a death wish is not the same as devotion, even if they look alike.

Regardless, only Manuel Garcia is qualified to judge this new Christ, and it appears that he has arrived at his verdict, because he coughs again, wet and low, dislodges something deep in his throat, and spits it through a space in the fence so it lands just inches from Amadeo and his cross.

DRIVING HOME, AMADEO TRIES to regain the clarity he felt when pounding nails, but hand and foot and universe are no longer working together. When the gears scrape, he hits the steering wheel with his fist and swears and hits it again. This last week was the most important in Jesus's life. This is the week everything happened. So Amadeo should be thinking of higher things when his daughter shows up eight months pregnant. Angel sits in front of the house on the bumper of the old truck, waiting for him. He hasn't seen her in more than a year, but he's heard the news from his mother, who heard it from Angel.

White tank top, black bra, gold cross pointing the way to her breasts in case you happened to miss them. Belly as hard and round as an adobe horno. The buttons of her jeans are unsnapped to make way for its fullness, and also to indicate how it got that way in the first place. Her birthday is this week, falls on Good Friday. She'll be fifteen.

"Shit," Amadeo says when he pulls in and yanks the parking brake. She must not have seen his expression, because she gets up, smiles, and waves with both hands. The rosary swings on his rearview mirror, and Amadeo watches as, beyond it, his daughter advances on him, stomach outthrust. She pauses, half turns, displays her belly.

She's got a big gold purse with her, and a duffel bag, he sees, courtesy of Marlboro. Amadeo gets out. Her hug is straight-on, belly pressing into him.

"I'm fat, huh? I barely got these pants and already they're too small."

"Hey." He pats his daughter's back between her bra straps, then, because he is thinking of her stomach, thinking of her pregnant, steps away. "What's happening?" he says. He realizes it's too casual, but he can't afford to let her think she's welcome, not this week, Passion Week, and with his mother away.

"My mom and me got in a fight, so she dropped me off. I didn't know where you and Gramma were."

Amadeo hooks his thumbs in his pockets, looks up at the house, then back at the road. The sun is gone now, the sky a wan green at the horizon.

"A fight?"

Angel sighs. "I don't know why she's gotta be all judging me, trying to act all mature. Whatever," she says without bitterness. "What me and the baby needs right now is a support system."

"A what?" The clarity is long gone. He shakes his head. "I'm real busy," he says, like an actor portraying regret. "Now's not a good time."

Angel doesn't look hurt, just interested. "Why?"

She lifts her duffel and begins to walk toward the door. "My mom's not here," he calls. He's embarrassed to tell her, embarrassed by the fervor that being a penitente implies. "I'm carrying the cross this year. I'm Jesus."

"And I'm the Virgin Mary. Where's Gramma, well?" She holds the screen open with her hip, waiting for him to unlock the door.

"Over there in Vegas with her boyfriend."

Angel laughs, a raucous teenage laugh. "We're all *kinds* of Virgin Mary."

Yolanda is making her way across Nevada in a travel trailer with Cal Wilson, and, depending on how things go, she could be home tomorrow or in a month. As if to check if she's coming, Amadeo turns and sees Manuel Garcia standing in the road, watching him and his daughter.

The old man's ruined face spreads into a grin around collapsed teeth. Loose, dirty pants are cinched at his waist with a belt, his wounded hands before him. Amadeo's mouth goes dry.

Up on the step, Angel is saying, "I was all, Whatever, take me to Gramma's if you want to. She don't care."

Amadeo turns from Manuel Garcia. He takes the duffel from Angel's hand and pushes open the aluminum door. "Come on."

—

THAT NIGHT, ANGEL CHATTERS about food groups as she makes dinner—a can of chili dumped over an underdone squash and a package of frozen cheese bread—then takes over the TV. She talks to her belly as she watches *America's Next Top Model.* "See, baby? That heifer is going *home.* You can't be like that to your girls and win the game."

Amadeo sits at the other end of the couch, uneasy. He wipes his palms along his thighs, works his tongue inside his mouth. Three times he looks out the front window, but the old man is gone. With a sudden stitch in his gut, Amadeo thinks of Tío Tíve. He can't know that Angel's here and pregnant for all the world to see.

"So," Amadeo says. "Your mom's probably gonna want you back soon, no?"

"Nah. I'm staying here with you and Gramma awhile. I gotta teach her she's not the only one in my life."

Amadeo kneads his thigh. He can't tell her to leave. Yolanda would kill him. He just wishes that Yolanda were here.

She and Angel are pretty close; Yolanda sends the girl checks, twenty-five here, fifty there, and a couple of times a year the two go shopping at the outlets near Santa Fe. Amadeo tries to remember the last time he was alone with his daughter, but can't. Two or three Christmases ago, maybe; he remembers sitting awkwardly in this same room asking Angel about her favorite subjects while Yolanda was at the grocery store or the neighbors'.

Amadeo is having trouble breathing. "Maybe you could

visit when my mom gets home." A needle of guilt slides into his side.

Angel doesn't seem to have heard him. "I mean, the woman's all preaching to me about how I messed up and why couldn't I learn from her mistake, but what am I gonna do now, huh? I mean, I get it. It's gonna hurt like hell and I'm missing prom and did you know I probably won't get to sleep a whole night until it's three years old? I'll be *eighteen* by then."

Angel looks like her mother. Amadeo doesn't remember Marissa acting this young back then. Marissa was sixteen, Amadeo eighteen, but they felt old, he is sure of that. Her parents had been angry and ashamed, but had thrown a baby shower for the young couple anyway. Amadeo had enjoyed being at the center of things: congratulated by her relatives and his, handed tamales and biscochitos on paper plates by old women who were willing to forgive every-thing in exchange for a church wedding. He stood to sing for them, nodding at Marissa: "This is dedicated to my baby girl." *Bendito, bendito, bendito sea Dios, los ángeles can-tan y daban a Dios.* They all clapped, the old ladies dabbing their eyes, Yolanda blowing kisses across the room.

Later, of course, after there was no wedding, no mov-ing in together, after Angel was born and learned to walk and talk—with no help from Amadeo—he was relieved by how easily the obligation slipped from his shoulders. The old women shook their heads, resigned; they should have known better than to expect anything from Amadeo, from men in general. "Even the best of them aren't worth a darn," his grandmother used to say. ("Not you, hijito," she'd say kindly to Amadeo. "You're worth a darn.") By the time Angel was five and Amadeo had moved with his mother back to the little town where he'd grown up and where their family still lived, he felt lucky to have been let off the hook.

As though answering a question, Angel says, "I didn't drop out of school for real. I'm gonna start back up after the baby comes, so don't worry." She looks at him, waiting.

Amadeo realizes that he forgot to worry, forgot even to wonder. "Good. That's good." He gets up, rubs his shorn head with both hands. "You got to have school."

She's still looking at him, demanding something: reassurance, approval. "I mean, I'm serious. I'm really going back." Then she's off, talking about college and success and following her dreams, the things she hears at the parenting class she goes to at the clinic with other girls her age. "I got to invest in myself if I'm gonna give him a good life. You won't see me like my mom, just doing the same old secretary job for ten years. I'm doing something big." She turns to her belly. "In't that right, hijito?"

This depresses the hell out of Amadeo. He opens a beer and guzzles half of it before he remembers who he is this week. "Fuck," he says, disgusted with himself, and pours it down the drain.

Angel looks up at him from the couch. "You better clean up your mouth. I don't want him hearing you say that. He can hear every little thing you say."

"Fuck," Amadeo says again, because it's his house, but he says it quietly, and thinks about the sound passing through his daughter's body to the child inside.

—

THE TEACHER OF ANGEL's parenting class has arranged for someone to drive her into Española at two-thirty every afternoon. Angel is up by seven. Amadeo can hear her, clattering dishes, the TV going. Midmorning, she's in the shower. The pipes hiss and gurgle in the wall near his head. He flops over in his limp bed, tries not to think of her, the naked lumps of flesh, but he can't help it. *Christ's pain*, he reminds himself. *Think of that.* Each day, Amadeo practices his face in the bathroom mirror after he showers, water running down his forehead. He spreads his arms, makes the muscles in his face tighten and fall, tries to learn the nuances of suffering. To think of his daughter makes him queasy. It makes him queasier to think about whoever got Angel this way. This is not a detail that made it into the story Amadeo heard from his mother, but he doesn't need facts to picture it: some Española cholo dealing meth from the trunk of his lowrider. When he finally hears Angel leave, Amadeo gets up. He watches from the kitchen window until the teacher's car is out of sight, then sinks into the chair in relief and eats the cold eggs and bacon she has left out for him.

He's on the couch with a Coke and the remote balanced on his thighs when Angel comes home. As she swings her backpack to the linoleum, she looks at him, surprised. "Aren't you working?"

"It's Holy Wednesday," he says.

"Where you working now?"

"It's slow. I'm waiting to hear."

"Huh." Angel drops to the couch, then scoots down so her neck is cricked and her belly high.

Who is she to criticize? "I'm getting something together with Anthony Vigil. We're doing a business, outfitting cars for the races down in Albuquerque." Actually, this *was* the plan—Amadeo enjoyed working with Anthony, and was good at it, reboring the engine, replacing the metal front and sides with fiberglass, removing what wasn't essential. Yolanda had been glad that Amadeo was "getting involved" and had offered to give them what she could afford to start them out. But in the end Anthony partnered with his cousin. "No offense, man," Anthony told Amadeo, "but in a business you gotta know your partner's going to show up."

"Huh," Angel says again. After a moment, "You still sing ever?"

"Nah." Not for years, though at one time he'd thought he could actually go somewhere with it. He's grateful to Angel for remembering; Amadeo offers her his Coke.

She shakes her head. "It'll dissolve his baby bones."

From eleven on, Angel was a little shit: surly, talking nasty, applying dark lip liner like she was addicted to it. Amadeo remembers when she was younger; he looked forward to when she'd come from Española to stay with him and his mom, enjoyed taking her out for the day, showing her off to his friends. He felt like a good influence, teaching her how to check the oil and eat ribs and not to listen to Boyz II Men. She was sweet then, eager to please, riding in the truck, fiddling with the radio, asking him at each song, "Is this good? Do you like this one?" When he'd nod, she'd settle back and try to sing along, listening hard, each word coming a little too late. Sometimes Amadeo would sing, too, his voice filling the cab, and Angel would look up at him, delighted.

Now she resembles that child again—her cheeks full and pink—but there's something frightening about her. It's as though she's reentered the world, proud to be a member in good standing. Now she regales Amadeo with facts she's learned in her parenting class, facts about fluids and brain stems and genitals. "Like, did you know he had his toes before he even got his little dick?"

Amadeo looks at her, surprised, then back at the TV. "Why you gotta tell me that?"

Angel faces him enthusiastically, grinning around her big white teeth, one foot tucked under her belly. "Weird, huh, that there's a dick floating around in me? Do you ever think about that? How Gramma is the first girl you had your dick in?"

"The fuck. That's disgusting." Amadeo is horrified; this is his *daughter.*

"Jesus, too," she says, singsong. "Jesus had his stuff in Mary." She laughs. "Couple of virgins. There's something for your research." She settles back into the couch, pleased.

Angel has seemed only mildly interested in Passion Week, which is a relief to Amadeo, and an irritation. "So it's like a play?" she asks.

"It's *not* a play—it's real. More real . . ." He doesn't know how to explain it to her. More real even than taking Communion, Tío Tíve had said months ago when he sat with Amadeo at the Lotaburger and offered him the part. Tío Tíve looked at him severely. "You got a chance to thank Jesus, to hurt with Him just a little."

Angel asks, "They're going to whip you and stuff? Like, actually hard?"

He's proud, can't keep the smile from creeping in. "Yeah."

"My friend Lisette cuts, but she just does it for attention."

"It's not like that. It's like a way to pray."

Angel whistles low. "Crazy." She seems to be thinking about this, turns a pink crocheted cushion slowly in her hands.

Amadeo waits, exposed.

"So it's gonna hurt."

He tries to formulate the words to explain to Angel that the *point* is to hurt, to see what Christ went through for us, but he's tongue-tied and shy about saying these things, as shy as he'd be if he were explaining it to his old friends. And he isn't even sure he's got it right. But here it is: his chance to prove to them all—and God, too—everything he's capable of. "But it's a secret, right? You can't go tell nobody back in Española."

"Why?"

"The Church don't agree. You just can't say anything."

"Can I see it? The morada?"

He'd like her to see it, to see what he's at the center of. "Tío Tíve don't let women in there. You can go to Mass at the church. You can be in the procession."

Angel scrunches her face. "Can't I just see it? Once? You're *Jesus*, aren't you?"

"Tío Tíve would kill me."

She's good-natured in her pleading, all smiles. "Come *on*."

"Women can't go in. And besides . . ." Before he can stop himself, he glances down at her belly. Her face slackens and she turns back to the TV. When Amadeo looks again, she's crying soundlessly, her face blotchy and ugly, mascara running down her cheeks.

It's not his fault. He didn't tell her to be a girl. He didn't tell her to get knocked up. They were doing so well, she was showing some interest, he was feeling so good. "It's just a building. It's mostly empty, anyway."

But now Angel's shoulders rock. She has her fist pressed over her mouth, and she's still not making a sound.

"Hey. Hey, don't cry." He turns awkwardly on the couch, pats the shoulder near him.

When she speaks, it's with a gasp. "You think I'm too dirty for your morada. Is that it? Too dirty for your morada, too dirty for prom, too dirty for everything."

An image flashes: Angel naked, sweaty and grunting with some boy. "You're not dirty," he says.

Guilt thick as tar bubbles in his gut, and suddenly he's nineteen again and it's summer, and he's with Marissa in her parents' backyard. They stretch out by the kiddie pool, beers warming in their hands and in the sun, while Angel slaps the water. Amadeo holds a plastic dinosaur, and he's making it dance on the surface of the water, while Angel, with her damp black curls and lashes, slick red smile and swollen diaper, laughs her throaty laugh. They're talking about Marissa's older sister's new trailer—two bedrooms, full bath, cream carpet—and Marissa says she wouldn't mind a trailer, they could get a trailer, used at first, and beside them Angel splashes, a blade of grass stuck to her chest. Amadeo says, "You won't catch me living in no trailer. Besides, they just lose value," and Marissa says, stubbing out her cigarette emphatically in the grass, "It's not that I wouldn't rather have a house, but when? And we gotta be saving if we ever want to have a place of our own—are you even saving *anything*?" This is when the fight starts, escalates. Amadeo accuses Marissa of getting pregnant just so he'll have to take care of her, and he calls her *dirty, dirty whore*. (She isn't, he knows that, hasn't done any more than he has, but ever since she slept with him he can't look at her the same way.) Then they're both on their feet, and he slaps her, hard across the upper arm, which is bare and exposed in her sleeveless shirt. Marissa staggers back, reaches behind her into air to steady herself, finds no hold, falls.

Amadeo looks at his hitting hand, horrified. But if he were honest he might admit that even as he moved to hit her he knew he could stop himself and knew he was going to do it regardless. The real surprise is the shock on her face, proof that he can act on the world.

Marissa stands. The skin on her arm turns white then red where his palm made contact.

"You asshole! Don't you ever hit me again." She screams at him, throwing plastic buckets and toys. Some strike him, some miss and fall to the grass. Amadeo wishes she'd kill him. But she keeps yelling, "Don't you ever hit me again!"

And it is that word, *again*, that terrifies him, as if by uttering it she opens up the possibility that he has it in him to do this again—even, somehow, makes it inevitable. From the kiddie pool, Angel looks up at her parents, eyes wide and black and unwavering.

"Don't you walk away!" Marissa yells, and Amadeo turns just long enough to see her grab the baby, too roughly, Angel's head jerking back as Marissa swings her onto her hip, water from the baby's sodden diaper spreading dark across her shirt, her denim cutoffs, down her short brown legs. She's yelling at him, calling him names, and he's thinking of how loud her voice must be so near Angel's soft pink ear. Even as he starts the truck, Amadeo doesn't think he'll go through with it. His breath is ragged, he's shaking, and he's on Paseo de Oñate before he realizes he's somehow still gripping the dinosaur.

Now, fourteen years later, Amadeo turns to Angel, who cries into her hands. He looks at his watch. Almost eleven. He touches her shoulder again. "Come on. Let's go."

THE MORADA IS NOT much to look at. Outside there's still the dark skeleton of a sign on a pole from when it was a filling station, the bright plastic panels long gone, and two blank pumps. During the day, strangers passing by will pull in for gas and look around, confused by the trucks parked in front, before heading straight through town to the Shell station on the highway. Tonight the parking lot is deserted.

Inside, the cinder-block walls are painted white, and a few benches face the front. The only thing worth looking at is the crucifix, and Amadeo watches Angel take it in. She walks the periphery of the room, stopping at various points to gaze at the man on the cross. This Christ is not like the Christ in the church: shiny plastic plaster, chaste beads of blood where crown meets temple, expression exquisite, prissy, a perfect balance of compassion and suffering and—yes, it's there—self-pity. No, this Christ, the wooden Christ nailed up on the morada wall, is ancient and bloody. There is violence in the very carving: chisel marks gouge belly and thigh, leave fingers and toes stumpy. The contours of the face are rough, ribs sharp, the body emaciated. Someone's real hair hangs limply from the statue's head. The artist did not stop at five wounds but inflicted his brush generously on the thin body. And there are the nails. Three. One in each hand, one skewering the long, pale feet. Amadeo feels his own palms throb and ache.

When he hears a noise, for a moment he thinks it comes from outside, but it is closer, inside the morada. A rustle. Amadeo looks from his daughter to the statue.

The suffering is garish under the buzzing fluorescent bulb: blood flows down Christ's pale neck and torso and knees, smears the cross and the wall behind Him, every wound deep and effusive. This statue's pain is personal and cruel, and He's not bearing it with perfect grace. Suddenly, Amadeo knows that the statue on the crucifix is a living man, a living witness to his transgression. He looks wildly from the statue to Angel, then back, heart pounding and hands trembling.

"There aren't no Baby Jesuses here, are there?" Angel observes. No Blessed Mother, either, no audience of saints. "I guess it's not a good idea for Baby Jesus to have to see hisself later." Her voice is tired. She taps her belly distractedly, walks a few steps, stops. "I wouldn't want my baby to know."

Amadeo waits in dread for the statue to move, to lift His head. To fix Amadeo with His eyes.

Angel makes her slow way around the room again, stopping every few feet, head tilted. She turns to him, face pale and slack, and he's startled when she asks, "So you really want to know what it feels like?" With her finger she traces a trickle of blood down the bound wooden feet. "Why?"

He can't say it, but his answer is this: he needs to know if he has it in him to ask for the nails, if he can get up there in front of the whole town and do a performance so convincing he'll transubstantiate right there on the cross into something real. He looks at the statue. Total redemption in one gesture, if only he can do it right.

Angel, no longer waiting for his answer, shrugs and turns to the door. As he watches it shut behind her, a longing wells in him so rich and painful that he must touch the wall to steady himself. At the front of the room, Jesus hasn't moved, wholly absorbed in His own pain.

Amadeo switches off the light, checks the lock on the morada door. Angel heaves herself into the cab of the truck, looking like a kid in her too-large jacket. She yawns, makes an effort to talk about other things all the way home, and Amadeo does not tell her what he sees that keeps him silent: Manuel Garcia, standing on the other side of the road in front of the dark windows of the drugstore, watching.

Since early morning, Manuel Garcia has been sitting on a lawn chair in front of the house, scratching his balls with his stiff-curled claw. When Amadeo gets up after eleven, Angel is planted at the table with a glass of milk, watching the old man watch the house. She doesn't shift her eyes from the window when Amadeo ambles in, rubbing his head with the heel of his hand. "Who is that, well? Is he retarded or something?"

Amadeo considers pulling on a shirt, then decides not

to. He bangs out the front door and across the yard, working his fists, limbs loose with adrenaline. "Hey, man. Go on home. You're scaring my daughter."

Manuel Garcia gazes up through pink eyes. "The puta whore. No Jesus never lived in a house of putas."

"You watch your mouth, viejo."

"Puta whore mama y puta whore daughter." Manuel Garcia smiles, because he knows he's an old man and cannot be hit. He's spent his whole life making people uncomfortable. He scratches his balls again and squints into the sun behind Amadeo.

"Go on home," Amadeo says again, suddenly afraid, as if the old man had the power to work evil, though, of course, he doesn't.

"I seen you last night. You know I seen you. Bringing her in the santuario."

Amadeo considers denying it, then considers pushing the old man into the dirt, grinding the lumpy skull beneath his heel.

As though he'd read Amadeo's mind, Manuel coughs and spits, nearly hitting Amadeo's work boot. Amadeo flinches, and the old man laughs. "Hija de Jesús, shaking her nalgas until someone gives it to her good."

Amadeo steps toward Manuel. "Shut your mouth."

"I'm thinking what your uncle will say when he finds out a whore been in the morada." He blinks red-rimmed eyes, smiles blandly. Suddenly he lunges forward, pointing his finger at Amadeo. "You watch how quick they cut you down from that cross," he hisses. "They'll cut you down fast."

Amadeo thinks he might throw up. He kicks the dirt.

"Don't you come here again," he says, and turns back to the house.

Manuel Garcia calls to Amadeo's retreating back, "No Jesus never defiled the santuario!"

Amadeo lets the screen door slam. "What'd he say?" Angel asks, still watching out the window. Sitting there, plump and content, she seems inviolable in her impending motherhood. He tries to remind himself how young she is. But he's furious at her, for giving Manuel Garcia something to sneer at, for tainting his Passion Week with her pregnancy and her personality.

Amadeo goes to his room. The bed is unmade, clothes piled on the floor. He's angrier now—look at him, living here like a surly teenager—and comes back out to reclaim the living room. He doesn't know what to do with his hands. Hit a wall, break something, put his daughter in her place. "Don't you even got a boyfriend?"

Angel turns and looks at him like he's stupid. "What do you think?"

"Didn't your mom never teach you not to sleep around?"

"All the girls in my parenting class, not one of them has a guy that matters. Not one. You think you mattered?"

Amadeo is shaking. "You shouldn't have come here. You think you have a right to just barge in my house and make yourself at home."

Angel's eyes widen, and then she narrows them once more. Slowly, enunciating every word, she says, *"It's not your house."*

Amadeo thumps the table with his fist and retreats to his room.

———

THAT EVENING, the phone rings, and Angel calls to him, "Dad?"

When Amadeo emerges, his pulse throbs in his neck, and he avoids her eyes as he accepts the phone. Someone mutters a blessing and hangs up without identifying himself. It takes a moment for Amadeo to recognize the priest. The priest will spend tomorrow at home; he said his Mass this evening, and will have no part in what happens on Calvario. Amadeo replaces the receiver. He wonders if the priest can sense Amadeo failing everyone.

Angel has heated a sausage pizza for dinner. She's already in her spot on the couch, eating. She raises her plate. "Dinner? Dairy, meat, grain, vegetable. All four groups." Her voice is conciliatory.

Amadeo considers sitting next to his daughter and trying to eat, but he isn't hungry, and he has to practice. There is so little time left.

In the bathroom he works on his Christ face, but his downturned mouth and drooping eyes are mawkish and ridiculous. Through the pink polyester lace at the window, he sees Manuel Garcia in his lawn chair, and he tries to picture how it will be tomorrow, the hermanos all dressed up, everyone watching Amadeo Padilla pretend he has what it takes to be Jesus.

When the screen door slams, Amadeo watches from the window as Angel picks her way in bare feet down the drive to where Manuel Garcia sits, gazing at the house. She hands the old man a paper plate: the leftover pizza. Amadeo cannot see the old man's face under his hat, but he's saying something. She waves him off dismissively and turns away.

Manuel says something else, and she stops, turns, walks back to him. She looks angry, glances at the house, and for a moment Amadeo wonders if she's going to betray him to Manuel, tell the old man everything he's done: left her to rental after rental, money always tight, the long series of Marissa's boyfriends—some worse even than Amadeo—around his daughter.

But she doesn't say anything, just shakes her head slowly and is still.

She stands before Manuel in her bare feet. The old man sets the paper plate in the dirt beside his chair, then gestures, impatient. She takes a step closer. Her face is stony; she looks away from Manuel to, it seems, a spot across the road in the Romeros' yard. Manuel leans forward.

Amadeo is still watching when his daughter lifts her shirt above her belly, then higher.

Her breasts are too big for the black lace bra, her maternity jeans low. Her belly glows red in the sunset, impossibly round and swollen. Amadeo sees her belly button protruding and remembers the same thing with Angel's mother, how toward the end he'd tongue the lump of it while he touched her down there.

Angel doesn't blink.

Manuel extends a gnarled brown hand, places it against her belly. Reaches out with the other. Cups her belly in both his hands, moves them over the surface of it. Angel stares at the Romeros' yard.

Amadeo could go outside now, put a stop to the terrible

thing that is happening, but he stays, one hand touching the pink lace. His legs are weak. When the old man closes his eyes, so does Amadeo.

ON THIS LAST NIGHT, he is supposed to stay awake, walking outside through the Garden of Gethsemane, thinking about his soul and about salvation. He is supposed to fast, to steel himself, to be betrayed, to hear the cock's crow. In houses all over town, hermanos are on their knees, leather thongs bound around their thighs, murmuring about suffering and gratitude, yearning for pain.

But Amadeo focuses on the sick sensation of his dick in his jeans, on willing it to shrivel up and fall off as the scene replays in his head: Manuel's hands on his daughter's body. Pacing the length of his room, he finishes a six-pack, then moves on to the next, and the image still won't dissolve.

The television is off, the house silent. In the living room, Angel sits on the couch, staring at the wall. She doesn't look up at him. "He's not gonna tell. You can have your Jesus day."

"I never asked you to do that. I never asked you for nothing." His voice wavers.

Angel sighs. "It doesn't matter."

He can't tell if she believes this or if she is saying it for him, and he doesn't know which is worse. Angel points the remote at the TV, and the bright sound of a commercial floods the room. "Just forget about it, okay?"

"I never asked you to do that." It's a plea, too quiet to hear over the sound of the television.

Amadeo realizes he's drunk.

"We can't be fighting." She pats the couch, glances quickly at him. "Look, it's *Law and Order.*"

Amadeo hesitates, then drops beside her, grateful, exhausted. He takes a handful of chips when she passes him the bag, thinking about the new feeling swelling in him: he's warm and swaddled, buoyed by forgiveness, suddenly too tired to sleep, too tired to move. They watch the show together, then a second and a third, until Angel goes to bed.

AMADEO WAKES TO ANGEL calling him and the sun streaming through the window. Good Friday.

They gather at the base of Calvario. Nearly two miles to the top, and Amadeo will walk barefoot, dragging the cross. He trembles and his upper lip sweats, though the morning air is cool. The hermanos help Tío Tíve unload the cross from the bed of his Ford, three of them sharing the weight. All the Lenten preparations are for this: the hermanos have washed their white pants, braided their disciplinas the old way, from the thick fibers of yucca leaves, mended rips in the black hoods they will wear to insure their humility in this reenactment. When the pito sounds three times—the cock's crow—Tío Tíve steps forward, Pontius Pilate giving his sign, and the hermanos seize Amadeo.

It starts as acting, soft punches, and then they're slugging him, tearing at him, shouting the worst curses of two languages and two thousand years. Amadeo splutters and cries out under the barrage, surprised that it is actually happening.

When they fall back, Tío Tíve places the crown of thorns

on Amadeo's head. Amadeo turns and hoists the enormous cross onto his right shoulder, stooping under the weight, and the procession starts. The hermanos walk in two lines behind Jesus and begin to whip themselves. Manuel Garcia follows, bearing no load except his own hands, and then the women and children, the bright clattering colors of them, so distinct from the neat dark and white of the hermanos. Amadeo cannot see her, but he knows Angel is there.

After the first mile, the cross grows heavy. He tries to get into the part. He was up all night, he tells himself, in the garden, crying out to God. He remembers to stagger: his first fall. The crown of thorns is pulled tight, so it pierces the skin at his temple, and the stinging sweat slides down, but Amadeo is just not feeling it. He's too heavy and slow, his brain hung over and filled with static.

Angel comes up alongside her father on the right, panting in her sneakers and tank top. "Shoot. I can't believe I'm hiking at eight months. This must be a record." She pats her belly. "Your mama's breaking the Guinness world record, baby." She swigs water, holds the bottle out to Amadeo. "Want some water? I got water."

Amadeo shakes his head fiercely and heaves the cross up the slope after him, wishing she'd leave him alone, wishing he didn't owe her. He can pay her back, but only if he can blot her out.

Manuel Garcia hobbles his way up the procession on the left, huffing and stinking like a dying man. Amadeo stumbles; Manuel Garcia wheezes laughter. The old man will turn back—he'll have to turn back—and leave the day to Amadeo.

Manuel leers past Amadeo at Angel and spits, "Puta."

Angel looks up, startled, then to Amadeo. "Dad—"

Rage wells in him—Amadeo nearly drops the cross and bludgeons the old man—but then turns inward. He calls between heavy breaths to the hooded men behind him, "Whip me!" And then, because they do not respond, louder, "Whip me!"

When the lashes come, Angel clamps her hands over her mouth.

Amadeo grinds the soles of his feet into the sharp stones, scrapes his shoulder under the edge of the cross. He feels the rough wood break skin, the hot blood rise, his own blood, his own heat. He must leave his body, become something else.

Manuel laughs so hard he begins to cough, spits in the dirt under Amadeo's bare feet. Suddenly it comes to Amadeo: this mockery is a gift! The filthy old man is playing his part and doesn't even know it. Amadeo laughs out loud, tears streaming down his cheeks. He's getting stronger on Manuel Garcia's mockery!

And Angel isn't a distraction—she's the *point*! Everything Jesus did He did for his children!

"Get away from me," Angel yells at Manuel. Her eyes redden and well with angry tears. "Leave me alone!"

"Just wait," Amadeo whispers, but she doesn't hear.

His second fall is not intentional; neither is his third. He has forgotten to pick up his feet, and he stumbles over a numb knot of foot, the cross crashing down with him.

Angel kneels beside him, her eyes worried, Manuel forgotten. "You gotta have water." She opens the little plastic top and pushes the bottle into his hands, but he doesn't take it.

In the brush, birds chirp and little lizards dart, then freeze, from rock to rock. He watches Angel follow one with her eyes. Inside her, the baby twists and turns—he can almost sense it—hot in her flesh and under the sun. For the first time he's glad she's here: more than anyone, he realizes, she's the one he wants with him today.

At the top of Calvario, the hermanos lift the cross from his shoulders and rest it on the ground. Amadeo straightens, and the word *good* thrums in his head with each step: *good, good, good.* The hermanos help him down, position his arms along the crossbeam, his feet against the block of wood that is all he'll have to stand on. Amadeo spreads his arms and looks up into wide blue sky; there is nothing in his vision but blue. As they bind his arms and legs against the wood, lines once memorized surface: *With a word He stilled the wind and the waves.* But the wind skates over his body, drying the sweat and blood at his temples.

Then the hermanos lift the top of the cross, and Amadeo's vision swings from sky to earth. Upright, his weight returns; his torn heels press into the wooden block. Below him, on the highway, a few glittering cars move slowly, oblivious. The hot air tastes of salt, and dust sticks in his throat.

Angel stands before him, holding her hands under her belly. The nails, the nails. He isn't sure if he says it or thinks it. But Tío Tíve nods as if this was what he expected and reaches into his pocket for the paper bag. A hooded hermano steps onto a stool and pours rubbing alcohol over the wood and Amadeo's hot hands. The alcohol burns cold and smells sharp and clean.

—

THIS IS THE MOMENT they've been waiting for, and the people crowd closer. Parents nudge their children to the front, turn their babies to face the cross. These children will remember this their whole lives. Perhaps one of them, one day, will make the town proud. For now, though, the people are proud of themselves, because they were right about this Christ. True, a few of the onlookers might have hoped for a more artistic arrangement of blood, but no one can deny that he looks awful up there; he is exhausted. The man has put himself through Hell for them. Flies land on Amadeo's cheeks and neck, and—mira—he's too tired even to shake them away.

The Hermano Mayor cleans each nail. Alcohol splashes into the dust. Someone in the crowd thinks, This is like our time on earth, just a splash, then we rise into Heaven. The Hermano Mayor wipes each nail with his white handkerchief, then hands them one by one to the other hermanos. The people's hearts fill with joy for Amadeo, glad it's his uncle who will do this for him. Family is important.

Some of the people watch Manuel Garcia. They hope he doesn't feel too bad, but really it's time, and the old man has rested long enough on his laurels. Manuel Garcia's back is to Amadeo. He gazes down the hill he's just climbed.

One or two of the people glance over their shoulders at Angel, to see how she's taking it, to see if she's proud of her daddy, to see if some of the bad girl is getting washed out of her. But her face is blank, and she's standing there with her hands dangling dumbly at her sides, her big cheap belly hanging low.

—

AMADEO HADN'T EXPECTED FEAR, but here it is, hammering in his heart. What he sees from up here are eyes, and though he knows these people, knows all their names, they are like the eyes of strangers. He sees the back of Manuel's head and knows that the old man won't turn around. He seeks Angel with his gaze, and when he finds her he rests there. He leans into her across the distance, her body supporting his own. Just wait, he wants to whisper to her. Just wait.

They pound the nail through Amadeo's palm.

IN A MOMENT, PAIN, but for now he thinks, *This is all wrong,* and he has time to clarify the thought. *I am not the Son.* The sky agrees, because it doesn't darken. Amadeo remembers Christ's cry—*My God, why hast thou forsaken me?*—and he knows what is missing. It's Angel who has been forsaken.

All at once he sees her. He is surprised by the naked fear on her face. It is not an expression he knows. And she feels not only fear—Amadeo sees that now—but pain, complete and physical. Nothing he can do will change this, and soon it won't be just her suffering, but the baby, too.

Angel cries out and holds her hands aloft, offering them to him. This is when the pain makes its searing flight down his arm and into his heart. Amadeo twists in agony on the cross, and below him the people applaud.

NIGHT AT THE FIESTAS

FRANCES WAS PRETENDING TO BE SOMEONE ELSE, SOMEONE whose father was not the bus driver. Instead, she told herself, she was a girl alone in the world, journeying to the city. With every gesture, she pictured herself: turning the page of her book, tucking a sweaty lock of hair behind her ear, lifting her chin to gaze out the bus window. Except Frances wasn't alone, and her father, evidently thinking she'd come along today for his company, kept calling back to her with boisterous cheer over the exertions of the engine.

"Broke down here in '42, Francy." He indicated the endless yellow grass, summer-dry and dotted with cows and the occasional splintered shed, and Frances sighed and lowered her book politely to meet his eye in the rearview mirror. "Had a busload of fellows all on their way to training at Fort Bliss. Every day for three years I picked up two, three boys from each town and brung them south." He chuckled at the memory. "You wouldn't believe how many ideas twenty ranch boys have about a bus engine."

Not counting Frances, eleven passengers had boarded early that morning in Raton, many of them also heading to Santa Fe for the Fiestas. Frances's father had offered each and every one of them a jolly greeting. "Glorious day, isn't it?" "Got my girl with me." "Getting off in Santa Fe? So's my Frances." Each time a lady boarded—three did—he took her bag and followed her to her seat and stowed it in the net above while she removed her gloves and arranged her purse. Then he stood aside with his bulk pressed into the seats to let other passengers by. Frances had found herself looking away from his sad, obsequious displays of friendliness, embarrassed.

The day of the breakdown must have been a good one for her father; it must have been a thrill to share in the camaraderie with fellows his own age, part of a brotherhood, if only until the gas line or distributor or whatever it was got fixed. Frances pictured him twenty years younger, standing among the uniformed boys, grinning and eager and tongue-tied. Pity and affection welled in her.

Frances hadn't been born then, but she was aware that the war years must have been hard for him, strangers looking him up and down, wondering why he wasn't in Europe or the Pacific. Frances had felt the shame herself as a child when kids at school talked about their fathers' service. They'd traveled to incredible places, those fathers— Japan and Singapore, Italy, England, France—and they had souvenirs in their houses to prove it: flags, medals, a Nazi helmet, a tin windup rabbit found in the pocket of a drowned Jap.

"My dad was a conscientious objector," Frances had said at school when she was eleven. "We're pacifists." She'd shrugged, regretful, smug. "We just don't believe in fighting." But she'd had to stop saying that when it got back to her mother, who'd pinched her hard on the upper arm.

"Do you know what it would do to your father to hear you spreading those lies? He isn't a coward. He has a condition."

The condition in question was a heart murmur, and, as far as Frances knew, the only ill effect he'd ever suffered was fainting once on the football field in high school. Now, nearly an adult, Frances no longer judged her father for those war years, but it did strike her as darkly amusing that, not trusting his heart to hold out in the army, someone saw fit to put her father in charge of a busload of civilians careening down the highway at fifty miles an hour.

Now, an hour and a half into the trip, the passengers were scattered throughout the baking bus, dozing against the windows or reading newspapers; across the aisle, a stout woman was crocheting something in pink acrylic. Even with the windows lowered, the air blowing through was hot and dry, and Frances was worried about the state of her hair, which she'd tied up in rags last night. She lifted the limp curls off her sweaty neck and shifted in her seat and tried to concentrate on *Tess of the D'Urbervilles*. The frieze upholstery was scratchy through the cotton lawn of her new dress.

Frances was sixteen years old and twitchy with impatience. If Frances's life was to be a novel—as Frances fully intended—then finally, *finally*, something might happen at the Fiestas that could constitute the first page.

She'd spend the weekend with her aunt and cousin in their little stucco house on Marcy Street. Tonight they'd watch the burning of Zozobra, the enormous gape-mouthed effigy of Old Man Gloom, and then walk back to the Plaza for music and dancing that would last all night. And Saturday there'd be the Hysterical Parade and night dances at the La Fonda and the Legion Hall with mariachis imported all the way from Mexico. "We'll be out until morning," her cousin Nancy had assured her on the telephone. "We might not even go home then." Frances believed it. A widow dying to remarry, her aunt Lillian was fun-loving and young-dressing, lax and indulgent of her teenage daughter, which was exactly why it had been such a feat for Frances to convince her mother to let her go.

"Lillian's got absolute feathers for brains," her mother had said again last night of her sister-in-law. "If having your husband drop dead before your eyes doesn't pull you up short, I don't know what will. Man crazy, the two of them. That girl's going to end up in trouble, and Lillian will be too busy batting her own eyelashes to notice."

"Mother," Frances had said with superhuman forbearance, which was the only way she could bring herself to speak to her mother now. "Nancy's not going to end up in trouble." But Frances didn't actually believe this, which was why Nancy was so appealing to be around, even if she was a year younger and made Frances feel dull and wholesome, an actual country cousin.

Frances was also hoping to see some beatniks and artists, who, Nancy had told her, lived in such unimaginable filth it would make you sick, and they actually *liked* it, didn't even try to better themselves. "Ugh," said Nancy. "A painter rents the shed behind my friend Sally's neighbor's house, and he's so poor he trades his paintings for dog food. Sally says he eats the dog food right alongside the dog."

Frances had somehow missed these characters in previous visits to the state capital, but apparently they came out in droves for the Fiestas, high on their drugs and flouting conventions left and right. Maybe one of these artists would take her back to his dingy house with the mattress on the floor and ask to paint her. Frances considered herself, like Tess, *a vessel of emotion untinctured by experience,* and Frances very much wanted to be tinctured.

So in preparation, she'd spent her carefully hoarded babysitting money on a new pink lipstick at Rexler's and, at Barton's, this emerald-green dress, with its low, square neck and matching belt. Frances was sorry that she hadn't been able to afford a discreet weekend valise, too, powder-blue leather stamped to resemble alligator skin, like she'd seen in an ad for face cream in one of her mother's magazines. Instead, she'd had to pack her clothes in her orange sun-patterned swimming bag, embarrassing and childish and completely inappropriate for this weekend.

"Fancy-Francy, I ever tell you about the time a lady left a baby on the bus?"

Frances tamped down a surge of irritation, closed her book, and gave her father a tight, tolerant smile in the mirror. "You have."

Of course he had. Twice a day for twenty years he'd driven the same dusty two hundred miles between Raton and Santa Fe, never even stepping off his bus to walk down the faded main streets of the towns he passed through.

Every single day, the landscape changing in the same ways: deepening or rippling, shading greener here, flatter there, from high plain to chaparral to woodland plateau and back again, the vistas unbroken except for the occasional herd of antelope or deer or, more rarely, elk. Of course he'd told her about the baby.

"You're kidding," said the crocheting woman. "Blessed be."

"Yep," her father said with enthusiasm. "She gathered up all her packages and boxes, but left the baby."

He told it again, how another passenger had discovered the baby fast asleep on the seat when they were only a few miles outside of Maxwell, how he'd slowed the bus, made an excruciating many-pointed turn on the empty blacktop highway, and drove back to the depot in town. They found the woman without much trouble; it was a small town, and the man behind the ticket counter pointed her out, sitting on a bench outside the station, surrounded by her luggage.

Frances could understand wanting to abandon a baby; the mystery was why the woman had only left it on a bus and not in the boondocks where no one would find it. Frances babysat, but just because there were things she needed: beautiful, transformative clothes, a typewriter, a powder-blue valise. Above all, Frances needed to get out of Raton for good. She wanted to go to college, to take her place among the fresh-faced young men and women at UNM, skirt swinging and books clutched to her chest, her face raised to the warm possibility of romance. This weekend was practice for the day when she would board this bus again and never return.

"My God," said the woman. "She must have been out of her head with worry."

"Claimed it was a mistake and practically tore that baby from my arms. But I'm not sure she convinced me, wasn't crying or anything. Who's to say she didn't pull the same stunt on some other guy's route?" Still, the story had a happy ending: "All that, and we arrived in Santa Fe only nine minutes behind schedule."

It was an excellent story made stupid by his telling: for instance, when he'd told it the first time at dinner, it was the turn that had seemed to interest him most; he'd demonstrated on the tablecloth using his knife as the bus.

Frances looked at her father in the driver's seat—his round, sloping shoulders, the stubble on the back of his neck. He held the big wheel with both hands as if it were a roasting pan. He used to be a frustrated man, a shouter and a spanker. But he'd mellowed as Frances got older. Now he sought her company with a sort of sodden sentimentality that left her at once touched and galled.

"Shame I can't go with you," her father called. "To the Fiestas. It would be nice to see Lillian, spend some time with you girls."

Frances kept her eyes on her book, pretending not to have heard. The swell of power this gave her was like an electric charge.

"Would you look at that," he tried again, sweeping his hand across the windshield. "You don't get views like these from an office, Francy."

"Daddy, I have to do some reading. For school." She held her book up to the mirror and sighed dramatically. "I'll just move back. You two enjoy your conversation."

"Smart as a whip, my girl," her father told the crocheting woman, but Frances could hear the hurt in his voice.

She stood, lifted down her bag, and as she did, her dress ripped at the armpit. From her new seat she examined the tear. "Goddamn it," she muttered, digging in her swimming bag for her cardigan. Up front, her father had fallen silent, his shoulders hunched. He needed to get used to her absence, Frances reasoned, because soon she'd leave for college, and then what would he do? She'd be kind to him when she got off in Santa Fe. She'd tell him she loved him. Frances put on her cardigan, and then, hot, sat back and opened her book.

IN WAGON MOUND, three people boarded. A thin red-cheeked woman in a gray dotted sundress sat across the aisle from Frances, and a man swinging a lunch sack took the seat in front of her. He smiled from under a bristly caterpillar of a mustache. Frances, aware of his eyes on her, looked out the window at the road blurring below. She pictured herself: her slow blush, lashes lowered against her cheek.

"Whew. Hot, isn't it?" The thin woman lifted off her straw hat, and her hair came with it, loosening from her chignon, then falling around her face in lank, damp strands. She pulled a pencil and a crossword from her purse and set to work.

All the while, Frances examined the man in her peripheral vision. He was sitting sideways, leaning against the window. He craned to see Frances over the backrest. Brown checked suit, agate bolo tie cinched tight under his collar.

He was thirty, maybe. His hair was a little long, parted down the middle.

"Hey." He stretched a narrow hand toward her, flicked her book. "Pretty girls should smile."

People were always telling Frances to smile; apparently her face in its natural state was pinched and sulky. "Well, you aren't beautiful," her mother had said thoughtfully this summer. "But you're perfectly fine when you smile." Frances hated the implication that she ought to appear good-natured for someone else's benefit. Who did this man—some ranch hand in his absurd city best—think he was? Still, he had called her pretty, and that was something. She raised an eyebrow in a way she hoped looked disdainful and queenly. "If I felt like smiling," she said, "I would."

He laughed, not unkindly. The man's breath was damp and garlicky from, Frances imagined, some massive ranch breakfast eaten in a hot kitchen. Greasy yellow eggs, beans, fat sausages splitting their burned skins. The thought was nauseating, and Frances turned her head.

"You don't make yourself sick, reading like that?"

Frances shook her head. She had absolutely no desire to talk to this man. She would not talk to this man. But her silence hung between them, unmistakable and rude. "No," she said finally. "I never get carsick."

"Lucky. I was in the Navy, and I never did get used to the seasickness."

"Well," said Frances, "it can't help, sitting backward like that." *Rude*, her mother would call her; Frances preferred *spirited*.

"What are you reading?"

What could Thomas Hardy possibly mean to him? Frances displayed the cover, feeling superior.

"So you're a smarty-pants," said the man. "Huh."

Frances had begun *Tess of the D'Urbervilles* that summer with trepidation, and she was proud of herself for making it as far as she had. Even more than the story, Frances enjoyed the image of herself reading this fat book with its forbidding, foreign-sounding title. It was a prop, exactly the book a girl with a powder-blue valise would be reading. And apparently, as a prop it was working.

The fellow lit a cigarette, exhaled, still watching her. "I'm not much for reading. Myself, I'm a painter."

Frances brightened and set the book in her lap. "Really? What do you paint? Figures?" She blushed.

"Nudes, you mean? That's what you're asking, isn't it?"

Frances's blush deepened. She didn't deny it.

He laughed. "I'd say I'm more of an action painter." He scratched his mustache with a finger, eyes on her, then took another drag.

Did that mean what she thought it meant? Was Frances being propositioned? He *was* thinking of her that way, wasn't he? Certainly he wasn't talking to the woman across the aisle. And why was that? Because the woman across the aisle was plain and had an entirely untended mustache. Frances ran her finger over her own upper lip, plucked last night in preparation for Santa Fe.

And now Frances wasn't just a girl going into the world, but a girl whose virtue was being tested. That it might not withstand the test was a thrilling prospect. Frances suddenly felt deeply certain that something momentous *would* happen this weekend. Not with this fellow, though he really wasn't bad-looking, despite his breath, and it was possible that the breath was just a result of his devil-may-care artistic lifestyle. Too many reefers, maybe.

Men in Raton utterly overlooked Frances. Only two boys had ever asked her on dates, both pitiful specimens still awaiting their growth spurts. And now what Frances had always suspected was true: She *did* have sex appeal. *Under her bodice the life throbbed quick and warm.*

Frances couldn't wait to tell Nancy. Nancy was involved in endless drama with bevies of boys, while Frances, with her modest clothes and overprotective mother, had to play the supporting role to her younger cousin, probing for details, shaking her head in scandalized admiration, offering advice on matters she had absolutely no personal experience with. At least Frances lived in Raton; Nancy didn't know how little she knew.

"Are you going to the Fiestas?" She smiled in a way she hoped was coy. "You must be, dressed like that." *Handsome,* she probably should have said, but it really was a terrible suit.

"You'll be there?" His green eyes—lovely eyes, now that she was looking—were bright and amused. Was he laughing at her? "Are you asking me out? Maybe you'd like to get a drink with me."

Frances straightened her sweater; she wanted to remove it, show off her arms, but was aware of the hole in her dress. "*You'd* like that, wouldn't you?" Who knew she had it in her, this sauciness!

"You should be careful." The painter twisted to stub his cigarette out in the ashtray, and Frances noted that his nails were clean. She would have thought he'd have paint around his cuticles. "You don't know a thing about me."

"*You* don't know a thing about *me*," Frances retorted.

The painter shook his head, bemused, and faced front. Frances kept waiting for him to turn back—he'd spoken to her first, after all—and once she nearly said something, but he bundled his jacket for a pillow and fell asleep against the window.

For the rest of the ride Frances went over the interaction, and she didn't forget her pique until they entered Santa Fe. As they approached downtown, the traffic thickened and tangled; at every street, it seemed, they stopped for crowds of happy pedestrians to cross. The passengers watched from the windows, and laughter and shouts rose above the rumble of the vehicles. Frances's spirits soared.

When they pulled up in front of the bus depot on Water Street, the painter stood before they'd even stopped and reached for his canvas bag. Then he leaned over her and squinted out Frances's window, as if scanning the crowded sidewalk for the person who'd come to pick him up. Frances braced herself for the smell of his breath, and then it came. "Little whore," he said in her ear, so softly she wondered if she'd imagined it, and before she'd even lifted her gaze to him, he was moving quickly down the aisle, stepping off the bus.

Frances flushed and for what felt like a long time couldn't move. Had anyone heard? But they were all disembarking now, straightening hats and shirt collars. Up at the front of the bus, her father was shaking hands and tipping his hat, helping the woman with the crochet down the steps.

Frances took a deep breath to compose herself. That

painter was nothing, no one. He probably wasn't even a painter. She could see him on the sidewalk. He'd bought a paper from the newsstand by the depot and was paging through it. Go away, go away, go away, thought Frances. She would not budge from this bus until he'd disappeared down the street.

Heart pounding, she arranged her purse and her swimming bag on her shoulders, straightened her cardigan.

"Enjoy the Fiestas," said the thin woman, setting her hat back on her head.

It was then that Frances noticed he'd left his lunch sack on his seat. Suddenly she was filled with rage at this man who'd had the gall to speak to her in the first place, to tell her to smile and then to insult her when she did. She would step off the bus, call to him, smiling and sunny—"Sir, your lunch!"—wave the paper sack over her head, make as if to hand it to him. And then, when he reached for it—shamed by her kindness—Frances would open her hand, drop it in the street, and grind his sandwich under her heel.

She leaned over the seat, snatched the sack. She was so angry she was trembling.

When Frances looked inside, there was no sandwich wrapped in waxed paper, no apple or jelly jar of milk, no food at all. Inside the bag was a fat stack of bills.

She walked stiffly down the aisle and submitted to her father's kiss goodbye. She flushed, hot and ashamed, as if her father somehow knew what she'd done, knew what the painter had called her.

"Be safe, Francy. Be good." He pulled her in for an extra hug, and Frances, with the paper sack stuffed in her purse, responded, "Of course."

Then Frances was down the bus steps and into the arms of Nancy and Aunt Lillian, who shrieked and clung and jabbered at her. They each took an arm and waved gaily with their free hands as her father's bus pulled into the Water Street traffic, then dragged her along the crowded sidewalk between them. "The Plaza's already full!" cried Nancy. "I thought you'd never get here."

"She's been beside herself all day," said Aunt Lillian. Behind her, the painter was still reading the paper. Every once in a while he scanned the street.

"Wait," said Frances, stopping. "I'd like to drop my things at your house."

"We can't go home!" said Nancy. "Everything's already started. Plus, I'm starving. The Elks Club is selling hot dogs and Frito pies!"

Frances felt she was walking strangely. Her purse was barely heavier, but it had tipped her off-balance and her gait was self-conscious and labored. "I have to go to the bathroom."

The bus depot restroom was vile, the floor wet around the toilet and dirty with footprints. Ordinarily, Frances would have hovered over a toilet like this, and even then only in an emergency. Today, though, she sat right down.

One hundred and forty dollars. An enormous amount of money, all in ones and fives and tens. Nearly what her father was paid every two weeks, more than she could hope to make in a year of babysitting. Enough to fund her escape.

Strange that he should keep it in a paper sack. Perhaps he'd just sold a painting or had intended to buy something, something illicit that required a discreet handoff. Drugs, stolen goods. She wondered if the painter was still outside, waiting to twist her arm and throw her onto the sidewalk and wrench her purse away.

Someone knocked on the bathroom door, and Frances sat still. The person knocked again. If she were the kind of girl to cry, she might now. But why? She'd had a tremendous stroke of luck. She was glad she had the money, glad she'd taken it. She needed it. He *owed* it to her, calling her what he had.

Frances smoothed the bills and slipped them into her wallet. But the stack was too fat and the wallet wouldn't close. Also, she'd be a draw for criminals with that kind of cash spilling out. So she removed all but twenty dollars, folded the rest of the money back into the sack and stuffed it into the bottom of her swimming bag.

The thought—the foolish, embarrassing thought— crossed her mind that maybe the man was an angel, but that was idiotic, something her mother would say. Frances was now pretty certain the man wasn't even a painter. His nails were one clue. And if he were a painter, what would he be doing in Wagon Mound? No one lived in Wagon Mound. And no one kept money in paper bags. More likely the man was a grifter who'd come to Santa Fe to spend his ill-gotten gains and cheat others. Unless he really was just a hardworking ranch hand and Frances was now holding his entire life's savings. But no: if there's one thing she knew, it was that even before he'd opened his mouth, there'd been something sleazy about the man, something underhanded and insinuating.

When Frances emerged from the depot into the sunlight, the painter was gone. She smiled at Nancy and Aunt

Lillian, slung her purse over one shoulder, swimming bag over the other. "I'm starving," she said.

THE PLAZA WAS SWARMED with people and packed with booths, everything buzzing and festive. Banners rippled in the hot breeze, and the grass was sun-dappled through the tall cottonwoods. The costumes! There, drinking a Coke on the bleachers was the Fiesta Queen in her frothy white lace, her mantilla and high comb, surrounded by her court. And there, Don Diego de Vargas with his crested helmet and cape. Conquistadors and Mexicans and bandidos, Indians, nuns, cowboys. Fringed vests and enormous sombreros, Spanish shawls and elaborate headdresses. Several people wore lush Navajo velvet, big blouses for the men, long skirts for the women. Frances most admired the fiesta dresses, though, silver-trimmed gauzy cotton the color of ice cream: pink, turquoise, green, yellow. She would buy one herself, she decided.

A large white-haired man came up behind Aunt Lillian and lifted her off her feet. "George!" she cried, and he kissed her on the mouth. When he set her down, Aunt Lillian patted her updo, and Frances thought of her mother's verdict: *featherbrained.*

Aunt Lillian's friend George was a cowboy, complete with leather chaps and lasso. "In real life I'm a banker." He pulled his card from his pocket and gave it to Frances. Then, back in character, he roped Nancy and pulled her to him. "Git along little dogie."

"Get off!" Nancy yelled. She wriggled free of the rope and threw it back at him, then yanked Frances away and marched her across the crowded grass. Behind them Aunt Lillian laughed.

"I hate him," Nancy said. "He's always ogling me."

Well, of course he was, Frances thought. Everyone was always ogling Nancy, and Nancy intended that they should. Look at her today, for instance. Her soft light hair, low-cut dress, silver rickrack glinting in the sun, the long strand of turquoise beads caught in her cleavage. So like Nancy to make herself look that way and then complain when people noticed. Frances squared her shoulders and touched her own hair; her curls had fallen completely. So what? If she cared about those things, she'd get her hair done professionally at the beauty shop. She could afford it.

As they walked the periphery of the Plaza, Frances looked in every window for a valise. No luck. The money stuffed in her bag seemed such an obvious presence, banging at her side. It marked her, and Frances couldn't believe people weren't staring. It would almost be a relief to spend it, to transform it into clothes her size, items that reflected who she was. But it wasn't to be spent, not yet, anyway. She pictured herself at college, opening a new notebook in the hum of a full lecture hall.

"Banker," spat Nancy. "Ha. *Works* in a bank, more like. He's a creep. I really don't know what she sees in him."

Frances shrugged. "Well, she's always been a little man crazy."

She paused to look in the plate-glass window of the Trading Post. Several kids about eleven or twelve also clustered on the sidewalk, peering in. There, surrounded by tooled-leather saddles and woven blankets, a Navajo girl in traditional velvet skirts stood stock-still, an enormous silver belt in her frozen outstretched hands.

"She *is* real," insisted a boy. "She blinked. There!"

The Navajo girl was remarkably good, stone-faced and flat-eyed.

The kids started banging the glass. "There! She did it again!" A few made faces and wagged their tongues.

"She's probably going to marry him," said Nancy bleakly. "I'll probably have to live in the same damn house with him."

At the Elks' booth, they ordered cold Cokes and Frito pies. Frances rifled through the bills in her wallet, but Nancy wasn't even paying attention.

"My treat," said Frances.

Nancy shrugged. "I won't say no."

They ate sitting on the back of a park bench, feet on the seat. It felt good to put down her swimming bag. Her dress was dark with sweat where the strap had pressed against her.

"God, it's hot," said Frances. She couldn't stand it a minute longer. She took off her cardigan and clamped her armpit shut.

"I know." Nancy licked chile from the heel of her hand. "What're you doing wearing a sweater, anyway?"

"I met someone on the bus," Frances said. "A painter. And not like your friend Sally's painter with the dog food. *This* guy is famous. He has shows in Paris and London, all over."

"So?" said Nancy, still sulking.

"So? So he's rich." Frances couldn't have been more

indignant if she'd been telling the truth. "And he asked me to dine with him tonight."

"To *dine*? What is he, an aristocrat?" But Nancy was looking Frances up and down, impressed.

"Of course I told him I couldn't. He must be nearly thirty. Still, it's never fun disappointing someone like that."

"Nancy!" somebody called, and Nancy brightened. Suddenly they were flanked by boys. They introduced themselves politely to Frances, and one even asked what Raton was like, but soon they turned back to her cousin. They jostled each other and joked about people Frances didn't know, and Nancy sat glowing in their midst.

For a while Frances made a point of smiling and nodding along, but that got old, and no one was looking at her anyway. She felt unbearably dull. Two of the boys started slapping at each other, and one boy put the other in a headlock, all for the benefit of Nancy. What *was* it about boys? Frances thought angrily. Couldn't they keep still for a minute?

"So? Isn't Mike a doll?" Nancy asked when they'd gone.

Frances put her hand on her cousin's arm. "Just be careful, okay? I'd hate to see you getting into trouble."

Nancy snorted. "You should talk, with your middle-aged painter. Anyway, you have a hole in your armpit."

"Burn him! Burn him! Burn him!" The crowd was chanting, and Frances chanted along, but self-consciously. Her own voice seemed flattened, droning in her ear.

It was night at Fort Marcy Park, and the baseball field was crowded with cars and trucks, spread blankets, abandoned picnics. Zozobra, the looming white marionette, bellowed as the flames climbed his gown. His face, with its scowling eyes and gaping mouth, flickered orange against the black sky; when he swayed, sparks rained down over the crowd. Above, fireworks whistled and exploded.

Nancy had Frances by the wrist and was dragging her through the press of people at the barricade. Here the bonfire's heat was a solid, smothering presence, pulsing under her skin like a sunburn. The sweaty seams of her dress were tight and chafing. Frances held tight to her purse and her swimming bag.

"They said they'd be here!" called Nancy. "Would you hurry?" She was looking for her friends, the boys from the Plaza among them, but Frances couldn't imagine how they'd ever find anyone in this mass of people. The air was weighted with the smell of gunpowder and sweat and toxic, chemical smoke.

Zozobra bawled, arms flailing uselessly, body rooted in the flames. The people's excitement seemed sadistic, medieval. Frances had a sudden vision of the painter stepping from the flames like Satan to collect his due, and the thought made her sweat still more.

"Can't we just watch from back there?" asked Frances, but Nancy didn't hear her over Zozobra's moans.

When the flames reached Zozobra's face, the crowd cheered. His head was stuffed with paper, records of divorce proceedings and legal wrangling and failed exams and paid-off mortgage documents. And now all those troubles were being burned away. It seemed these people really felt released, but Frances kept glancing all about, her shoulders aching under the strap of her bag. Zozobra thrashed and wailed in anguish, shaking off flaming paper that drifted around him.

In no time at all, Zozobra collapsed with a cascade of sparks, gloom defeated once again, and the cheer of "Viva la Fiesta!" rose from the crowd. You could already hear the music from the Plaza, rousing and joyful. Everyone streamed through the streets to join it.

The crowd in the Plaza was even louder and denser than in the park, people spinning and writhing to the mariachi band playing from the lit bandstand. The dark crush was thrilling and terrifying, unlike anything Frances had ever experienced. Nancy whirled, laughing, sipped from an open bottle of beer handed to her. She handed it to Frances, and no sooner had Frances taken a sip than another bottle was passed to her.

They hadn't found Nancy's friends, but it hardly mattered; everyone was friends on the Plaza. The gaiety swirled about them, but though Frances tried, she simply couldn't find her way into it. She danced and laughed, but her rhythm was off, her voice false and harsh. She gulped the beer until she felt the disembodied sensation of drunkenness, but the feeling only made her less a part of the crowd, untouchable and remote.

She tried to spin a story about one of the boys from earlier—the one in the leather vest, say—who couldn't get her out of his mind, who'd been looking for her all night, waiting to lift her chin, but the scenario was hollow and unsatisfying.

Maybe if Frances had a costume she'd be feeling it all more. She wished she had a Spanish shawl, black embroidered with red and gold chrysanthemums. She wished she could buy something—anything—now. What a joke, to have all this money in the middle of Santa Fe and nowhere to spend it. Mostly, Frances wanted to put her bag down. But it was still strapped to her, cumbersome, banging into everyone every time she moved.

Next to her a fight broke out, two sweaty men lunging at each other, their teeth bared, their rage clumsy and grunting. Frances gaped, but Nancy just rolled her eyes and pushed her deeper into the crowd.

By one in the morning, the bands had changed. Drunk men commanded Frances to *dance! Dance!* "Why so gloomy?" one asked and flicked her nose.

Nancy's dress had slipped off her shoulder, exposing a dingy bra strap. She weaved among the men, pinching one on the bottom. He retaliated by squeezing her breast. Another reached for Frances's breast, but she batted his hand away.

"S'okay," he said. "Not much there anyway."

Those men, their hands were everywhere, and Nancy couldn't stop laughing. Laughing with abandon, Frances thought. She was so envious it hurt.

Someone grabbed her upper arm and spun her around. "If it isn't Smarty-Pants."

The painter. Frances gasped. But he didn't strike her and he didn't throw her to the ground to be crushed. He was dancing, feet stomping, fingers snapping. "Enjoying yourself, I see."

He was drunk, unfocused in the eyes, slack around the mouth. His shirt was unbuttoned, his bolo tie gone. At his sweat-glazed temples, his hair was curling. Frances's hand tightened on the strap of her bag.

"And you?" she shouted over the noise. "Are you enjoying yourself?"

"More now." He swigged from his bottle, held it aloft. "To the kindness of strangers."

Could he know? He couldn't possibly. All those people on and off a bus; any number of people could have taken the sack. It might have remained on the bus, to be discovered by someone in Las Vegas or Watrous or Springer. Her father might have picked it up during a trash sweep, and, knowing him, thrown it away without looking inside. The fact was that Frances would have overlooked the sack if she hadn't been so angry. *Little whore.* But *angry* wasn't quite the word. She was shocked, yes. Hurt. Embarrassed.

And also—strangely—released. She stood a little straighter and swung her bag by the strap, and for the first time in hours her smile didn't feel forced. All around her people were fighting and kissing and dancing wildly. The music soared and slipped under her skin. Her feet found the beat.

Perhaps the painter had left the money for Frances intentionally. Perhaps he'd known she'd see the bag; it was a test, and by taking the money, she was admitting she was what he'd called her. In taking it she'd sullied herself, and he knew it and was laughing at her.

If that was the case, if he'd spent the whole night looking for her, this was a game she could play. She took his sweaty hand and danced toward him, swaying her hips, her purse and bag knocking against her.

"Here," he said, lifting the strap of her swimming bag. "Take a load off. Makes dancing more fun."

"No," said Frances, jerking back, ready to claw and scream and bite if need be. Then she smiled. "I'm fine, thank you." He slid his arm around her waist, and Frances felt a glorious sensation of free fall.

Nancy appeared at her elbow. "Who's your friend, France?" She stuck her hand out, mock formal. "Nancy. Frances's cousin." Nancy stumbled over the *s*'s and tried again more deliberately. "Frances's." She was drunker than Frances had thought.

The painter released Frances to shake her cousin's hand. "Charmed," he said and brought it to his lips.

"So you're the painter. Frances said you were incredible."

He grinned at Frances, a wide, knowing grin. "I am incredible. Not to be believed."

Nancy laughed, and Frances did her best to mirror her cousin, to look like a high school girl cheerfully celebrating 268 years since de Vargas's retaking of Santa Fe. Nancy lost her balance and started to stumble. The painter caught her and didn't take his hand off her elbow after she'd steadied. He winked at Frances, and just like that the music drained out of her.

Under the west portico, some kind of commotion. A man on horseback pumped his arms, then nudged the horse forward and into the Plaza Bar, ducking as he passed through the door. Catcalls, cheers, and a moment later, man and horse backed out; whooping, calling patrons spilled after him.

The band struck up "La Cucaracha" for the third time

that night, and the crowd sang along, mumbling and braying through the lyrics.

The painter grabbed Frances's wrist. "I think you owe me a drink. You and your cousin both."

"No, thank you. We can't." Frances detached herself and took her cousin's hand, intending to draw her into the crowd and away from the painter, but Nancy shook her off.

"She doesn't talk to boys," said Nancy, laughing. "They terrify her."

"Not me," said the painter. "I don't terrify you, do I? This afternoon I didn't terrify you a bit." He turned to Nancy, whose elbow he was still holding. "She's not really so hopeless. We had a terrific conversation all the way from Wagon Mound. I told Frances all about my painting."

"Tell me," said Nancy, canting her head in the way she thought was sexy and probably was. "What do you paint?"

He regarded her, thumbing his mustache. "All kinds of things. Portraits, for one—especially of beautiful women." He smiled. "I get paid a lot of money for my portraits. Isn't that right, Frances?" His smile vanished.

"We need to go, Nancy," she said, but her cousin ignored her.

"And you have shows in Paris and London?"

The painter laughed, returning his attention to Nancy. "Oh, yes. I'm always on the lookout for models."

"I bet you are," said Nancy, laughing. "I bet you look high and low for pretty girls. But I'm listening."

It would have been so easy now to say, "I found something of yours," to hand over the lunch bag and slip into the crowds with Nancy, but Frances said nothing. Really, there was no question of giving back the money. It was already a part of her, or not of her, but of the Frances she was becoming. Already the money had transformed into Frances's future: her next year and her year after that, and all the years that would take her away from the tongue-tied, stiff-legged person she was now.

When the painter leaned in to say something to Nancy, Frances broke away and pushed through the crowd toward the bus depot. She weaved around people, forcing her way through their laughs and protests. At the edge of the Plaza she turned, expecting to see the painter at her heels, but the crowd was oblivious, caught in its own net of drunkenness.

She ran, her heels catching on the uneven sidewalk, dodging a group of men with painted faces and massive feathered headdresses. They called to her with war whoops, but she didn't stop until she reached the depot.

There Frances waited, but her father's bus didn't come. Of course not; he was fast asleep now, at home in Raton. He wouldn't even wake up for another four hours, and it wouldn't be until noon tomorrow—today—that he'd pull in at the depot. Still, a part of her thought he'd somehow know she was waiting for him, or that fate would intervene with a breakdown or a baby left behind, anything to disrupt his route and send him back. She thought of her father's jabber on the bus and her irritation, then remembered that she hadn't told him she loved him. Her eyes welled.

She could hear the music from the Plaza. That pounding, tireless mariachi cheer! A group of revelers passed noisily on the sidewalk, and Frances braced herself to fight them off if need be. No one looked her way.

For the first time it felt like September; the air had that chill. Frances tightened her cardigan and rifled through her swimming bag again. But there was nothing warm there, nothing she needed, just some clean underwear, her short summer nightgown, another flimsy sundress. Nothing else except the money. She began to count it again. It was all there, minus two Frito pies. She shoved it back into the paper bag, feeling sick.

Frances opened her book, but it was too dark. She could barely see the words, couldn't have followed the story anyway. Frances would not think about Nancy and the painter. She would not think of what he was doing to her cousin—her younger cousin, a child she ought to be watching out for. She wouldn't think of them on the mattress in his dingy one-room shed, Nancy stretched out lush and pink, waiting to be painted. As he moved toward her, the painter would tell Nancy how beautiful she was, even though he didn't have to, not now that he had paid for her. Poor Nancy would close her eyes and listen. Frances could almost smell his breath as he leaned in. Nancy, who didn't understand how the world worked, who didn't understand that people could be cruel, would believe everything he said.

As if conjured, the painter appeared at the top of Water Street, and Frances's heart stilled. He was walking slowly toward her, head bent as if absorbed in thought. He seemed to have lost his jacket now, too. A beer bottle swung between his fingers.

Even if he lifted his head, from this distance he might miss Frances sitting on her bench in the shadows, his paper bag in her lap. He wouldn't see her until he passed directly in front of her. She wondered if the painter, too, had been drawn to the bus station by the promise of return, if he, too, was counting the hours until he could head back north, though he'd be leaving without his bolo tie, without his jacket, without his money. He rubbed his arms, seeming to feel the cold.

The street was empty now but for the two of them, the painter at the top of the block, Frances waiting like his bride. As he approached, she clung to the sack, her heart sloshing in her chest. If he looked up, he'd see her. Frances imagined the scene: the dark windows of the depot, the framed schedules, and a young girl, defenseless on her bench. Except that she wasn't defenseless; she was solid and powerful and rich. Frances held still, her grip cold on the bag. As he neared, his progress intolerably slow, the hairs on her bare legs lifted. Surely he saw her. Twenty feet, ten. Now if she reached out from the shadows she could almost touch him, and then, like a breath, he was beyond her.

Frances rose, the sack still in her hand. She stepped from the shadows into the center of the sidewalk, under the yellow streetlight. There she stood, bereft and disbelieving, watching the painter's unsteady progress away from her. Past the newsstand, the stationer's, the pharmacy, and then he turned the corner and was gone. On the Plaza, the music suddenly stopped, and in the pause between the music and the cheers, the endless night settled across her shoulders.

THE GUESTHOUSE

✦

JEFF STANDS WITH HIS SISTER IN THEIR GRANDMOTHER'S kitchen, still in his funeral clothes, but barefoot now. He heard the stroke had been painless and decisive, yet, judging from the state of the house, his grandmother had clearly been in decline even before the clot wedged itself into that tight corridor in her brain. She was always tidy, but the place looks awful: the floor is sticky and grainy, the sink full, and on the stove smelly water stagnates in an egg pan. In the cupboard beneath the sink, there is a leak. The wood is buckled and soft, stinking of spores and damp garbage. He thought his grandmother was doing fine, and his obliviousness pains him.

"Why didn't you tell me things had gotten this bad? Didn't you ever check up on her?"

"Excuse me?" says Brooke. "Are you blaming me for Grandma dying?"

"Of course not," Jeff says, although he is. The house is ten minutes from UNM. Brooke couldn't stop in once? He blames his mother, too, and himself, even if he does live two thousand miles away, because he should know better than to expect anything of the two of them. He forces a laugh. "At least the house is standing. At least it hasn't been pillaged by obit-scouring meth-heads."

"Yet," says Brooke. She takes a handful of cashews from the cut-glass candy dish that has been on the counter since Jeff can remember. It occurs to him that it's a little creepy, eating a dead woman's nuts, but he doesn't say so. Brooke is squeamish about these things, and if she's not thinking about it, he won't point it out. She wears a baggy linen skirt with a bunched elastic waistband, wrinkled everywhere except at her bottom. Nineteen years old and already middle-aged.

"You okay?" he asks, his concern for his sister a reflex. "You can leave if you want."

"I'm fine," she says. "Quit asking if I'm okay."

He nods and flips to a new page in the steno pad, refusing to linger on the lists and notes and telephone numbers in his grandmother's looping cursive. Jeff is awash in an enervating, aching nostalgia, his limbs thick with it. There's so much that needs to be done before he flies back to New York: he has to cancel his grandmother's cell phone and credit cards and order more copies of the death certificate for the insurance companies, sort through her files. And he'll need to get in touch with a real estate agent. Not that the house will fetch much in this market. It's just a slump-block two-bedroom ranch with brown carpet, ratty grass in the yard, and a few scraggly potted geraniums on the concrete porch. Jeff's grandmother was certain the land would appreciate—and it should have—other neighborhoods on the edge of the city did—but instead, trailer parks sprouted around her. Occasionally there are shouting matches, drug busts and gunshots and sirens, misery constantly turning over.

It'll be awful to sell. Everything about the house is suffused with significance, Jeff thinks, looking around: the orange enameled pots and pans, the brown velveteen throw pillows, the bedspreads with their polyester ruffles. Everything touched by her, everything bereft. In the shadowed living room, the coral couch waits, fabric rumpled where she used to settle under the lamp. They spent hours deliberating here, Jeff and his grandmother, the adults of the family, sorting out his mother, sorting out Brooke. Jeff and his grandmother were the doers, the fixers, and now Jeff is alone. The fact is, he doesn't know if he'll survive the loss of her.

Brooke tosses her head and shakes a handful of cashews into her mouth. "If Grandma was here she'd point out how fattening these nuts are. We should have buried her in her jeans with that patent leather belt cinched tight." She draws herself up and strikes a Vanna pose. "*I've* used the same notch since 1960," she mimics in a voice totally unlike their grandmother's. "You'd think by eighty she'd have grown out of that kind of vanity."

"You're being mean," says Jeff, then softens. Their grandmother could be hard on Brooke. Brooke isn't pretty like their mother and grandmother—she is plain and pale, small-breasted, with a cap of short dense hair and a loose paunch. She is regularly mistaken for a lesbian. He wishes she were one. Women are so much more forgiving, it seems to him, so much more likely to let his sister be a little ugly.

"Lisa couldn't come?" Brooke asks.

He listens for a trace of spite in her voice, but doesn't detect any. Brooke chews blandly. This fall he flew her to New York to stay with him and his girlfriend. The trip wasn't a success. Lisa was hurt by Brooke's reserve, but soldiered on, cracking terrible jokes, insisting on standing in line for hours at the Empire State Building and the Statue of Liberty, efforts that made Jeff feel self-conscious and faintly embarrassed by his girlfriend. Now he wishes he'd had the chance to introduce Lisa to his grandmother.

"She couldn't get away," he says. "But she says hi."

Brooke licks her finger and runs it through the salt in the bottom of the bowl. "Weird how you quit seeing stuff, you know? I never realized just how much crap Grandma had." She flicks at a souvenir tea towel pinned to the wall. It features a coy brown child in a hula costume with one suggestive hip cocked. "Like, this is so offensive on so many levels."

Jeff nearly defends the tea towel, but catches himself. He forces a smile. "You know Grandma and her finely tuned ironic vision."

Initially, Jeff thought they'd rent out the house—the extra income would be good for his mother—but he doesn't think she has the emotional wherewithal to be a landlord. She doesn't have the emotional wherewithal to handle most things, really. She's in England now, on a walking tour of the Lake District. When he asked when she was coming home so they could arrange the funeral, she cried, "But I've been saving for this trip for years!" Then she added resentfully, "Besides, my mother would rather you be there than me," as if the church could accommodate only one of them. She'd told him to go ahead with the funeral, claiming she couldn't bear it, claiming she'd rather mourn alone, neither of which stopped her from calling all morning and texting throughout the service to tell him about her devastation. He sees her gesture for what it is, a last childish assertion of her independence, despite the fact that the intended audience—his grandmother—is no longer paying attention. Honestly, he's glad to have his mother offstage, and he's glad for the time difference, too, which means that for the next seven or so hours she'll be safely asleep in some chilly floral B&B in Grasmere.

Jeff has heard it said that teachers reach only the emotional maturity of their oldest students. His mother, then, is a kindergartener, launching out stubbornly on her own, and then rushing back, crying, for comfort. She calls Jeff nearly every day, unless she's feeling fragile, in which case Jeff is supposed to call her and to keep calling until she picks up. Small problems loom large for Jeff's mother and require endless discussion—whether or not to replace the microwave, what to do about the stray cat that has begun to linger at the patio doors. Just a few months ago, she called Jeff in tears because she'd run into Jeff's father at the gas station. She hadn't even talked to him, just glimpsed him, or thought she had. Almost twenty years they've been divorced, and she's still ready to fall to pieces.

Jeff thinks, not for the first time, that maybe he should move back to Albuquerque and finish his dissertation here. Lisa wouldn't be happy, but she couldn't object, not with his suicidal sister and bereaved mother needing him. He could live right here—or, better, in the guesthouse out back. That would make a certain kind of sense. He's always felt proprietary toward the guesthouse. When he was a kid he played out there among the remnants of his grandmother's New England life: his dead grandfather's clothing, his mother's childhood toys, everything she'd dragged with her across the country. It occurs to him for the first time how unlike her it was to save all that stuff, since he'd never known her to be sentimental, unlike Jeff himself, who mourns even memories that aren't his. "Can I live here when I grow up?" he asked when he was ten, and his grandmother laughed. "Consider it yours."

Jeff swallows hard and thumps his list. "We've got to unload this place, pronto."

"Maybe we should discuss it?" There's something rigid in his sister's tone that makes Jeff look at her more closely.

"What's to discuss? Mom needs the money."

"Well," says Brooke, straightening a pile of junk mail, "I don't want to sell, and I don't think you do, either. Also it's not your decision."

Jeff exhales. "You think *Mom's* going to step up?"

"You know, being the favorite may have meant something when Grandma was alive, but it doesn't grant you total authority now." She raises her head in challenge.

"Oh, stop." This is an old accusation, made by both Brooke and, less frequently but with more bitterness, their mother. But it isn't fair, attributing Jeff's closeness with his grandmother to favoritism—unearned, undeserved— given how much Jeff put into that relationship. For years he stopped by most days after school and, once he'd left home, called every other day. By comparison, Brooke and their mother barely tried. "You want to find renters? Deal with inspectors and repairs and leases? Run a little property management company on the side while you finish up your gen-ed requirements?" He pushes the steno pad at her so hard the pages riffle, then immediately feels foolish.

"You know," Brooke says, "Grandma would have hated that service. The preacher or whatever looked at his notes before he said her name."

The funeral, which took place in a flat-roofed brick monstrosity moored in an expanse of crushed rock, *was* terrible, dreary and sparsely attended. "I did my best." Jeff's voice cracks, and he's glad, because his sister should feel bad about giving him a hard time.

Brooke's tone softens. "You did a fine job." She leans on the counter with her knuckles, rocks back and forth, then laughs a single harsh bray. "But if my funeral is like that, I'll kill myself."

"Christ, Brooke," Jeff starts, but he's stopped by the ringing phone.

She answers, listens a moment, then says, "Talk to Jeff." He gives her a puzzled look as he takes it, but her face reveals nothing.

"Jeffy, honey. I'm real sorry your grandma died. She was a great lady."

His stomach seizes even before Jeff consciously places the voice. Victor, their father: unemployed and undependable, obstinately friendly, chronically drunk.

"Don't you recognize me? It's your *papa*, man."

Jeff closes his eyes. "We appreciate your thoughts, Victor."

"Listen, there's stuff we got to talk about."

"I'm afraid now's not a good time. As you've pointed out, my grandmother just died."

A silence follows, through which Jeff can almost hear his father scheming. Victor says, "Well, I'm probably dying, too. Cancer."

Jeff laughs. Brooke's hands on the counter are still; she watches him, impassive. Jeff half-turns, leans into the receiver, as if to protect her from the conversation. "I can't help thinking this is a coincidence, Victor. Your calling now." His grandmother's phone is equipped with a foam shoulder rest, which Jeff crushes in his hand. With effort he relaxes his grip. "The funeral ended two hours ago."

"That's what I'm saying. A death really makes you think about mortality and all that. Man, *poor* Becky. I'm just saying you might want to see me. It's my stomach. They say that's a bad one."

"What's this about, Victor? Do you need money?"

"No." Victor sounds offended.

Jeff doesn't know why he asked. His father has never asked for money, not even after the divorce. He could tell Victor to screw himself, but part of him is curious to know if his father actually is dying. The man's history of manipulation doesn't exempt him from real cancer, Jeff supposes. He wonders if his father's illness will trigger grief and catharsis, forgiveness and reconciliation. He shudders, then flips to a new page, clicks the pen. "Fine. We'll say our goodbyes. You still at the same place? Give me your address."

"No need!" His father's tone is cheerful. "I'm right out back."

"What?"

"Just look." And, indeed, there he is, their father, in the middle of the dry lawn in their grandmother's backyard. He waves sheepishly, cell phone pressed to his ear. "I could see you two standing there. I almost came in, but I didn't want to freak you."

Jeff hangs the phone on the wall but continues to steady himself against the receiver. "He says he's got cancer," he says, jerking his thumb at the window. "So make of that what you will." There's something almost pleasing in the anger Jeff feels toward his father. He feels beleaguered, wronged, and also energized, because once again he has to take charge.

Brooke turns and shrugs her hunched shoulders, crossing her arms over her breasts, matching Jeff's show of nonchalance. Her whole life she's had bad posture; she even slumped as a defeated little toddler. Outside, Victor is taking a leak in the tomato bed, squinting into the colorless sky.

"I should see what he wants. Care to join?"

Brooke looks at her stubby fingernails and shakes her head.

"How long do you think he's been lurking out there?" Again Brooke shrugs, and he feels his frustration mount. "Well, if I'm not back in twenty minutes, send a search party."

Jeff turns the deadbolt on the back door and steps outside.

—

THIS CALL SHOULDN'T BE a surprise. As if driven by an instinct for calamity, Victor pops up when Jeff and Brooke are at their most vulnerable. Two years ago, for instance, when Brooke was just home from the hospital, still trying to keep down clear fluids, Victor arrived to announce he was getting clean, moving to Alaska to work on a commercial fishing boat, and wanted to make amends before he left. While Victor wept and wrung the hem of his t-shirt, Jeff blocked the doorway, trying to prevent his father's voice from reaching his mother and sister at the back of the house.

Jeff remembers more of life with their father than Brooke does. He had eight years of it, while she was just a year old, too fat to walk, when Victor left. Jeff is glad she was spared the memories, but he knows she just feels excluded.

Victor has never been the kind of father to demand visitations or parental rights, and seems to accept his role as failed father and human with remarkable good humor, holding no one—not his ex-wife, not his children, and least of all himself—responsible.

Jeff encounters his father about once a year, never by choice. Now and then when back in town Jeff will bump into relatives of his father or see them on commercials or the evening news. Victor's family is immense and tangled: half of them are drunks and the others have had success in real estate and local politics. All their children go through the public school system, so periodically one ends up in Jeff's mother's classroom, where she guides its little hands, tracing letters on a table dusted with flour.

She came to Albuquerque from New Hampshire for college, hair in a long braid, full of enthusiasm for the desert flora, the vistas and dry air, what she called *the realness* of the place. That same realness presumably drew her to Victor, an electrician rewiring the Education Building, and they were married within a year. There are pictures from this time, his mother dragging playfully on Victor's shiny tanned arm, her braid swinging.

This was before Jeff was born, before Victor punched Jeff's mother in the throat and stomped on her hand, breaking six of those matchstick bones. This was before his grandmother moved to join her only child. "Your mom needed help," she said. "She's always needed help."

"HEY, MY MAN!" Victor comes in for a hug, but Jeff puts his arms up, absurdly defensive. Victor laughs and waves his hands in mock surrender, then slouches against the cinder-block wall of the guesthouse. He squints into the kitchen window, where Brooke's dim figure is bent over the counter. "Make your sister come out. I haven't seen her in forever."

Jeff shrugs. "She will if she wants."

Victor seems about to argue, but instead he says, "How's your mom?"

Jeff hesitates. "How do you think? She's a wreck."

Victor perks up. "She's not doing good?"

Jeff hooks his fingers in his pockets and pretends to survey his grandmother's backyard. Victor doesn't look sick, doesn't seem to have aged at all. His hair is wet and a little long, combed straight back, curly at the nape. The man isn't even balding, which Jeff finds galling, since his own hairline has been in retreat since college. Victor's undershirt is worn thin enough that Jeff can see his dark nipples, a queasily intimate sight.

"How's Lupe?" Jeff asks, then regrets taking responsibility for the conversation, making things easier on Victor.

"Didn't work out. She just wanted my money. But was she *fine*." Jeff's father purses his lips and bobs his head as though appreciating good music.

Lupe was Jeff's twenty-three-year-old stepmother. The one time Jeff met her, last year, she served saltines on a plastic TV table in the dirt outside their travel trailer. While Victor swigged his beer and talked about his plans for fixing up the place, building a deck—no mention of Alaska—she and two pit bulls watched Jeff sullenly as he sipped warm orange juice. When Jeff made to refill his cup, she moved the carton away.

"Yep," says Victor philosophically. "Went back to Chihuahua. Took the dogs and car and TV and everything." He shrugs. "She was mad the whole time, anyway. She married me 'cause she thought I had a pool. The city one was just down the street, but it wasn't good enough for her."

"So," Jeff says, because he doesn't have all day. "Cancer."

Victor bats the word away and turns abruptly to the guesthouse. He pushes hard on the door, and it scrapes along the concrete. He stands aside and extends a formal arm to let Jeff pass. "Come in, see my place."

Jeff steps inside automatically, but his brain seems to be taking a very long time to process the information before him. The dusty, comfortable jumble is gone, all of it. The boxes and bureaus, his mother's childhood dollhouse, the Victorian cabinet filled with his grandfather's mineral collection. Victor has robbed them. Sold their history. With real grief, Jeff remembers the pleasure of finding a set of little wooden village pieces belonging to his grandmother when she was a child, remembers how she'd brightened when he brought them to her.

The violation is astonishing. "What have you done, Victor?" Jeff's voice comes out strangled.

"I knew you'd flip out," Victor says, as though once again disappointed by the sheer uncoolness of his son. "Shit."

The dim air smells of urine. A square of brown shag covers the concrete between the couch and the TV. Daylight falls on an open microwave crusted with exploded food, a plastic trashcan stuffed to overflowing, a bag of pork rinds scattered across the floor. Three or four metal restaurant chairs with brown vinyl backs are covered in beer cans, clothing, fast-food wrappers, plastic empties of cheap vodka.

Victor is also surveying the place, and he looks a little uneasy. "I let it go a bit, I guess, but it's usually real cozy. Home sweet home."

Jeff turns to his father, disbelieving. His father in his grandmother's home. None of this makes sense. "You broke in. You're *squatting*."

"Would you quit?" Victor screws up his face in annoyance. "I didn't break in anywhere."

"Oh, God. You don't have cancer. Did you really think I wouldn't press charges if I thought you were dying?"

"Becky let me stay. She said if I cleaned it out it was all mine. I'm telling you, she's one nice lady."

There is no way his grandmother let Victor stay here. There is no way. She didn't even know Victor anymore; if they'd had any contact at all, she'd have told Jeff, he's certain. The last time they saw each other was when? Jeff's high school graduation? Almost ten years ago. He remembers them talking, briefly, smiling and standing apart like strangers, while Jeff kept his hand on his mother's arm and involved her in a conversation with his English teacher. "I'm calling the police," he says without conviction. Then he hears it: a snuffling, squeaking noise.

Along the back of the dim room is a huge terrarium. At first Jeff is under the impression that Victor has a dog living in there, one of his pit bulls, maybe. As his eyes adjust, however, he sees that the tank is filled with rats. A wire top is held down with bricks. The rats are glossy gray and brown and black, teeming behind the glass with their obscene naked tails and intelligent faces.

"Jesus," he breathes.

Victor grins proudly. "There's probably twenty or thirty now. They keep breeding—brothers and sisters, sons and mothers, every which way—but half the time they eat each other. I don't even have to feed them."

The rats scramble over one another's heads, impossible to count. Jeff is riveted. "Jesus," he says again.

"Disgusting, huh?" Victor says. "You should see them flip their shit when the snake gets near. You gotta wear special gloves or they'll bite through your hand. Even leather won't hold them back. I got to stun them"—he demonstrates dashing an imaginary rat against the concrete—"or they try to bite her."

"What do you mean, snake?" asks Jeff faintly.

Victor leads him to the bedroom, which is even darker and more fetid. Orange light slinks through the slats of the blinds. In the corner, heaped like laundry next to the unmade bed, is an enormous boa constrictor.

"She's digesting," says Victor, nudging it with his work boot.

The snake unwinds until it's stretched to full length. Jeff steps back. The boa constrictor is huge and butter yellow, shining like something moist that lives underground. It watches Jeff and his father through dull pinprick eyes. A black tongue as glossy as plastic flicks in and out.

Jeff has never been afraid of snakes; he's used to seeing them in the desert. Once he ushered a rattler out of his mother's garden with the tip of a shovel. But this is a monster.

"Hey there, Sabrina, honey." Victor squats, rocks on the balls of his feet, and lifts the snake. The muscles in his arms strain. "Want to hold her?"

Jeff shakes his head, a single jerk.

Victor seems hurt. "She's not going to go and strangle you. She's not hungry. And besides, she's gravid. That's why she's slow." He hoists the snake over his head and drapes it around his shoulders, stroking the thick creamy flank. It moves with muscular silkiness, lifting the weight of head and tail, curling itself around Victor's body. It's languid and sensual and Jeff is repulsed by the thought of his father and the snake living here together.

All at once he remembers something he hasn't thought of in years: staying overnight with his father soon after the divorce, being tucked into his father's bed, and waking in the dark next to him. On his father's other side lay a woman Jeff had never seen. He sat up, watching his father asleep on his back, belly high and bare, and the woman beside him, whom he knew was naked under the sheets. She opened her eyes and looked right at Jeff until he clamped his eyes shut and lowered his head to the pillow. In the morning she was gone; his father stood at the tiny linoleum counter making coffee, no mention of her at all. Jeff is sweating.

"She's my new business, Jeffy. Three thousand bucks every time this lady births. More even. You haven't seen anything cuter than thirty baby snakes."

Under the anger and revulsion, Jeff can't deny a thrill of fascination, because Victor is always, always surprising him. The marvel of Victor is that for all his malefactions—and after today, Jeff can safely add criminal trespass and animal cruelty to the catalogue—still he manages to play the role more of fool than villain. Even this scenario—Jeff shoots another glance at the tank full of incestuous, cannibalistic rats—is darkly, appallingly comic. The story would make for excellent entertainment at the bar with Lisa and his graduate school friends, except that telling it would be a public admission of Jeff's genetic link to this man.

"She's incredible, I'm telling you, a real miracle of creation. She lays eggs, but *inside*. Ovoviviparous! Shit, I love that word."

Jeff hears the door push open in the front room. It's Brooke, blinking in the dark. "Holy crap," she says.

Victor rushes forward, remarkably nimble under

the weight of the boa, his smile almost heartbreakingly eager. "Hey, Brooke, baby. Good to see you." He makes as if to embrace her, but Brooke backs up in alarm and presses against the door, arms crossed. Victor shakes his head with sad affection. "It's been forever, girl! When'd you cut your hair so short?" He turns to Jeff. "She's not a, you know?"

Brooke's presence shakes Jeff from his stunned inaction. "You've got to leave, Victor. Now." He gestures at the room, the rats.

"But that's what I'm trying to explain. Your grandma said I could stay."

"There is no fucking way she said that."

Brooke laughs.

"Jeffrey, your grandma always liked me. She used to tell me, 'Victor, you got potential. Victor, you need to make something of your life.'" Victor is talking like he's about to close a sale. "I'm telling you, every time I ran into her, she inspired me. Over the years we kept in touch on and off. When I saw her in Albertsons maybe six months ago, I'd of recognized her anywhere but she recognized me first, said, 'Victor, honey, how are you?' She told me how you two were doing, college and Columbia and everything, and you know, that was real considerate, seeing as you two never tell me nothing, my own kids. She offered to buy my groceries, but I told her, 'Becky, you keep your money,' and I carried her bags out to the car. Ever since, it's been great between us."

"Does *Mom* know about this?" Brooke steeples her hands over her nose, gaze fixed on the snake. "Oh my God, that thing is so creepy. Can I touch it?"

Victor brightens. "A beauty, isn't she? They're America's fifty-fourth most popular pet."

Jeff is tempted to slap Brooke's hand away. She extends an index finger, hovers, then makes contact. The boa regards her coldly and tastes the air.

"You need to leave now. A real estate agent is coming tomorrow. You need to clean this shit up and get out."

Victor looks stricken. "You're selling Becky's house?"

"We haven't decided," says Brooke.

Victor massages the snake's tail, which flicks obscenely between his fingers. After a moment, he says: "Tell you what. You can sell it, man, fine by me. I'll be your real estate agent, show it to buyers. I know all about property from my cousin Yvette. I'd keep the bathroom and kitchen real clean. I only got to be here until Sabrina has her babies, two months max, and then I can sell them off and get my own place." Victor is jittery, running his free hand through his hair, over and over. "It's the ideal setup, Jeff. You go on back to your school, and I'll take care of everything. You can't sell the house like this, anyways. It needs work. Have you seen under the kitchen sink? Must've been leaking for years."

"You think someone's going to buy this house with you and Animal Planet out here? No fucking way."

"Are you really dying?" asks Brooke.

"Of course I am! Where'm I going to go, Jeff? I don't have a deposit or nothing."

Jeff tries to picture the cancer coiled in his father's abdomen, but he can't make himself believe it. The man is indestructible.

Victor swivels to Brooke. "You want to know the truth,

I'm scared. It was awful seeing your grandma get weak like that. Know what I found in her closet?" Victor lowers his voice to a tragic whisper. "*Depends*. God, poor Becky."

"I didn't know that," Brooke says softly. "That's so sad." Her eyes fill, her first real sign of grief, and Jeff is almost annoyed at her for allowing herself grief at a time like this.

"You went inside the house?" Jeff demands.

"The bathroom out here hasn't been working too good. Would you relax? I didn't go and sell nothing. I'm no criminal. Listen, Jeff, what you got to understand is that I'm not the same guy I was when you were a kid."

Jeff is bilious at the thought of Victor in his grandmother's house, moving with a snake among her belongings. "So you exploited her? You threatened her? Did you punch *her* in the throat?"

Victor is perfectly still for a moment, and when he speaks his voice is careful. "I made mistakes in the past, Jeff. That's on me. Your grandma *gave* me a key. I helped her out, it wasn't just a one-way. Dishes, vacuuming, I did it all. Every single day I made her breakfast."

"I don't believe you," Jeff says. His grandmother was supposed to be hardheaded and practical. She used to say, enjoying her own bawdiness, "You can't bullshit a bullshitter." He supposes she might have been capable of a shrewd calculation: an unused shed for the presence of a grateful man. But what's more impractical than trusting *Victor*?

"I believe him," says Brooke. "I do. Grandma loved having a man around worshiping her."

"Would you stop it, Brooke?" Jeff snaps.

"She never respected me or Mom. You just didn't want to notice."

"You're being a child. She loved you." Brooke is right, though. His grandmother liked her men. But to allow her daughter's abusive ex-husband to move in because she *liked* him?

Maybe. Maybe she told herself she was being broad-minded, not letting social conventions or her family's narrow ideas about loyalty get in her way. It's horrible imagining his grandmother so weak: so hungry for attention that she would turn to a man thirty years younger, so cruel that she would choose Victor.

Victor puts a hand on Jeff's shoulder. "I'm sorry, son. She was old." Jeff can smell his soap and cologne, and he understands that his father showered in preparation for this encounter. "She was sick. Things weren't easy for her."

Jeff smacks Victor's hand away harder than he means to. This is the first time he's touched his father in years.

Victor grins mirthlessly. He rubs the snake's head with his thumb. "You think she needed your permission, Jeff? Where were you? Off at your fancy university, with your fancy girlfriend. Oh, Becky had lots to say about you."

Jeff wants to scroll back to a time—less than an hour ago—when he was mourning the grandmother he knew. Victor is telling the truth, Jeff understands this. His grandmother betrayed him, betrayed all of them. Once, not long after the divorce, he walked in on a conversation between his mother and grandmother. "Maybe he'll take you back," his grandmother was saying, and Jeff had known how wrong she was to say it even before he saw his mother's stricken expression.

"You know, maybe I'm sad, too," says Victor. "Ever think of that? Ever think how you're not the only one who lost an important person? Don't you think I wanted to be at Becky's funeral? I only stayed away for *you* two. You and your mom." He turns his attention to the snake, stroking his thumb across the flat shiny skull. "I wanted to say goodbye."

Brooke's mouth twists. "You and Grandma, you weren't, like, in a *relationship*, were you?"

"I'm not going to apologize." Victor draws himself up, but won't look at them. "She helped me out. She helped me with my drinking."

"Not much, she didn't," says Jeff viciously. He kicks a beer can harder than he means to, and it rattles across the concrete, bounces off the glass front of the terrarium. The rats freeze, then resume their scrambling.

"You mean you *loved* her?" asks Brooke, and her tone is more wondering than disgusted.

"Brooke," Jeff says. "Let me handle this."

"Will you quit bossing everyone?" Her voice is low, her cheeks reddening. "I don't need you handling things. Always calling me—'Are you okay, Brooke? Are you dead yet, Brooke?'—fishing around until you find something to handle. *Mom* doesn't need you." She laughs meanly. "And apparently Grandma didn't need you either. What do you think we did all those years you were off getting your degrees?" She clenches and unclenches her fists, looking helpless and pathetic.

Jeff is stung. Two years ago, when his grandmother phoned with the news that Brooke was in the hospital, Jeff flew home immediately. He can picture his sister exactly, despite the fact that he hadn't been the one to find her, had in fact been two thousand miles away: unconscious in her giant sleep shirt, cheek pressed into the bathmat, some of the pills undissolved in the Technicolor vomit. The image still pains him.

The animal smell in here is so rich and awful, Jeff thinks he might throw up.

"Oh, that's right," Brooke says, "stomp off. Go nurse your precious ego."

Jeff pushes past her to the door and bursts into the yard and the sun's assault. Shaking, he gulps at the clean, dry air.

IN HIS GRANDMOTHER'S KITCHEN, Jeff circles the table, trying to locate her presence in this house. But she is gone. He feels wet and heavy. Years ago, when his grandmother's aunt died, he'd caught her here weeping. "Well, I'm up next!" She laughed through her tears and dragged a Kleenex hard across the fragile skin pouched around her eyes. He watched the skin slide back into place, not knowing how to comfort her. "And that's not the scary part. The scary part is there's no one to turn to. Who will take care of me?"

Mother, sister, Jeff. His family is just too small. Someone should have foreseen that this would be a problem, someone should have made other arrangements. Jeff senses isolation waiting for him, a yawning, sucking nothingness, a dark wind blowing at the edges of this bright, solid world. He can feel its gust.

When Brooke came home from the hospital, Jeff knew he had to talk to her, but had been too afraid. So instead, his grandmother sat Brooke down and said, "No more of this nonsense. This can't happen again." And miraculously, it hasn't. All the while Jeff lingered in the kitchen, a coward, safe in the knowledge that if he, like his sister, should ever let slip his grip on life, his grandmother would be there to boss him back into shape.

Jeff knows he has to go back out there, deal with Victor, untangle this mess, but instead he wants to cry at the injustice. No one should have to be responsible for these lives. "You love it," Lisa told him once. "Who would you be if they didn't need you?"

WHEN JEFF OPENS the guesthouse door, Victor is on the couch, leaning over his thighs. The snake is on the ground, making her deliberate way across the concrete to the terrarium. Jeff shudders, seeing her in motion like that, and when he steps into the house he positions himself behind one of the vinyl-covered restaurant chairs.

"Jeffrey," says Victor, his voice subdued. "Your grandma and I didn't, you know. If it makes you feel any better."

This does, in fact, make Jeff feel better, but he resents the ebbing of his outrage.

"I don't want to hurt you, honey. I'm asking a favor. Please."

"You can stay, Victor," Brooke says. "Jeff, you don't want to sell, I know you don't. Victor can help get the house ready to rent, and then he can manage the place."

"Manage." Jeff's voice is flat. The snake has arranged herself into a pile next to the terrarium. She gazes through the glass. The rats watch her warily, motionless.

"Thank you, baby," says Victor, his voice slack with

relief. He exhales and drops back against the couch. "I thank you."

"When Sabrina gives birth," Brooke continues, "he can sell the babies, and then he can pay Mom rent, too. It's the solution that makes the most financial sense. And apparently Grandma was okay with it." Her expression is bland and controlled, but she keeps tucking the same short piece of hair behind her ear. "So."

"Mom will never go for this."

"I'll convince her." Brooke watches him steadily. It's the same expression Jeff imagines she wore when she stood before the mirror with her full glass of water and smorgasbord of pills. He imagines she held her own gaze as she swallowed.

"I cannot believe you're taking his side, after everything he's done."

"I'm not taking sides."

The snake's head glides closer to the glass, and the rats scramble and squeak.

It won't work. Brooke will make a hash of it, Victor will disappoint, their mother will weep and rant, and Jeff will be called in to set things straight. He laughs acidly. "You're as bad as Grandma, trusting him."

His sister's tone is calm. "People change, Jeff. *I* changed, not that you notice. I'm not still seventeen years old and suicidal. Grandma changed. Maybe Papa has, too."

Brooke doesn't even know Victor, not really, but it seems she sees some other version of their father, the version, perhaps, that Jeff himself missed so desperately after the divorce. For over a year after, Jeff cried soundlessly in his room, longing for his father: his father of the infectious exuberance, his father of the surprising generosity. Possibly this is the Victor Jeff's grandmother saw, too.

Gently, Brooke says, "You shouldn't always have to deal with everything," and Jeff feels that something essential has been wrenched from him.

"Come on, son," says Victor. "We're family. We're all still family."

Jeff whips around, pulling the chair with him, the metal legs scraping the concrete. He understands that somewhere deep in his reptilian brain, he is still afraid of this man. "You're not family, Victor. You forfeited that right." He holds the chair before him like a shield. Rage catches inside him. He wants to maim and destroy, like Victor, like Brooke. He and Brooke, they're both their father's children, Jeff thinks, his heart crashing around behind his sternum. The snake adjusts her head imperceptibly and eyes him. He thinks of his father's hands on her body, that revolting gentleness. He lifts the chair over his head.

For once the man isn't grinning, isn't smiling and sliming his way through life. Maybe *this* is the Victor his grandmother knew: open and vulnerable.

"Oh, no," says Victor. "Please."

Jeff understands how Victor must have felt just before his fist met the frail give of throat. But even as he throws the chair, Jeff is aware that he intends to miss the boa constrictor, because even now, feeling as he does, he can't hurt an animal, can't give himself so fully to this destruction.

"No!" Victor cries in anguish.

The chair does indeed miss the snake. The shock flashes across the glass of the terrarium and the whole sheet pauses, holding its shape and breath. The rats freeze for a single stunned moment. Then the spell breaks, the pieces rain down, and the rats spill like river water from the terrarium.

As if they've waited for this moment, the rats swarm the snake, plunging their sharp teeth and snouts into her flesh.

The boa contracts and strikes outward, over and over, whipping across the cement, trying to fling them loose, and though some of the rats are cast off by the force of her panic, most hold fast. The boa constrictor throws back her head and opens her fanged mouth wide, and Jeff sees all the way down her pale blue-white throat.

F A M I L Y   R E U N I O N

"**W**HAT'S AN ATHEIST?" THE GIRLS AT SCHOOL HAD ASKED Claire at recess when she was ten and a new kid and too dumb to know when to shut up. They were sitting on the grass near the fence, finger-crocheting. Claire was desperate to be liked by these girls with their neat ponytails and jean skirts and coordinating socks. Her strand of finger-crochet looked dingy and tangled, nothing like the smooth braid Josie Lewis produced.

"It means you have faith in the fossil record," Claire had explained, which was how her anthropologist stepfather had explained it to her. Really what it meant, Claire knew, was that you were from the wrong kind of family, a family that rented and wasn't from Salt Lake City and was disfigured by divorce. It meant that instead of a minivan you had a father in San Diego who drank Fosters for breakfast. It meant you weren't Mormon. "Basically it means you believe in *Homo habilis*."

"Ooooh," breathed Lindsay Kimball, whose grandfather was the prophet. "You said *homo*. I'm *telling*." She brushed grass off her skirt and trotted over to the playground monitor.

Claire sighed and followed. Once again, she'd have to sit out for recess.

Claire was always in trouble for swearing, usually for saying "Oh my God." It popped out without her noticing and was hard to control because no one could explain to her why Mormons thought God was a bad word. She thought they were supposed to *like* God.

It was particularly galling to get in trouble for swearing, because her mom didn't even allow *stupid* or *hate* or *shut up*, which all the other kids got to say. And her mother didn't care whether these words were directed at people or not; Claire couldn't even say, "I hate eggplant," which she did, passionately. "So you want me to lie?" she'd asked her mother over ratatouille. "You want me to lie for the sake of appearances?"

"Try *detest*," her stepfather Will had suggested. "Try *loathe* or *abhor* or *execrate*."

Claire's mother shifted Emma to her other breast and smiled across the table at Will, shaking her head. "Thanks, sweetie. That's very helpful."

As far as Claire was concerned, none of these people knew what real swears were. If the girls at school knew the kind of words her father said, they'd never speak to her again. *Mother-fucking-cocksucker-piece-of-shit* and *stupid-cunt-*

bitch. Sometimes he screamed these words at strangers—cashiers at the supermarket, for instance, or other drivers on the stalled freeway. Last summer, he'd taken Claire to the pound to adopt Zark the dog. The day had been a good one, until there'd been a problem with his credit card, which had culminated in him kicking a chair, throwing pens and animal-care pamphlets around the room, and screaming at the poor woman cowering behind the counter.

But her father didn't even have to be mad to say those words. Or even that drunk. Sometimes he said them when he was telling a joke. Claire didn't know their exact meanings, but preferred not to delve too deeply. Every July and August during her six-week visitations, she tried her best to shut the words out. After all, she had her innocence to preserve.

By age eleven, Claire understood that the best way to overcome her disadvantages was to convert. And so she was a frequent visitor to her friends' houses in the upper Avenues. The families of her school friends were moral and prosperous and safe. Their houses had wide hallways, white carpets, rubber trees with leaves that the mothers dusted.

On Sundays, Claire began to accompany friends to church, where she solemnly plucked her square of Wonder Bread and paper cup of tap water from the wire basket as it was passed around. She sang with exuberance in Primary. When she visited people's houses for Monday night Family Home Evenings, she sat up straight and raised her hand and answered questions about the Pearl of Great Price and purity of body, while the other kids squirmed.

At church and school, Claire hid the truth about her own family: the foreign films, the ratty hand-me-downs from the kids of Will's dissertation advisor, and the hikes. Her two-year-old sister's nose was perpetually chapped and snotty from dust allergies. They didn't take baths every night, or even every other night. Instead of mashed potatoes and mac and cheese, they ate dahl with asafetida and rotting cheeses and baba ganoush, all kinds of wet, spicy foods that stank up the house while they were cooking and stank up the bathroom even worse after.

Claire became adept at playing Mormon, and while she never fooled anyone, at least she didn't offend anyone, either. Claire hoped they thought about her soul, and discussed what a credit to the Church it would be. One day, she prayed, they'd recognize her as one of their own and invite her to convert for real.

But despite Claire's efforts, no one did invite her. And there was always some other group, some other activity Claire wasn't a part of. Sure, she might attend church, but then there were Mutual and Young Women's—clubs you actually had to be Mormon to join. And recently Young Women's was absorbing her friends entirely. They now wore deodorant and knee-length khaki skirts and crossed their feet at the ankles. They talked about Firesides and Beehives and Standards Nights and Personal Progress. Claire felt her tenuous grasp on social acceptance slipping away.

AT THE BEGINNING OF JUNE, Claire's mother signed her up for a Girl Scout overnight, even though Claire wasn't in a troop. From what Claire could tell, Girl Scouts was a sort of consolation prize for girls who weren't preparing to be defenders of Zion. There in the damp bunkhouse she met Morgan Swanson. Though Morgan was sturdy and grubby-looking, she had the mannerisms of a sitcom girl: hands on hips, looking out from under her bangs, she'd say "Well, s-o-o-o-*ry.*"

Morgan lived six blocks down the Avenues and went to a different school. For two weeks they spent day after day together, laughing hysterically, whining on the phone until their parents let them spend the night. In the afternoons they'd meet at the corner store halfway between their houses. They'd buy Dots and Pixy Stix and then walk to the cemetery, where they'd eat the candy sitting on gravestones. Morgan tossed the wrappers on the ground; Claire wadded hers into tight balls and tucked them into divots in the lawn.

Afternoons following sleepovers, Claire lolled on the living room carpet, snapping at her mother and Will, snatching toys from Emma. When she was reprimanded, Claire tried out her new comebacks—"Right, I am *so* sure"—and was exiled to her room.

Claire had been stunned to discover that Morgan's family was LDS. She considered herself something of an expert on Mormons, and Morgan's family was nothing like the families who lived in the upper Avenues. Their house was narrow, their stairs cluttered with laundry and toys and *Good Housekeeping* magazines. Claire had only met Mr. Swanson once; he'd nodded at her, then loosened his tie and went to watch TV in the cramped master bedroom. Morgan's mother Patsy, however, was enchanting and given to loud hooting fits of laughter. She fed them frozen chicken nuggets and ice cream. Morgan's family was small: just Morgan and her parents and two little sisters.

"I smell birth control," said Claire's mother.

"Gross," said Claire. "I don't know what you're talking about." She pressed her lips and looked away.

ONE EVENING IN THE MIDDLE of dinner, the phone rang. Claire felt nauseated. She knew who was calling.

Her mother stood. "Hello?" Then her voice hardened. "She's eating right now. Yes, the ticket arrived." Will was watching her mother. Only Emma still shoveled couscous around her plate.

Even though Claire had actual memories of the time, she still had trouble imagining her parents married: sharing a bathroom, running errands together, laughing. They'd been divorced for most of Claire's life, but her father had only begun insisting on visitations a few years ago, when Claire's mother had begun dating Will. "It's my legal right," he said, "and besides, I'm on the wagon."

When her mother handed her the phone, she patted Claire on the back.

"It's your papa!" Today he was in a good mood. He'd once called her mother a fucking bitch and said she was brainwashing Claire, which Claire had found offensive. As if she wasn't intelligent enough to think for herself. Still, even a good mood could turn. She could feel blood thumping in her neck.

"Are you having fun this summer?"

She'd learned it was best to keep her answers short. "Sure."

"I bought your ticket. Are you excited? Do you miss your papa?"

"Sure."

Once Claire had told him the truth, that he was scary and she didn't want to visit and she didn't love him, but he'd said, *Yes you do*, and when she'd countered, *You can't read my mind*, he'd answered, *Yes I can*. She'd been so angry she'd sobbed in her mother's lap for over an hour and hadn't stopped shaking for a long time after that.

That night while Will and Emma read books in the living room, Claire's mother made Mexican hot chocolate, crushing the tablet with the mortar and pestle, stirring milk and sugar in a saucepan. Usually, Claire loved Mexican hot chocolate, but her stomach was still unsettled and something was lodged in her throat. Sad light reflected off the kitchen windows.

"You know he isn't really on the wagon, right?" Claire demanded.

Her mother didn't turn from the stove when she spoke. "When you're a teenager, the law says you can decide for yourself whether you want to visit him. Only two more years." She poured chocolate into Emma's two-handled frog mug and dropped in an ice cube.

"I don't think an alcoholic is a good example for a kid. I would think that you'd agree."

"I do agree, Claire." Her mother sighed, strain showing on her face. "You know I do. But I have to follow the law. At least he doesn't drive when he's like that."

"How would you even know?"

Her mother snapped to attention. "You'd tell me if he did, right?"

Claire shrugged. She couldn't always even tell when he was drunk. He wasn't always angry, of course, but Claire couldn't help feeling that even his high spirits were threaded with danger. Last summer at the pound, the woman behind the counter had run his credit card again and again with shaking hands. Claire had never seen an adult look so frightened. She'd pitied the woman, but she'd also been amazed that the woman had let him take both Claire and the dog home with him.

"Right, Claire?"

"I guess," Claire said, and was disheartened by the comfort her mother seemed to take in this. "Can you put lots of ice in mine? Hot drinks are bad for you."

Her mother dipped her finger in the saucepan. "It's not hot, Claire. Really it's pretty tepid."

"It doesn't matter. Hot drinks burn your insides."

"Sweetie, if it's hot enough to burn your insides, it'd be too hot to drink."

"Mother," Claire explained, her voice rising. "It says so in the *D and C.*"

"*D and C*?" Her mother smiled to herself. "Dilation and curettage?"

"*Doctrine and Covenants*, Mother."

"Ah." She looked at Claire a moment, then cracked the ice cube tray and dropped four into the mug.

Claire took a sip. The chocolate congealed around the ice, coated her tongue in a thick, cold scum. Her stomach clenched. She set the mug on the counter. In the living room, Will and Emma laughed and shrieked.

"Don't you like it?" asked her mother, arranging three cups on a tray. She carried the tray to the living room.

Watching her mother's straight back, Claire was suddenly so filled with rage that she couldn't breathe and her
vision blurred. She poured the chocolate down the sink and
let the mug clang hard against the metal.

WHEN MORGAN CALLED one morning with an invitation to
her family's cabin for their reunion, Claire was thrilled.
She'd never been to a cabin. She pictured logs and woods,
a lake and a canoe. She pictured deer gamboling, squirrels
chattering, friendly raccoons sniffing a red-checked picnic
blanket.

"It's an old church," Morgan said over the phone. "It's
really fun. We're leaving in twenty minutes."

"Please?" Claire asked her mother, hand against the
mouthpiece.

"I don't know." Her mother looked up from the living room
floor, where she was doing an animals-of-the-rainforest
puzzle with Emma. "It's really last-minute. And you haven't
demonstrated that you handle slumber parties very well."

"Mom!" Claire wailed, then caught herself. In her most
adult voice, she said, "I understand I have made mistakes in
the past, but I am responsible now."

Her mother frowned. "You're sure? Five days is a long
time, honey. And you don't know Morgan very well."

"I'll be ready," she told Morgan.

Claire packed all her coolest clothes: jeans with the flowers stitched on the pockets, her yellow and blue plaid shirt
with ruched sleeves, her Swatch with six different bands
you could change depending on your outfit. She brought

eleven pairs of underwear and every color scrunchie she owned.

At family reunions, Claire knew, there were cousins, and some of those cousins were bound to be boys. And since she would be the only one who wasn't a relative, the boys would have to have a crush on her. They might play Truth or Dare.

She wished she had a duffel bag or a rolling suitcase; instead she had to use her stepfather's dusty backpack that he brought on his field trips overseas. It still smelled gamey from his last trip—the smell, Claire was sure, of Ethiopia.

WHEN THE MINIVAN pulled up, only Morgan and Patsy were inside.

Claire's mom came out with her to meet them. Emma, in a saggy diaper and rubber pants, crouched on the sidewalk and prodded a roly-poly. Claire wished her mother had spent a little time on her appearance. She had on her giant thick glasses and a t-shirt with a hole in the shoulder.

"Good morning!" called Patsy, leaning over Morgan. Her red hair was pulled into a sporty ponytail, and she was wearing lipstick and sparkly eye shadow. She was lively, thin, with dry creases around her eyes. The skin between her neck and the top of her shirt was speckled red under a gold locket.

Claire's mother squinted into the car. "Thank you for inviting Claire, Patsy."

"Oh, I'm so glad she could come. We'll have a super time!"

Claire slid open the door and threw her bag in. She turned for a hug, but her mother had squatted beside Emma, who was gumming something in her mouth.

"Emma! We don't eat bugs." Her mother fished around in Emma's howling mouth.

Claire slid the door shut, and Patsy shifted into drive. "Nephi City, here we come!"

Morgan twisted in her seat and made a face at Claire. "It's *not* a city," she said. "So don't get your hopes up."

The cup holders in Patsy Swanson's minivan were gunky, and the backseats were full of naked Barbies and Happy Meal toys and the plastic backings of Fruit Roll-Ups.

"Where's your dad?" Claire asked. "And your sisters? I thought they were coming."

Morgan put her bare feet on the dashboard. "They'll meet us there." She looked at her mother. "Right, Mom?"

Patsy kept her eyes on the road. "Oh, there's going to be lots of people—my sisters and brothers, all their kids, my dad. We'll have a barbeque and everything. It'll be a blast!"

From Salt Lake to Sandy, Morgan played her Paula Abdul tape turned up loud. Morgan and her mother knew all the words. Claire knew only one or two songs, but she sang along anyway, a fraction of a second too late. This was *fun*, the kind of fun girls in movies had with their mothers. Claire's mom only listened to NPR, and sometimes Will turned even that off, saying he needed quiet.

Morgan was clearly her mother's pal, ranked above her younger sisters, and now Claire was Patsy's pal as well. Claire was emphatically not her mother's pal; Will was, and Emma was pal to both of them. Right now they were all probably at the shallow end of the city pool, clapping and cheering as Emma swam the three feet between her parents. Sometimes Claire felt like nothing more than a reminder of an unhappy time in her mother's life, the unfortunate consequence of an unfortunate marriage. Claire supposed if she were her mother, she'd want to forget it all, too—the shouting, the smashed chairs—to inhabit completely this calm, fresh life with her new husband and new child. Still, it wasn't fair that her mother could divorce her father and never see him again, while summer after summer Claire was sent to pay for her mother's mistakes.

Outside Provo, Patsy pulled off at a convenience store. "Whew," she said. She arched her back, stretching long and slow, and Claire saw a crescent of pale skin at her waist. "Let's get some snacks." At the door, she gave Claire and Morgan each ten dollars. "Pick what you want. I'll get drinks." Morgan didn't even exclaim over the amount, just started browsing, and Claire wondered if the Swansons were secretly rich.

She chose M&Ms, then couldn't decide between potato chips and pretzels. "What do you think?"

Morgan had already paid and was munching on bright orange chips. "Come *on*," she said. "Just get it all."

Outside, Patsy was waiting for them at the picnic table with a six-pack of fruit drinks. Claire had never had anything so delicious, sparkling and bright and fruity. They didn't even drink soda at her house, and this was something else altogether. She took tiny sips to make it last. This was probably the kind of thing they drank in France. She sipped again and inspected the glass bottle with the bunch of fruit embossed near the long, tapering top. *Fruit Coolers.*

"Hey," Claire said. "This contains six percent alcohol by volume!"

"Oh my heck!" shouted Morgan. She looked at her bottle. "How do you know?"

Patsy took a long drink, nearly emptying her bottle, then inspected the label. "So it does. I can't believe I made that mistake." She collected the bottles from the girls and stood.

Morgan clamped her hand over her mouth. "We just broke the Word of Wisdom."

Claire looked longingly at her bottle—still nearly full—as Patsy carried it to the trash, wishing she'd gulped it, wishing she'd kept her mouth shut. She'd probably never taste anything so wonderful again.

In the car Morgan was quiet for a while. Then she turned to Patsy. "Mom, what are we going to do? *We broke the Word of Wisdom.*"

The Word of Wisdom was a very big deal. At the beginning of the year, Lindsay Kimball's dad had bought a Cherry Coke. "With *caffeine*," Jessica Beckstead had reported. Listening, Claire had mirrored the other girls' dropped jaws. When he got home, Lindsay's mother had made him get right back in the car and return it, even though he'd already opened the can. "Did they take it back?" asked Josie Lewis, voice low, and Lindsay Kimball's eyes had filled with tears.

But Claire never expected that Morgan would respond like this, mouth tight and worried, forehead creased. The Morgan Claire knew pocketed candy at the corner store and said, "What the H-E-double-hockey-sticks."

Patsy sighed. She gripped the steering wheel with both

hands. "Would you stop overreacting, Morgan? We didn't do it knowingly. You don't get in trouble for an accident."

Morgan chewed her lip. "How do you know?"

"Listen, I once dated a guy who did his Mission in Peru. Someone gave him a drink, and he had a few sips before he realized there was alcohol in it. It's not a big deal if it's an accident."

"I've had wine," Claire offered tentatively. She'd never told anyone this. "On special occasions my parents give me some mixed with water. That's how kids in France have it." She paused. "Wine can actually be healthful. It's only bad if you abuse it."

"See?" Patsy said to Morgan. "Not a big deal." Patsy looked at Claire through the rearview mirror. "Do you like wine? Do your mom and Will have it every night with dinner?"

Claire held Patsy's gaze in the mirror. "No, not that much. Definitely at dinner parties."

"Oh," said Patsy, voice even. "They have dinner parties? Fancy ones?"

Claire's parents sometimes had potlucks with Will's colleagues at the U—mostly professors and foreigners who brought their precocious children and third-world food. "The ladies get really dressed up and there's candles and stuff. Usually we have steak and lobster." She added helpfully, "It's called Surf and Turf."

Patsy looked over her shoulder. "And there's wine. And they're not evil, right?"

"No," said Claire, shocked. "Of course not."

"There you go. Claire's had wine and she's not evil."

Morgan faced front, but Claire could tell her shoulders were tense. In a low, hard voice, she said, *"Claire's not a member. Claire doesn't get to enter the Celestial Kingdom."*

Claire's face burned. She thought of how much she'd loved the fruit cooler, wondered if the longing she'd felt *was* a kind of evil, and then, sickened, if she was on the road to becoming her father.

"Morgan, Claire is your guest. I expect you to treat her like one. I apologize for Morgan. I don't know what's gotten into her."

Claire looked at the ground to avoid Patsy's eyes in the mirror. With her foot she prodded a topless Barbie in hot pants.

Morgan turned away, and for another hour no one spoke.

Morgan was right: Nephi City was not a city. It was a town surrounded by flat grassland at the foot of the Wasatch Mountains. The houses were small, some single- and double-wide trailers, with dry lawns and neat flowerbeds. The cabin was just off Main Street, across from 5 Buck Pizza and King's Hardware.

When Morgan had said the cabin was an old church, Claire had pictured a creaking bell tower and an overgrown cemetery. The Swansons' church was flat and built of long orange bricks. Instead of a steeple, there was an A-frame vestibule with cracked white trim. This building should have been tolerated, or torn down, or added onto with some equally hideous addition. Not bought. Claire pictured the person—Patsy's father—who passed by and thought he saw potential.

Inside, the church was dim and forbidding. Dwarfed by the space of the sanctuary was a cluster of orange institutional couches with hard blocky cushions. Dark paneling printed to resemble wood lined the walls; that and the brown carpeting made the room dusky, even in the heat of the day. Sunlight penetrated the gloom only at the far end of the sanctuary, where a vinyl accordion door was folded to reveal a yellow-tiled kitchen.

"Hey," said Morgan, apparently only now realizing the place was empty. "Where is everyone?"

"They'll be here soon," said Patsy. "Tomorrow, maybe." She dropped onto a couch.

The bedrooms were the offices and classrooms, ten down a hallway.

"We call the end room!" yelled Morgan, flinging open the door to reveal two single beds. The bedspreads were thin, one pink, one orange, the nubbled chenille stripes grimy. A window between the beds looked out on a dry lawn with picnic tables and a concrete basketball court. Beyond was a chain-link fence, and beyond that the yard of a small house, littered with faded toy trucks.

"I call the pink bed," said Morgan. "I mean, if that's okay. You're the guest."

"That's cool," said Claire, sitting on her bed. She smiled so Morgan wouldn't notice how disappointed she was by the cabin. It smelled like the dust on a window screen.

The hall was lined with shut doors. "Ta-*da*," said Morgan, pushing one open. "Wanna go in the boys' bathroom? We can."

Inside, instead of three bathroom stalls, like in the women's, there was only one, plus two urinals along the wall.

"Weird, huh?" said Morgan.

They peered into a urinal.

"They see each other's thingies when they go. They just pull them right out in front of each other. Gross, right?"

"Have you ever seen one?" asked Claire.

"Doy, on my little cousins."

"I mean on a grown-up. Like on your dad."

"No," said Morgan, shocked. "Have you?"

Claire's father walked around naked. He said it was natural. He even opened the front door naked, beer in hand. "You don't mind, do you?" he'd asked the neighbor who came to borrow jumper cables. The man had laughed nervously. "No problemo." Claire minded. A lot. She had to pretend to be absorbed by the television or her book, all the while being so aware of his hairy red penis swinging around.

"Of course not." Claire pressed the flusher on the urinal. As the water surged and swirled, it splashed Morgan's arm.

"Nastaroni!" yelled Morgan and ran out.

"MAKEOVER TIME," Patsy announced.

At the drugstore they put whatever they wanted into the cart. Mud masks, glitter polish, a massive bag of Laffy Taffy, a glass bottle of Jean Naté each for Claire and Morgan. Claire felt rich and glamorous. The three of them laughed and called to each other across the aisles, while all around them dull-faced townspeople were buying toilet paper and laundry detergent, sweat suits and packs of socks.

Claire picked up a package of barrettes.

"Put them in," Patsy said. She considered the blow dryers, then placed the most expensive model in the cart. "This is our vacation. We deserve quality."

Back at the church, they spent a long time in the bathroom, makeup and brushes and creams spread on the counter. Claire didn't know when she'd last been so happy. Shimmering teal eye shadow reached Morgan's eyebrows and her cheeks were nearly purple with blush. Patsy had given herself Cleopatra eyes and lined her lips in dark red.

"I could do your hair," Claire offered Patsy.

"Or I could," said Morgan.

"Super," said Patsy, handing Claire the brush.

Patsy's hair wasn't as soft as Claire expected, but beautiful still. Up close, two or three silver strands shone among the red.

"Girls," said Patsy, eyes closed, "you don't know it now, but these are the best days of your lives."

"Really?" asked Claire. Just yesterday this would have been devastating news. Her whole life she'd been banking on things getting better, but today, hair teased in a high, tight ponytail, makeup so thick her skin itched, Claire could almost believe it.

"Maybe," said Morgan grimly. She watched with narrowed eyes as Claire wrestled Patsy's hair into a messy French braid, then sprayed it all stiff.

The phone rang, its sound barely reaching them from the sanctuary at the far end of the long hall, but Patsy continued to apply her mascara.

"We should get it," said Morgan. "It might be Dad."

Patsy put a hand on Morgan's wrist. "Let it go." She blinked at her reflection.

THAT AFTERNOON, MORGAN and Claire sat in the shade on the concrete steps, watching cars pass. It was hot, and when Claire scratched at her face, the makeup gathered in gluey worms under her nails. Patsy had gone off in the minivan promising a treat, and without her there, all the day's liveliness seemed to have evaporated in the parched air. It was funny to Claire, this concept of setting up a vacation house—cabin (*why* would they call it a cabin?)—in a place where people lived their lives. In houses all around, women vacuumed and baked meatloaf, kids watched television, men left for work and came home.

"Don't worry," Morgan said. "It will be more fun when my dad and my cousins get here."

"I'm having fun," said Claire, listless.

Patsy returned with a bag of groceries and Rocket Pops. "You know what we need, girls? A sprinkler party!"

By the time the girls had changed, Patsy was already in her swimming suit, her towel spread on the dry grass. She lay on her back, stretched her toes and pressed her middle with the pads of her fingers, frowning. Her suit was magenta, a one-piece, but not the kind the mothers of Claire's friends wore when Claire accompanied them to the Deseret Gym, with legs and cap sleeves. It was a regular swimming suit, like Claire's own mother's. Morgan looked at Patsy, alarmed, then quickly over at Claire, as if to see if she'd noticed. Claire averted her eyes and pretended to be absorbed in catching the drips on her popsicle with her tongue.

"Go on, girls," said Patsy, indicating the sprinkler. "Play!"

Claire hooted and splashed, acting out an approximation of fun, trying to lift Morgan's mood. She was doing this for Patsy, Claire realized, and she laughed more vigorously, until she realized they actually *were* having fun. She grabbed the hose and aimed the sprinkler at Morgan.

"I'm gonna kick your trash!" yelled Morgan and charged her.

Finally, breathless, they dropped onto towels beside Patsy. Morgan's mascara had dissolved around her eyes, giving her a haunted, dissolute appearance. A woman in a long denim dress passed on the sidewalk and looked at them. Claire imagined how they must seem to her: idle, fascinating, privileged.

Patsy squinted into the sun. "This is nice. Reminds me of when I was a teenager, hanging out at the city pool." She turned onto her belly and wiggled out of her straps.

Morgan scowled at her mother's bare freckled back. "Where's Dad? You said he was coming."

"Something came up at work. So it'll be just us girls!"

Morgan glared. "Next time he calls, I want to talk to him." She stalked to the steps and sat hugging her knees.

Patsy rolled onto her side and smiled at Claire. "Morgan's very close to her dad. He's a really good man. He converted for me, you know." The skin on her chest was even redder than usual and the tops of her small breasts squeezed together.

"Really?" asked Claire. She paused. "Who's watching Morgan's sisters?"

"They're with our neighbor." Patsy's voice was suddenly sharp. "Do you think I'd just leave them alone?"

Claire opened her mouth to apologize, but to her relief Patsy smiled again.

"I met Mr. Swanson in college. I was a sophomore and he was a senior. I had lots of boyfriends back then, but he fell in love with me immediately. By the end of the year we were married. Now he's even more devout than me!"

"Wow," said Claire. Patsy was talking to her as if she were an equal, a friend. She looked at Morgan, who was glowering on the steps. Morgan swiped at her face, smearing her makeup still more.

"So Will's your stepdad?" Patsy asked.

Claire inhaled. "Uh-huh."

"Your mom got a divorce from your real dad?"

Claire nodded. Pieces of grass were stuck to her ankles, but when she tried to pick them off, they clung to her wet fingers. "But it was because he could be really mean."

"Mr. Swanson's not mean." Patsy rolled onto her back, eyes closed to the sun. "So . . . did your mom have boyfriends before Will?"

Claire looked at her thighs. The water was beginning to dry. She felt sticky. "A couple."

"Did they ever spend the night? Did Will spend the night at your house before they got married? Did they sleep in the same bed?"

Claire didn't say anything. Her eyes felt hot and she couldn't have raised her head if she'd wanted to.

Patsy patted her leg, left her hand there, and Claire felt a warm rush in her thighs. "It's okay, honey. I'm not judging."

Her voice was so kind. Somehow Patsy understood the shame and was forgiving her.

Morgan stomped over and grabbed Claire's wrist. "Come on. We need to go for a walk."

Patsy squinted up. "I'll come with you."

Claire didn't want to leave Patsy's side.

"No," said Morgan and yanked. "Why can't you leave us alone?"

Patsy blinked, her face naked and hurt.

"Ugh!" shouted Morgan, throwing a towel over her mother. "Get *dressed.*"

They walked around the block, but they were barefoot and the pavement was hot. In some places the sidewalk gave way entirely and they had to pick their way through burning dirt. Morgan walked three steps ahead and never said a word and never turned around.

Claire tried to pretend to be interested in the neighborhood: small houses, a boarded-up garage, some little kids in a yard who eyed them suspiciously as they passed. At the next corner, Morgan waited for Claire. She seemed to have softened.

"So when's the family reunion starting?" asked Claire conversationally.

"Stupid. There *is* no family reunion."

"What?" asked Claire. "Your mom lied?"

Morgan turned away. Her pale shoulders were hunched and the straps of her bathing suit cut into her soft skin. "She didn't lie. There must be some mistake."

Claire hesitated before asking, "Morgan, is your mom Mormon?"

Morgan whirled around. "Of course she is," she snapped. "Her father is a *bishop*."

"Oh," said Claire, suddenly aware that she liked Morgan less. "Why are you so mad?"

THAT EVENING AS PATSY was laying out the fried-chicken dinner from the restaurant near the highway, the phone rang again. "We'll let it go," Patsy said. She put a hand on Morgan's shoulder a moment, then continued setting the plastic sporks on thin paper napkins. The phone stopped.

"I want to call Dad," said Morgan. They'd washed their faces, but Morgan's eyes were still shadowed.

Patsy shook her head. "Let's not bother him. He's very stressed out with work."

After a moment she turned to Claire and said, "Maybe you should give your parents a call, let them know you're okay."

"It's fine," Claire said, feeling Morgan's glare. "I can do it after dinner."

"Now's good," said Patsy. "Just to check in."

Claire dialed carefully. Her mother picked up. "Did you call me, Mom? Just now?" Claire could hear Emma and Will laughing in the background.

"No, honey, but it's great to hear your voice. Are you having fun?"

Claire said she was, then waited for her mother to ask if everything was okay, but she didn't. "Morgan's dad couldn't make it."

"Oh? That's too bad. But you're having a good time?"

There was so much she wanted to tell her mother—about the wine coolers, about how sad Patsy seemed, and how Morgan was angry with her and she didn't know why—but Patsy and Morgan were both watching. "We did makeovers today. We ran in the sprinklers."

"That sounds terrific, sweetie."

"Yeah." Claire allowed a silence, into which her mother ought to have read that everything had gone wrong.

Instead, her mother said, "I better go, honey. I've got to put Emma to bed, or she'll be a grouch."

When Claire dropped the phone into its cradle, Patsy said, "Bon appétit!"

The fluorescent ceiling panel seemed very far from the table and the flickering dim light made Claire sad. Morgan was silent as they ate. Claire kept glancing at her, but she didn't lift her gaze from her mashed potatoes.

Morgan was a brat. She was spoiled and didn't know how good she had it, having Patsy as her mother. At least Patsy wanted to spend time with Morgan. At least Patsy *tried*.

"This is delicious," Claire told Patsy. She paused. "I think you're a really good mom."

"Thank you, Claire." Patsy smiled gratefully and looked more beautiful than ever. They both considered Morgan, who appeared not to have heard.

But when Patsy took the dirty paper plates to the kitchen, Morgan looked right at Claire. "Just so you know, you're going to be cast into Outer Darkness."

"Outer Darkness?"

"That's where the bad people go, the people who deny Jesus. There's nothing there. Just dark." Morgan's gaze was very still and certain. "*We'll* be in the Celestial Kingdom. My mom and dad and my sisters and me."

"That's not true," said Claire. Surely she'd have heard of this before.

Morgan pressed her lips and nodded, as if to say it was a shame, but it wasn't up to her. "It's definitely true."

Claire thought of her conversations with Will about galaxies beyond the Milky Way, how when he explained infinity she felt so queasy and anxious she had to push the idea from her mind. The notion that she could end up in that emptiness was terrifying. Panic tightened around her chest.

She imagined them all, Morgan and the girls from school with their pretty haircuts and orthodontia and ironed floral dresses, all of them being lifted above her, led through the Celestial Curtain, which glowed white with warmth and life, while she, with her tangles and off-brand Keds and too-short jeans, was sucked into the cold dark-ness of space. Floating around like an astronaut who had come untethered, without even stars to orient herself.

"Ice cream!" sang Patsy, sweeping in and placing a paper bowl in front of each of them.

Claire felt close to tears. "Maybe it's just a story."

"It isn't a story," Morgan said. "It's revelation. God told Joseph Smith personally."

"Morgan," warned Patsy. "What are you talking about? We don't need to talk about that."

"Yes," Morgan insisted, "we do need to talk about it."

Patsy bit her lip. "This isn't really dinnertime conversation."

Morgan whipped around and looked at her mother. "Why shouldn't we talk about the teachings of the Prophet? Revelation is important. You *know* that." She stood. Claire could feel her rage vibrating around them. Morgan pointed at her mother. "You'd *better* know that!" she shouted, then ran down the hall. At the far end, a door slammed.

Outer Darkness. There was no such thing, thought Claire. She was an atheist, so there couldn't be.

If Claire were away from her family when the end came—say, if it happened tonight while she was in Nephi City—she would be cast out alone, with no one to hold her as she drifted around in the vast, airless blackness. Her mom and Will and Emma might be destined for Outer Darkness, too, but they'd have each other.

She pictured the three of them as they were now, probably reading books on the couch at home, the lamplight warm and yellow. They'd be reading *The Mammoth Hunt*, Emma's favorite book, laughing at the antics of Fern and little Sam, the Ice Age siblings. Emma, with her dimpled hands and silky honey-brown curls, surrounded by her mother and father, all their heads touching. They were perfect, the three of them: related, joined. A triangle, the strongest shape there is.

LATER THAT NIGHT, Claire found Patsy and Morgan lying together on Morgan's bed. Morgan's face was pressed into her mother's chest, and Patsy's fingers were twined in her hair. Claire stood in the doorway, watching them. Four more days. She missed her mother with an intense, full-body longing that hit her so hard, so squarely in the chest, she couldn't breathe. She knew she'd begged to be allowed to come here with Morgan; why then did she feel she'd been sent away?

Much later, when Claire woke in the night, Patsy was gone and Morgan was sleeping. Claire opened the bedroom door. At the end of the long hall, a light was on.

In the sanctuary, Patsy was in a long rose-printed nightgown, hunched over the phone. Claire stood in the dark of the hall, watching.

"It has been a while!" Patsy laughed gaily in the way Claire loved. "Three kids, yeah. I've been thinking about you a lot lately. A lot." Her voice dropped, and then Claire realized that something was wrong. Patsy was drinking Fruit Coolers. She had a box of them, and there were four empties, the one in her hand half-full. Her voice rose and tightened. "Anything you wanted. I'd do it now." She listened for a long time. "I know it's late. I'm sorry. I know."

Patsy hung up, then threw the bottle against the wall. It hit with a crack but didn't break. Claire watched the bottle empty itself into the carpet, and thought again of Outer Darkness. She could feel it gusting inside her, cold and vast, as if she'd swallowed a bite of it at dinner and it had swelled to fill her.

Patsy dropped her head into her hands. "Oh my gosh." She hit the floor with her fist. "Fuck," she wailed softly. Then: "Jesus. Jesus. Jesus *Christ.*"

When she lifted her head, she looked directly at Claire, as if she'd known she was there all along. Patsy's mascara was smeared, her eyes dark and red.

"I'm sorry," Claire croaked and backed down the hall.

Patsy caught up with her and put an arm around Claire's shoulder. "You poor thing. You're sad. I've made you sad. Are you sad?"

Claire shook her head.

Patsy kneeled before her, dragging on Claire's hands. "I was just talking to an old friend, but I'm okay now. Everything's okay."

"Is it true about Outer Darkness?" And as if responding to its name, the emptiness inside Claire dilated. "Is it true I can't be with my family in the Celestial Kingdom?"

"Oh, gosh." Patsy looked stricken, and her eyes welled with tears again. "It is true," she said. "I'm so sorry, honey. I don't know what to tell you." She dropped her head, then looked up suddenly. "But it will be okay!" She jumped to her feet and steered Claire down the hall with both arms.

She pushed open a swinging door. The dark room was empty but for a pool sunken in the floor, a huge square expanse of tiny bathroom tiles. Four steps and a metal handrail led down.

"This is the baptismal, Claire."

"Wow," said Claire. She thought baptismals were supposed to look like birdbaths, or grander, more sacred-looking, like the marble-edged pools in the book of Maxfield Parrish paintings her parents had. This was so ordinary, like a drained swimming pool, except smaller and cubic.

Patsy descended the steps, put the stopper in, and turned the faucet.

While the baptismal filled, the two of them stood at the edge. Patsy held Claire's hand so hard it hurt. Outside the pebbled glass windows a phosphorous streetlight shone. The water was black, the pool too deep for its proportions.

Patsy shut off the faucet. "Do you know what this means?"

Claire listened to the quiet of the church and the sounds of water dripping and a gurgle in the pipes. This was it, the moment her life would change. Claire's chest was tight, her mouth dry. What surprised her is how accidental this all felt: imagine if she hadn't woken up, imagine if she'd slept through her chance. She nodded.

Patsy led her by the hand into the warm water. Claire had never been submerged in her clothes; her pajamas dragged around her legs as she took each step. When they were in the center of the pool, they stood facing each other until the black water stilled around them. The water was high on Claire's chest. The line of wet climbed Patsy's nightgown, and where the thin fabric clung to her breasts, the rosebuds looked like welts.

Claire breathed in the steam and the scent of Patsy's lotion. Her mind was quiet, waiting.

"It's okay, honey," said Patsy. "Deep breath."

Patsy cupped one hand behind Claire's head and held both Claire's hands in her other, then tipped her back into the water.

Claire's eyes flew open. She couldn't see anything in the warm dark, except, somewhere, a shifting haze of orange light. For a moment she felt bodiless, as though she'd become the water, but then the weight of it pressed around her, squeezing her lungs and throat. Claire opened her mouth to scream, but before she could, she had surfaced. She sputtered and coughed and blinked the stinging water from her eyes.

"Now do me," said Patsy, and she settled herself in Claire's arms.

Claire cradled her awkwardly, aware of the slippery warm skin at Pasty's neck and of the sucking of her own t-shirt against her belly. Patsy's gown drifted beneath the water as graceful as mermaid hair. Claire gazed down at Patsy's calm face and her closed, waiting eyes.

"Do it *now*, Claire."

When Patsy came up, water streamed from her face. She was smiling. "That's what we needed," Patsy said softly, the ends of her red hair dripping. "A new start."

Claire smiled back. For a long time, it seemed, they stood smiling at each other, like people in a movie in love. Then Claire remembered the strange phone call.

"Are you okay?" she asked. "Why were you so sad?"

Patsy pulled her close. "You could be my daughter," she said. "I feel like you are." Patsy kissed her on the mouth.

Warmth and happiness flooded Claire. "I know," she said. "Me, too."

Patsy pushed Claire's hair back, and shivers went down Claire's spine in wave after wave. It was almost too much, this happiness.

Patsy cocked her head, coy. "Can I tell you a secret? Promise not to tell?"

The sense of her loyalty brought tears to Claire's eyes. She wanted to do something for Patsy, to sacrifice, to obliterate herself for this woman. "I promise."

Patsy put her face close, and Claire could feel her breath on her lips when she whispered. "No one knows where we are. Not Mr. Swanson. Not your mother. No one."

Claire realized she'd already known this, but as soon as Patsy spoke the words, she was afraid.

Patsy put her wet forehead against Claire's, and though she wanted to, Claire didn't step back. It seemed only the pressure of the water surrounding her kept her on her feet. "You and I have a bond here that is really special, Claire. You may not recognize it now, but you will."

In Patsy's lopsided smile, her misty eyes, her affection, there was a ripple of something dangerous that Claire hadn't noticed before.

The Fruit Coolers.

"Patsy," she said. "I need to tell you something." Claire took a deep breath. "My father is an alcoholic. My real father. He screams and breaks things. Once when he was drunk he kicked the dog and she threw up blood." In Claire's mind her voice was strong and clear, but when they came out, the words were small and whimpered in the dripping vastness of the baptismal. "I need to tell you that the Word of Wisdom is right."

A shadow passed over Patsy's face. For a long moment she regarded Claire. Then she drew away and set the current swirling. She rose grandly up the steps, water flowing from her nightgown, and wrapped herself in a towel. "Of course it is." Her shape loomed black against the orange glow from the windows. "I know that." Patsy held open the door. "Get out," she said sharply. "It's bedtime."

Suddenly, Claire didn't want to leave the pool. "I want to go home."

Patsy laughed harshly. "Oh, you're going home. Tomorrow first thing."

In the dark bedroom Claire peeled off her soaking pajamas, hunching to hide herself while Patsy watched. She didn't have another pair, so she pulled on a t-shirt and shorts, shivering.

In ten days, Claire was scheduled to fly to San Diego. Six weeks would stretch on as if forever. She would have to relearn how to be careful, how to call him Papa, how to smile when he was in a good mood and make herself small when he wasn't. She would have to gauge how much he'd had to drink, to pretend not to notice when he raged. And all the while she would carry the vast darkness inside her. Meanwhile, life at home would go on. Emma would continue her Little Guppy swimming lessons at the Y, her friends would become more and more adult, more and more the ladies Claire would never be. Her mother and Will would do puzzles with Emma, their three heads bent together. Safe in their ignorance, her family would close around the space she left, and when Claire came back in August, she'd be a stranger to them.

Patsy patted Morgan's bed. Morgan breathed open-mouthed, her neck angled so that it looked almost broken. "Lie down."

Claire looked uncertainly at her own bed, but obeyed. She tried to read Patsy's expression, but the moon had shifted and her face was in shadow. Morgan rolled in her sleep, her body hot and soft against Claire's own, and Claire felt ill.

"You needed this time with us, Claire. A child drinking wine. Disgusting." Patsy tucked the blanket under her chin and pushed it hard into her throat, then lifted Morgan's heavy arm so it lay across Claire's chest. "Sleep tight."

Patsy crossed the dark room, stood for a minute at the threshold, and then shut the door.

JUBILEE

WHEN ANDREA PULLED INTO THE DIRT LOT BY THE ORCHARDS that adjoined the blueberry fields, she saw she'd timed their arrival just right. Where the farmworkers normally parked their beat-up sedans and rusting pickups, the Volvos and Mercedes and Audis were lined up, a faint scrim of dust from the dirt drive on their hoods. Usually, Andrea was embarrassed by her mother's old Chrysler with its missing wood panel, but today she parked it among the luxury vehicles with a sense of vindication.

"Nice rides," said Matty, nodding appreciatively.

"I told you, they own everything. Like three hundred acres." She gestured at the trees and at the sky, too, as if the Lowells actually did own the whole wide world. "Not just blueberries, either. They grow practically every stone fruit ever invented. Even the dumb ones, like nectarcots."

For several years, the blueberry industry in California had been expanding, and the Lowells had been early adopters. In honor of their eleventh annual blueberry party, the field-workers—a few of whom Andrea had known her whole life—had been given this Saturday off, paid. "Wouldn't want the precious guests to have to pick alongside Mexicans." She snorted, picturing the Lowells' friends in their Brooks Brothers chinos and silk skirts and strappy heeled sandals making their way down the rows.

Matty shrugged. "I wouldn't mind a paid day off."

"You'd have to have a job first," said Andrea, then glanced at him, worried she'd offended him. But it wasn't even clear he'd heard; he was looking, as usual, at something that wasn't her. Andrea wished he'd shaved that wormy black mustache or had at least put on a button-down. He looked so good in a button-down. But whatever, she reminded herself; she didn't actually care what the Lowells thought.

Andrea had dawdled in a gas station off the highway so they wouldn't be on time. She'd bought Matty a forty— rather, he bought it with his fake ID and her cash—then lingered, trying to distract him. She flicked a plastic bottle of pheromones near the checkout. "Imagine the kind of guy who thinks Sexxx Juice is going to improve his prospects," she said. Andrea was always bringing up sex around Matty so she could demonstrate how cool she was with it. At the magazine rack, she dragged on his arm, trying to look game and easygoing as she pointed out details in men's magazines. ("Guys really think that's hot?" "Yes," Matty said.) Finally, though, Matty had pitched his bottle—still half-full—and asked if they were going to this party or not.

Technically, Andrea had been invited to this party. Rather, her parents had been invited. Technically. But she was certain that the Lowells didn't actually expect them to come. After all, they'd never been invited before. This invitation—letterpress-printed on thick, soft paper—had been a gesture of goodwill, and not even that, Andrea was sure, but something the Lowells had felt they had to do, given that her father would be there anyway, with his taco truck.

The truck was a highlight of this year's party, according to the invitation: "Tacos provided by our own Salvador Romero and his El Primo taco truck!" And there, instead of blueberries on sage-colored sprigs, was the truck itself: a festive little line drawing debossed in red and yellow.

The taco truck was a recent acquisition. Andrea's father had saved for four years, plotting, cobbling together loans (including a pretty substantial one from William Lowell), driving the family crazy with his exuberance. The truck would pay for itself, he said, would give him something to do. All week it was shuttered, parked in the driveway while her father worked as a supervisor in the Lowells' orchards, and on the weekends he drove it to the park, where he served egg burritos and Cokes to young men famished after their soccer games, tacos and tortas to families out for a stroll. Her father never said so, but Andrea suspected from her mother's strained silence on the subject that the taco truck wasn't as lucrative as he'd hoped.

"Are they kidding?" Andrea said when she heard the Lowells were hiring her father for the party. "You'd think they'd want something fancy."

"Oh, you know these wealthy people," said her mother, shaking her head in bemusement. "They get their ideas."

Her parents had been delighted to see the truck fea-

tured on the Lowells' invitation and had gushed about how
touched they were to have received it. Her mother turned
the invitation in her hands and shook her head in wonder.
"They didn't have to think of us, but they did."

Andrea was hijacked by the image of her mother in her
teal dress with the gold chain belt, trailing the Lowells all
over their party. "You're not actually thinking about going,
are you, Mom?"

Hurt flashed in her mother's face, and Andrea bristled
at the Lowells for causing this hurt. "I work on Saturdays,"
her mother said stiffly and dropped the invitation in the
trash. Later, in spite of herself, Andrea had plucked it out
and squirreled it away in her room, saving even the enve-
lope (yellow lined in red—why was she so impressed with
the invitation?—she hated that she was so impressed).

Well, if the Lowells wanted Mexicans at their party,
that's what they'd get.

The day wasn't ideal for an outdoor party, Andrea saw
as she unstuck herself from the driver's seat. The leaves
of the peach trees were dusty silver in the hot afternoon
light, and a breeze stirred the dry soil. "You won't believe
these people," she told Matty, shutting the car door. She
told him about the framed photograph she had once seen
in their kitchen: the redheaded brother and sister as children in their green velvet coats, the Eiffel Tower lit and
snowy behind them. "Can you believe that? Matching
coats! And she was actually wearing white gloves. What a
waste to bring little kids to France. They probably planned
the whole trip just for that one stupid picture of their kids
being adorable in Paris."

"Annoying," conceded Matty.

"Tell me about it. They probably read *Madeline* every five minutes. They probably couldn't stop themselves."

Andrea still remembered the children's expressions: the boy flashing a showy television-child smile, little Parker scowling at her patent-leather toes. She'd seen the picture years ago; Andrea had come with her father when he'd stopped by to pick up paychecks. She remembered the kitchen, too, large and gleaming, the row of pale green porcelain bowls as thin as eggshells stacked in the open shelves. Mrs. Lowell had given Andrea three still-cooling ginger cookies wrapped in a napkin, which Andrea had made last for over a week, tasting in the increasingly stale nibbles the calm and security and beauty of this home.

"I'm pretty sure Parker Lowell isn't even that smart. She's too *sweet* to be smart." Andrea fingered an aching pimple on her forehead.

"Do you think she's easy? In my experience lots of rich girls are easy."

Andrea ignored the pang in the center of her chest. "I'm pretty sure she only got into Stanford because she's legacy," she said, even though she didn't believe it.

"Why are we here?" asked Matty. "If you hate them so much."

Matty was here because Andrea had strong-armed him into coming; she intended for people to assume he was her boyfriend. It was the least he could do, after all the essays she'd written for his classes at Chico State.

And why was Andrea here? Driving, she'd felt full of the brazen courage she would need to crash this party. She would show up full of breezy, sparkling confidence that would startle these people. Andrea was an equal now, a

Stanford student, poised and intelligent, no longer just the daughter of one of their laborers, no longer an awestruck kid worshiping their cookies, and if the Lowells wanted to trot out her father and his taco truck to provide a little kitsch, then they'd have to do it in front of her. By her very presence today, she would prove to them their snobbery and make them ashamed of their entitlement and their halfhearted acts of charity toward her family. Admittedly, her plan was vague, but it involved making Parker eat a taco in front of her. And she would have Matty at her side, handsome bad-boy Matty Macias, whom she'd loved since eighth grade. Matty, with his gelled hair and warm, thick-lashed eyes and the cords of his scapular showing at the neck of his t-shirt. Matty would not fail to disconcert.

"We're here because I was invited. I can't just snub them. Parker and I are classmates."

Andrea smoothed the wrinkled back of her new sundress (J. Crew—the most expensive dress she'd ever bought, and she did not intend to keep it; the tag still hung, scratchy and damp now, down her back, and she hoped, should Matty touch her, that he wouldn't notice it).

"Just, you know, be polite," Andrea told him.

"—the fuck?" Matty said, shooting her an irritated grimace. "You think I'm an idiot?"

"I think you're not used to being around people like this."

Andrea strode past him, clutching the invitation. Only now did it occur to her that maybe she ought to have brought something: Flowers? Wine? Already she could hear laughter through the trees.

———

ANDREA HATED IT, the constant alert hunger for every possible chance to move up in the world. "He's lazy," her father
would tell Andrea's mom in the evenings, referencing one
or another of the farmworkers. "He might as well go back
to Mexico. Work hard, get ahead. Look at me."

Over and over, the same conversation. "You should talk
to Bill about law," her father would urge, pronouncing his
name *Beel*. "Maybe he could help you."

"He doesn't practice," said Andrea.

"Still," said her mother, "it's nice to show interest."

"We'll have to get the girls together," William Lowell had said after Salvador told his boss with tears in his
eyes (Salvador's eyes had filled even relating the exchange)
that Andrea had been accepted at Stanford. "Maybe lunch
at the house, and they can swap notes." But though Mr.
Lowell asked after Andrea (Salvador always told her when
he did), and remarked over and over how wonderful it was
that she'd gotten in, and on full scholarship, too, they never
did get the girls together. And thank goodness. It would
have been strange and awkward. As children they'd played
together on a few sporadic summer afternoons—Andrea
remembered running after Parker through the orchards,
bashful and grinning—but the girls hadn't seen each other
in years.

Stanford, Stanford, Stanford. There were weeks last
summer when Andrea couldn't sleep, so thrilled was she
by the sense that her life was blooming into something
marvelous. She'd tremble in bed, eyes darting around the

dark familiar shapes of her room, which was really just an alcove off the kitchen, amazed that she would actually be leaving this home she'd known her whole life: goodbye to the rippled linoleum, goodbye to the Aladdin-print curtain that was her bedroom wall, and beyond it, goodbye to the refrigerator's intestinal gurgles. Oh, the success and wealth and greatness the future held for her! It actually made her breathless to think of it. Parker Lowell was the single blight on her joy. During freshman orientation, as Andrea was herded through White Plaza with others from the Chicano student association, she found herself looking with dread for Parker among the clumps of happy milling students. It was only a matter of time, Andrea knew, before they ran into each other at a party or on the Quad, and when they did, Parker would smile and make small talk and, through her very graciousness, expose Andrea as she truly was: cheap, striving, unworthy. Maybe, Andrea thought, Parker would get mono.

But the campus was sprawling and Andrea's freshman dorm mercifully distant from Parker's. The first quarter passed, and nearly the second, before Andrea saw her, in the winter production of *Once Upon a Mattress*. She'd sat tense in the audience, searching the actors' faces, and felt oddly thrilled when she finally spotted Parker. As Parker, lady-in-waiting to Queen Aggravaine, curtsied and twirled and warbled on stage, Andrea considered pointing her out to her roommate, but didn't.

Her whole life Andrea had been subjected to her parents' slavish interest in the Lowells' affairs, so she shouldn't have been surprised that all through freshman year they kept her apprised of the Lowell family news. "I really don't care," Andrea said, but she listened anyway, thinking as she did that there were lots of interesting things she could tell them about power structures. They reported on leaf curl and how the Elbertas and Elegant Ladies were faring, and on the Lowell boy's job in the governor's office, and then in the spring they called with the news that brought Parker lower than any bout of mono ever could: Mrs. Lowell had left her husband for their landscaper—their twenty-eight-year-old *female* landscaper—and William Lowell, apparently unable to live for twenty seconds without a wife, had started up with the widow of his roommate from Exeter.

Andrea had been shocked. In the face of her mother's shock, though, she'd feigned total equanimity. "No one's really straight," Andrea explained, "not one hundred percent."

So it was that the Lowells, poised and affectionate and photogenic, now found themselves cut down by a crisis that had all the elements of a joke, and it seemed to Andrea that the balance between them had shifted. In Andrea's mind Parker underwent a faint oxidation, taking on a patina, for the first time, of vulnerability. Again Andrea found herself seeking Parker on campus, this time so she might extend her hand in friendship.

WHEN THEY STEPPED into the clearing between the orchards and the rows of highbush Jubilee blueberries, Andrea saw that her father's taco truck had inspired a whole Mexican theme. Gone were the sun-faded Porta-Pottys and the water truck; in their place, the Lowells had erected a tent festooned with fluttering papel picado flags. Elderly people in pastels sat in the shade and the younger people stood around drinking margaritas. White tablecloths rippled in the hot breeze. In the center of each table sat a little piñata on bright woven fabric.

And there, at the edge of the party, was the taco truck itself. From where she stood, Andrea could see her father's arms handing full plates out the sliding window. She remained out of his line of vision. He'd be surprised and proud and pleased to see her here as a guest, would probably think Parker had invited her personally, but she didn't feel like getting into explanations, and she didn't want to establish herself as the daughter of the cook, at least not yet.

The truck *did* look festive here, Andrea saw with disappointment, against the backdrop of trees. A colorful hand-painted sign announced a pared-down, classed-up menu: Kobe beef, wild-caught salmon, free-range chicken, and vegetarian, all on blue corn tortillas.

"A vegetarian on a tortilla," said Andrea. "Ha."

"Funny," said Matty. He scanned the crowd. "They know how to do it up."

Tacos were not the only option: caterers in white shirts presided over a vast spread of fresh, colorful food. Tin buckets were lined up on another table, a grosgrain ribbon tied around each handle. Already several beautifully dressed children were in the blueberry rows, picking.

And now, turning toward Andrea, in a floral shift and Converse sneakers without socks, was Parker. In one hand she swung a bucket, and in the other she held a massive sloshing glass of wine. "Andrea?" She tilted her head, her red hair shining in the sun and slipping over her shoulder.

"Your dad didn't say you were coming. It's so great you could make it!"

Was Parker going to hug her? Yes, she was. Andrea put her arms around Parker, and there was nothing casual about it, nothing breezy. She pulled away too soon, terri-fied Parker would feel the price tags.

"So," Andrea said, tongue-tied. She brandished her invitation. "Do I need to give this to you?"

Parker looked at the invitation, but made no move, and it remained there, large and clumsy in Andrea's hand. Stupid, to think she might be required to present it like a ticket. She waved it at the party and the field and the orchards. "It all looks great. I haven't been out here in years."

Parker stuck her hand out at Matty. "Parker. Great to meet you."

"Oh, sorry. This is Matty." Andrea smiled at him in a way that she hoped looked affectionate and familiar and somehow also conveyed the sense that they were having lots of spectacular sex.

"Matthew," said Matty.

Andrea smiled woodenly; Matty jingled the coins in his pocket with one hand and, with the other, thumbed the edge of his repellent little mustache.

Andrea had imagined cornering Parker near the truck, plying her with tacos, which Parker, too polite to refuse, would choke down in class-conscious misery until she was sick. Absurd and far-fetched, yes, but Andrea had gotten a grim pleasure from the image. Now, though, she felt pathetic for even thinking it.

As if reading her mind, Parker ran her hand through her hair, glanced at the taco truck, then back at Andrea. At least she had the grace to look uncomfortable. "It's so great of your dad to be here. His tacos are awesome. I ate like six already."

"Yes," agreed Andrea. "They are pretty great." How many times were they going to say *great*?

A gold Tiffany's heart dangled at Parker's throat. Something about the necklace combined with the Converse suddenly enraged Andrea. "Man," she said, "I was *really* sorry to hear about your parents. I mean, it must have really turned your world upside down."

Parker shrugged, but her throat beneath the gold chain splotched red. "They seem to have gotten over it." She jerked her thumb at one of the clumps of laughing adults. "My dad can't keep his hands off Judith."

And indeed William Lowell had his arm around the thick waist of a beaming woman who could only be the widow. She was short-haired and mannish, a silk scarf tied in the collar of her striped Oxford. It was no surprise she wasn't as pretty as Elizabeth Lowell, Andrea supposed; William Lowell had been burned by beauty. Still, she felt obscurely disappointed by the widow, as though William Lowell had been guilty of a lapse in taste.

"Weird that I hardly see you at school." Parker smiled. "We must travel in different circles." She turned to Matty and said seriously, "Andrea is *super* smart."

Matty snorted. "She thinks so."

Was Parker mocking her? *Encouraging* her? Andrea bristled. Parker didn't know how smart she was. Parker didn't know one thing about her.

"Seriously, I hear you're doing really well. Your dad tells my dad."

The thought of her father bragging about her was horrifying. Every term this year (and in spite of a B-minus in chemistry), Andrea had received honor roll certificates from the Chicano student association, which had made her proud until she realized they were just part of all the extra efforts made on behalf of minority students: the special dinners and study breaks and offers for faculty mentorship with junior faculty eager to bolster their tenure files. Still, she'd sent the certificates home to her parents, who didn't know the difference. Now, though, she had a hideous vision of her father flapping the flimsy sheets in William Lowell's face, William Lowell's indulgent smile. William Lowell didn't brag to Salvador about Parker's accomplishments, you could be sure of that.

"Last time I was out in the field I was nine, I think," said Andrea. "You were here, too. Do you remember?"

Parker shook her head.

"Why would you? It was so long ago. You were picking blueberries for your mom, and I wanted to help, too, so Isabel—Isabel Gutierrez?—you probably don't know her, she worked here for years—anyway, Isabel gave me a bucket. So I was out there picking away, happy as can be. Then your dad came down the row and yelled for me to stop." Andrea laughed heartily, mirthlessly. "He was worried about child labor laws! Wouldn't want anyone to come by and find a little Mexican kid picking blueberries!"

Parker tipped her head, laughed uncertainly. Her entire face was pink now. "Sounds like maybe he was being a bit too scrupulous."

Andrea shrugged. "I've just always remembered it. *You* kept picking. It wasn't child labor for you. You were just getting some berries for a pie." She smiled.

Even Parker's flushed face irritated Andrea. What was she, some swooning Victorian?

"Well, pick as much as you like today." Parker nodded at the children in the rows. "Today we're even allowing child labor."

Parker politely extricated herself, and then she was off to charm other guests with her straight teeth and easy personality. Matty stood watching her, jingling the change in his pockets.

"Would you just stop fidgeting for one minute?" Andrea snapped.

"What is with you?" Matty asked. "You're fucked up, you know? You're fucking obsessed."

Andrea turned on Matty. "Do you even know how much all this is worth?" Oh, yes, Andrea had Googled the land appraisal—she knew.

Matty gave her one long disgusted look, then headed for the beer. Andrea nearly ran after him—but to what? Grab his hand, beg him to support her? She winced sourly.

In the spring, in that lull after midterms and before finals, Andrea had finally run into Parker at a party at one of the co-ops. Andrea had arrived with some dormmates, who, once they'd all swigged their punch, had gone off in search of weed, leaving Andrea swaying at the periphery of the party. It had just stopped raining, and in the backyard several people were naked and dancing a formless hippy dance in the mud, ruining the lawn, which is what Andrea was watching—arms crossed critically as she envied their lack of self-consciousness—when Parker Lowell came up behind her and circled a thin arm around her neck.

"Andrea!" Parker cried and thrust her friend forward.

Parker was drunk, eyes damp and unfocused. "Meet Andrea! Andrea, this is Chantal. Oh my gosh, Andrea and I have known each other our entire lives. Our dads work together."

Chantal had glitter on her cheekbones and smeared black eyeliner. But it was Parker Andrea was staring at. "Imagine," her mother had told her just days before, "that entire family, ruined." But Parker didn't look like someone whose world had fallen apart. She looked breathless and happy. She was leaner, gorgeous hipbones poking out the top of impossibly well-fitting thrift-store corduroys. She wore a boy's AYSO soccer shirt, through which her braless nipples showed. Her bare face shone from dancing, and at her temples Andrea could see veins blue through her nearly translucent skin. Andrea wanted to speak privately to Parker, to tell her how sorry she was, how shocked they'd all been. She'd touch that lovely arm, speak sincerely, and they'd understand each other.

Instead, Andrea gestured at the mud dancers. "Insane, right? You couldn't pay me to do that. Not in a million years."

"Oh, I don't know," said Parker. "It seems kind of fun."

Feeling drab to her core, Andrea searched for something else to say but came up with nothing. Couldn't she even stand like a normal person? Parker and Chantal stood close with their arms looped around each other's waists, and their intimacy looked so natural that Andrea felt a pang. "I just meant they're probably getting mud in their cracks."

Chantal laughed, but Parker fixed Andrea with sincere attention. "What are your summer plans? Heading home?"

"I'm not sure. Probably I'll find an internship." Andrea

was heartsick at the thought of the months that lay between her and the start of the next school year: the chilly, buzzing shifts at Safeway, the hot Stockton nights. Most internships were unpaid, she'd learned, and she didn't know how to go about finding them anyway. "You?"

Parker laughed. "I'm totally embarrassed, but I'm just going to hang out." Her eyes flicked away; she was, it seemed, genuinely embarrassed. "Travel some, maybe. Mostly hang around home." She laughed nervously. "I figure I'll have to work the rest of my life."

Hope glinted in Andrea's chest. Maybe they'd get together this summer; maybe, with nothing else to do, with her college and boarding-school friends away on their European tours, Parker would reach out. Already Andrea knew that wouldn't happen.

Chantal was looking at Andrea. "What does your dad do again?" she asked Parker.

"He's a farmer." And Parker's voice was so easy, so unselfconscious, that Andrea knew she believed it.

A fierce rage rose from nowhere and spotted Andrea's vision. A farmer! As if her dad was Old MacDonald milking his cow. As if the Lowells were all out weeding in their overalls. William Lowell had a law degree, for God's sake.

Later, she would kick herself for not calling Parker on her shit, would cycle through the things she might have said: "Parker's dad *owns* farmers." Instead, she'd smiled hard and bright until the terrible conversation wound down and Parker and Chantal melted into the crowd arm in arm.

So, yes, this was Parker's crime: thinking her dad was a farmer. Now, while a three-piece mariachi band struck up at the edge of the clearing, Andrea watched with loathing as Parker greeted her guests. Where did this anger come from? Andrea wasn't one of these strident activists, with eagle eyes sharp on the lookout for injustice, leading grape boycotts and bus trips to Arizona. She wanted to become a lawyer, and not a civil rights or immigration lawyer, either. She wanted to be a lawyer in a slimming wool suit riding the elevator to the top of a New York skyscraper.

Yet if anyone mentioned the Lowells, people who'd only been kind to her family—it was, after all, a *nice thing*, hiring her father's taco truck—suddenly she was outraged. Andrea didn't blame the Lowells, not really—they couldn't help being who they were, having what they had. They weren't even snobby. And technically Mr. Lowell sort of was a farmer. Except of course, she *did* blame them, and it didn't matter that she knew it was unfair. Why did she want to embarrass Parker, dig into that rich guilt that was so ripe and close to the surface? Andrea flexed her fingers, imagined sinking them into flesh that would give as easily as the skin of a browning peach.

"Wine?" offered the waiter at her elbow. "This is a Sauvignon Blanc from the Pink Leaf Winery in Lake County."

"Oh," said Andrea. "Okay." She drank it quickly, then exchanged the glass when the next waiter came by.

She was hungry, and the smell from the taco truck was delicious. But she felt stuck here on the edge, without another person to walk with. Under a swinging piñata, Matty was chatting with an older couple, not caring, apparently, that in his t-shirt and work boots he looked like an employee. He should be right here beside her, laughing at what she said. That had been the whole point of bringing him.

Waiters supplied her with wine, elaborately speared vegetables, savory little puffs. And a beribboned bucket. She was warm, and the wine made her tight-faced and loose-limbed and tipsy. She didn't know if the bucket was to keep, but she'd just decided she'd keep it anyway when she felt a nail scrape gently at her neck.

"Tag's out, honey." It was the widow.

Andrea clapped a hand on the nape of her neck.

"You're a friend of Parker's? From school? Bill pointed you out."

"I must have forgotten to cut it off." She felt the miserable heat rise in her face.

"Don't look so worried, honey." The widow gave her a friendly scratch on the back and winked. "I won't tell. We've all done it. It's a nice dress."

Andrea smiled, and it felt so good that she realized it was the first genuine smile she'd smiled all day. "Thanks." The widow's hair was coarse and thick, a raccoon's pelt. It wasn't her fault she wasn't as pretty as Elizabeth Lowell. "My dad's the taco guy," she confessed.

"Lovely man. He must be so proud of you."

"Oh, well," said Andrea modestly, but she couldn't help smiling. "Lots of kids get in."

"I'm glad Parker has a friend here." The widow sighed, sipped her wine. "I guess the situation can't be anything but awkward."

"Oh, I *know*," said Andrea. "The power dynamics—"

"Between you and me, I don't actually know what I'm doing playing hostess. I don't even know most of these people." The widow withdrew a tube of lipstick from her pocket and smeared it on thin, tense lips.

"I think you're doing a great job," Andrea said.

"Both kids are angry, of course. It's worse for Parker, though, being the youngest." Parker and her father were standing arm in arm, entertaining a laughing crowd, and the widow watched them as she talked. When she splashed wine on her shirt she swiped at it without looking. "She keeps calling her parents to scream at them. She accuses her mother of being—of sleeping around. She doesn't think much of me, either, told her father he was pitiful and desperate." She laughed once, sharply. "She got both of us with that one."

It was impossible to imagine Parker raging about anything. She certainly didn't look angry with her father. She was smiling rosily. Mr. Lowell kissed the silky top of her head. It was like a Ralph Lauren ad. That's what this party was missing: a camera crew. Briefly, Andrea wondered if Parker's mother had taken the Paris picture when she moved out, or if it was still in that gleaming kitchen facing the widow as she made her mayonnaise casseroles.

Andrea was startled and flattered and uncomfortable to be let into the widow's confidence, and her heart went out to her. "It must be so hard for you."

"Do you know, he says he's not sure he'll even divorce her. Doesn't want to leave her in the lurch, he says." The widow's laugh was brittle, slightly unhinged. It occurred to Andrea that she was drunk. "He's too good, that man. Parker scared him to death with that little pill stunt. I told him that was the point. I was young once, too." The widow smiled brilliantly with magenta lips and played with the tails of her scarf.

That pill stunt. "Yes," said Andrea.

"I told him she should have a summer job, keep busy. My kids have always had summer jobs. I bet *you* have one, don't you?"

Andrea's head was cottony and the buzz of the wine drained, leaving a heavy, hot remorse. "Parker and I aren't actually that close. I didn't actually know about the pills."

"You get selfish if you don't work, I told him. If you never have to think about anyone else. It's not her *fault*, but that's what happens."

"Is she really so unhappy?"

The widow tipped her head and looked at Andrea as if for the first time. Her lipstick was thick, waxy and dry. "She's quite a performer, your friend."

"No," Andrea said with sudden savage energy that took her by surprise. "She's *not* a performer." Who did this widow think she was, spreading the Lowell gossip at their own party? She was an ugly, hateful woman. "For the record," she said with indignation, "the Lowells were the most beautiful family I have ever seen."

"Ah. I see," the widow said lightly. "I hope you'll be more discreet than I was. Do tell your dad how much I enjoyed his tacos. Excuse me." She gave Andrea's back another little scratch and moved unsteadily off.

AT THE BUFFET, Parker and Matty were laughing over a bowl of guacamole. Matty leaned forward in a way that meant he had designs on her. Of course he did. But Andrea didn't care about Matty just now.

Andrea was swollen with shame, her upper lip damp as

though the shame were actually oozing out of her. And yet, at the edges of the remorse and sorrow, she was obscurely jealous, too, as if with those pills Parker had established once again her supremacy over Andrea. But Andrea would rise above that, be the gracious, expansive person she'd always hoped she'd become. She hurried toward them.

"Parker," she said, generous, repentant. She composed her face into a semblance of sobriety, because what she had to say was important.

"Oh, *what* now?" asked Matty.

"Listen—I just met your stepmother."

"She's not my stepmother," Parker said warily.

Andrea laid a hand on Parker's bare arm. She could feel the tiny golden hairs, the heat of her skin, and affection welled in her. "She told me that you tried to kill yourself. And I just wanted to say I'm so sorry. So, so sorry." Why couldn't she get the tone right? She really was sorry.

Parker flushed so deeply that her eyelids pinkened, too, and Andrea wondered with a bleak horror if the girl was going to cry, here in front of everyone. "Why are you even here? You think I don't notice you hate me?"

Andrea tightened her hold on Parker's arm. That's not true, she wanted to say.

Matty grabbed the edge of Andrea's sleeve. "I think we should leave."

"Parker, I'm just trying to be nice."

"Let's go, Andrea." Matty put his arm around her, just as she'd always hoped he would, but she shook him off.

And then, on the other side of the party, the door of the taco truck swung open and her father descended the steps, wiping his hands on a towel. He looked around, smiling absently, before his gaze snagged on Andrea. Suddenly a dreadful thought occurred to her. If Parker chose, she could have her father fired, all because Andrea came here today. Her blood became very still and very cold.

He came toward them, smiling quizzically, head tilted. Andrea grinned, bright and tense, waved. She held the grin, looking, no doubt, maniacal, but she didn't know what else to do. "I'm really sorry," she told Parker. "This had nothing to do with my dad. He didn't even know I was coming."

Parker looked slapped. "Fuck you, Andrea. I *like* your dad."

"I only wanted—"

"Just shut up." Matty's tone was urgent, and it was this urgency, and the look of embarrassment on his face, that made her understand how far she'd gone.

Andrea turned on him. "Where do you get off? *You* said Parker looked easy."

Parker's expression was gratifyingly bruised. "What?"

Her father sped up. He gripped Matty by the shoulder. "Is he bothering you?" he asked Parker.

Matty widened his soft eyes in surprise.

"God, no," said Parker.

Salvador searched Andrea's face. "Is everything okay, mija?"

Andrea averted her eyes from her father in time to see Parker and Matty exchange a look. She saw them decide to protect her.

Parker smiled resolutely. "Everything's fine, Salvador. Your tacos are amazing."

Her father wouldn't be so easily reassured, Andrea

knew, though he also wouldn't argue with Parker. Still, Andrea didn't stay to find out.

She turned and ran into the trees. She slowed only when the mariachi music was faint at her back, then walked deeper down the rows. The branches were covered in tight green nectarines, hard and fierce. She ripped one off and threw it at the trunk, but it landed dully in the mulch.

God, how she'd wanted to get together with Parker for that lunch last summer. How she'd wanted to sit in that kitchen, eating vanilla ice cream topped with blueberries from those fragile green bowls. Feet swinging from the bar stools, she and Parker would marvel at how much they had in common. Astonishing that they hadn't been closer all these years!

The real astonishment, when the invitation never came, was how surprised Andrea had been—though of course she should have known. She imagined how it went: William Lowell suggesting lunch and Parker dismissing the suggestion, horrified by the prospect of starting the school year saddled with Andrea.

"You are the leaders of tomorrow," the university president had told them in September at their freshman convocation. Even then Andrea had known that he hadn't meant her. "Look around. Look at yourself. Every one of you has the unique talents that this world is waiting for." Probably he even believed it. But Andrea knew that whatever she was granted in life would be granted as a result of her wheedling. She'd forever be checking ethnicity boxes, emphasizing her parents' work: farm laborer, housekeeper. Trying to prove that she was smart enough, committed enough, pleasant enough, to be granted a trial period in their world.

Sure, she'd make a success of herself, more or less, but her entire life would be spent gushing about gratitude and indebtedness and writing thank-you notes to alumni and rich benefactors and to the Lowells.

Andrea cut across the rows, feeling the brush of the leaves against her arms. When she emerged from the orchard, she was at the far edge of the blueberry field. From here, she couldn't see the party, but the music skimmed over the bushes, the violin's manic dance softened by distance. The canes were taller than Andrea, and they bobbed in the breeze as if to the music, until, with a flourish of trumpet, the song ended. Brief, tepid applause, then the canes bobbed only for themselves. Her anger was gone now, and her shame, too. Andrea was left with just the sound of the wind in the leaves and a terrible sense of loss. This place had mattered to her, she realized—it still mattered to her—and now it was irretrievable. Never again would she be allowed to return.

Mr. Lowell hadn't actually yelled at her that day when she was nine. He'd called out, "Stop! Please stop!" as he jogged down the row toward her. Then he'd slowed and said more gently, as though approaching an escaped and not entirely tame pet, "Hi there, honey." He'd taken the scratched five-gallon bucket from her hands and thanked her for her help, and he gave her the cold Coke from his lunch cooler, settling her on the tailgate of his truck until her father emerged from the trees.

Before that, though, before Mr. Lowell found her, Andrea had been alone in the row of Jubilee blueberries, the leaves shining and swaying over her head.

Seek, pluck, seek, pluck. The percussion of the berries as

they dropped into the bucket. The berries firm and warm between her thumb and forefinger, their fragile dusty skin printed from her touch, the sweet burst on her tongue. The scent of the sun and soil and leaves.

Her head was pleasantly hot and fuzzy with a soft sense of calm and focus, of complete absorption in her task. She was covering the entire bottom of the bucket, a single even layer, and then she'd form the next layer and the next until the entire bucket was filled with that fragrance and sweetness and heft.

"Jubilee," she said, the word as mild and sweet as the berry itself. "Jubilee, jubilee, jubilee." Through the rows, she could hear the indistinct voices of the other pickers and the burble of the irrigation system.

Now, ten years later, she picked another berry and then another. When her hands were full, she made a hammock of her skirt and filled it, not caring that now she'd never be able to return the dress. She picked and she picked until she forgot there were other people around, and as the leaves rustled and the light scattered over her, she forgot herself, too.

ORDINARY SINS

✦

L AST NIGHT CRYSTAL DREAMED SHE WAS SITTING NAKED on the corduroy rectory couch next to Father Paul, who was snipping at her fingers with orange-handled scissors. In the dream she was holding a prayer card on which was printed, in place of a saint, a still from her sonogram. She felt stinging cuts on her knuckles and in the webbing between her fingers, saw the warm blood running down her wrists and beading on the laminated surface of the card, but she neither cried for help nor tried to get away; she was pinned to the couch by her pregnant belly.

If the dream hadn't been so unsettling, it might have been almost comical, Crystal thought now, Monday morning, as she updated the calendar of events for Our Lady of Seven Sorrows: Father Paul, so benign and solicitous and eager for approval in waking life, starring as the villain in her dream. She glanced down at her fingers typing, intact. If she were to tell Father Paul about her dream—though she wouldn't tell him anything about her life ever again—he'd be concerned and apologetic, as if it weren't Crystal's own warped brain that had cast him in the scene. Even the thought of his concern irritated her. Any minute, Father Paul would walk into the office, and when he did, she'd smile as if everything were just fine, as if their conversation on Friday had never happened.

Impressive, how efficiently her subconscious tallied, dismantled, and blended together her sins, molding them all into a tidy and disturbing little narrative as persistent and irksome as pine sap. First, on Friday, she'd been rude to Father Paul. Then, on Saturday, she'd gone to a party at a condo in a new development west of town with friends from Santa Fe High and had spent the evening sipping from other people's drinks. That was bad enough. But she'd also left with someone, a friend of a friend, ridden back to his apartment in his truck, knowing full well that he was drunk but not feeling an ounce of concern for the babies or for herself. "I've never fucked a pregnant girl," the guy had said softly, watching from the bed in his filthy bedroom as she pulled down her maternity jeans. He'd been cautious and attentive, and for as long as it lasted Crystal had felt deeply sexy and, for the first time in seven months, unburdened.

Only at dawn, once she'd slipped out into the chill and was waiting for a cab on an unfamiliar street in a tired, trucks-on-blocks kind of neighborhood, did it occur to her to worry about the babies, that they'd been squished or knocked about, polluted by his fluids. And Crystal might have been murdered, too—strangled, shot, beaten beyond recognition. Wasn't murder the leading cause of death for pregnant women?

With a pang of dismay, she thought of her last checkup. She'd been given a 3-D ultrasound, the latest in prenatal imaging, the technician told her, which they were offering free because they were still training on the machine. The images were terrifying and unreal: boy and girl, fists and ears and pursed lips, bent legs stringy with tendons, alien eyes swollen shut. Everything looked yellow and cold and shiny, as if dipped in wax. "Say hello to your cuties," the technician had said, and Crystal had watched in silence as they pulsed on the screen.

But today the babies seemed great, kicking up a storm, and she hadn't been murdered. Saturday had been nothing more than a last hurrah, Crystal reminded herself, a harmless attempt to pretend that her life was still her own, whatever Father Paul or her mother might say. Looked at another way, the dream was even reassuring: at least Crystal *felt* guilt. At least she might think twice next time. Yes, everything was fine, and it was even nice to be back at work, away from her weekend and her nightmare, in the close clutter of the parish office, where the day was predictable, the tasks manageable— where, in theory at any rate, earnest, hopeful work was taking place all around her.

Meanwhile, the real Father Paul was late yet again, this time for his eight o'clock premarital-counseling appointment. A young couple sat on the couch facing Collette's desk. The man plucked at one of his sideburns with sullen impatience; the girl sat upright and glanced nervously at him. Every few minutes, Collette looked up from folding the weekly bulletins and glared at them.

From her desk in the corner, Crystal sipped her Diet Coke and watched. Collette's bad temper was democratic in its reach and, when it wasn't directed at Crystal, could be very entertaining. Once, when they were alone in the office, Collette had startled her by pausing at her desk and saying, darkly, that Crystal was an example to young women, choosing life. For a moment Crystal had seen herself as Collette might: a tragic figure, a fallen woman, but, when it came down to it, contrite and virtuous, taking responsibility for her mistake. But then Collette had elaborated: "If girls are going to run around like that, they should pay."

The young man opened his cell phone, then snapped it shut. "Eight fifty-seven," he said. "Jesus. I got *work* to do."

"He'll be here," the girl said. She looked at Crystal and gave her a miserable, apologetic smile. She'd dressed for the appointment: black pants tight around the thighs, shirt made of a cheap stretchy satin. Her hair was down, sprayed into crispy waves around her face. A gold cross hung from her neck. Crystal imagined she'd dug it out so that Father Paul would think she was a virgin, which was what Crystal herself had done when she took the job two years ago.

Since the arrival of Father Leon, the young Nigerian priest, three months before, Father Paul had been sleeping past his alarm. Crystal enjoyed the thought of the priests chattering away late into the night like girls at a sleepover— but the idea of humorless, aloof Father Leon saying anything that wasn't strictly necessary defied imagination. Sometimes, to amuse herself, Crystal experimented by greeting him with wide-ranging degrees of enthusiasm, but Father Leon gave her the same solemn nod every time.

More likely, Father Paul stayed up late reading. In the afternoons Crystal cleaned the rectory, and Father Paul's study, with its crowded, dusty shelves and uneven stacks of books, was the most difficult of her jobs. Or it would have been, if she'd ever done it properly. Usually she swiped her paper towel along the edge of the shelves and vacuumed around the papers and wool cardigans and scattered shoes and books. Church histories, Pacific naval battles, CIA conspiracies. If she mentioned his books—how many he had or how busy they must keep him—Father Paul generally cracked some mild self-deprecating joke and changed the subject to television, as if out of consideration for Crystal. He loved crime shows, the same ones Crystal occasionally watched at night, in which naked young women showed up dead in hotel bathrooms. "My guilty pleasure," Father Paul said, shrugging good-naturedly.

Crystal didn't like thinking about a priest's guilty pleasures. But, actually, she couldn't see Father Paul being truly guilty of anything. Even the crime shows were part of an act, she suspected, to prove that he was a little naughty. Human. During Lent he'd made a big show of sneaking handfuls of M&M's from the glass bowl on Collette's desk, the woman's one concession to office niceties.

"Oh, you know me," Father Paul would say, jiggling the candy in his palm before tossing back a mouthful, and Crystal would smile gamely.

"Guess he has to have something," Collette said once after Father Paul left. "These alcoholics never get any better, just switch one thing for another. He better watch it."

Crystal had rolled her eyes. Twenty-eight years clean, Father Paul had announced last month, on his anniversary, and his air of celebration had seemed just as overblown as Collette's cynicism.

Father Paul would, as always, feel terrible about being late for the couple's appointment. He'd take off his glasses and press his thumbs into his eyes, and his lapse would probably show up in his homily, as his lapses always did. His sins were so vanilla that you almost had to wonder whether he committed them just to have something to talk about on Sundays. Even his alcoholism and his journey to recovery had been wrung of any possible drama by how thoroughly and publicly he had examined them. In the next several days he'd repeatedly bring up this morning's tardiness, and Crystal would have to tell him each time that it was an honest mistake, that everyone makes mistakes.

The young man bounced his leg, and the heavy heel of his work boot thumped. Finally, he stood. He planted his fists on the cluttered edge of Collette's desk and leaned in. "I'm not waiting around all day."

His fiancée widened her eyes. But, if he meant to intimidate, he'd picked the wrong person. Collette had worked in the parish office for years. Her tasks were menial and few, but she sat at her desk all day like a toad, grumbling in Spanish as she opened offertory envelopes and pasted labels. Though her desk was closest to the door, she did not greet people when they came in. If spoken to, she sighed, set down whatever she was working on, and looked so put-upon that, more often than not, people made hasty apologies and turned to Crystal for what they needed.

Collette jerked her porous, wrinkled chin at the young man. "You got things to do? So get away with you, then."

When he looked at her in surprise, Collette held his gaze. "I mean it. Get out. We don't want you here."

The man stepped back, glanced uncertainly at the door, then at Crystal.

"Please," the girl said, eyes filling, voice tragic. "We *have* to meet Father Paul. We're not even done with the premarital questionnaire. The wedding's on Saturday!"

Collette turned to Crystal. "Go find him."

Crystal fixed her eyes on the screen and clattered away at the keyboard. "Actually, I'm in the middle of something."

"And if he's not there, bring that Father Leon." Collette snorted, as she always did when mentioning the new priest.

The girl's face registered dismay, because Father Paul was beloved and Father Leon was not, but what could you do? A priest was a priest, even if he was just a pastoral vicar newly arrived from Africa, and you had to act grateful.

Now Collette said, "It'll do that man good to socialize him. You hear me, Crystal? Go on."

Crystal pushed herself up from her desk, tugging her shirt over her belly. "*Fine.*"

THE JOB WAS SUPPOSED to have been temporary, a pause before college, but here she still was, needing the money more than ever. When Crystal first started showing, she worried that she might have to leave, but to her relief her pregnancy had elicited surprisingly positive reactions, Collette notwithstanding. The ladies in the Altar Society had given her an array of miniature garments in pink and blue. Her mother, usually so needy and resentful, was pleased that Crystal had given up her apartment and moved back home. She talked incessantly about the babies, prepared plates of protein- and calcium-rich foods, loudly beseeched God to keep them healthy. Crystal was grateful—she was—but still hated that her mother had to be involved.

"Where were you, staying out all hours?" her mother asked when Crystal got home Sunday morning. "You know better. And me home alone waiting."

But no one was as sympathetic as Father Paul. Perhaps because she was young and pregnant or because she cleaned the rectory, he was always reaching out, thanking Crystal for her hard work, taking an interest. "Anytime you need an ear or a hand," he'd say as she Windexed the patio doors. He seemed eager for her good opinion, seemed to want her to confide in him.

Once she had admitted that the babies' father was out of the picture, though she hadn't revealed how little she'd known him—another hookup, another party. She hadn't revealed that whenever she was out, at the mall or the grocery store, she found herself looking more closely at a certain type of man—short, built, sandy-haired—despite the fact that he hadn't even been from Santa Fe, had been visiting from California. She hadn't revealed how often she wondered what traits in her children would bring the blurry, drunken memory of him more sharply into focus.

"I'm so sorry," Father Paul had said, his eyes soft and his voice rich with empathy. Then, after a moment, "You know, the sacrament of Reconciliation is such a gift."

When Father Leon's arrival was announced, Crystal had expected someone energetic and progressive and possibly tiresome, setting up basketball games and youth activities and regular soup kitchens in the hall. She'd thought that the new priest might joke with her, might offer real comfort that came from his contemporary understanding of how the world actually worked.

Instead of invigorating the parish, though, Father Leon's

arrival had strained its atmosphere. "Would you believe he told me to type up his homily?" Collette had hissed, thrusting a legal pad into Father Paul's chest. "Who does he think he is?"

"I'll talk to him," Father Paul had promised, but the same day he'd drawn Crystal aside and asked her to type it. "Please. As a favor to me." So, ever since, it had fallen to her to decipher Father Leon's slanted, feminine cursive. Each time Crystal handed Father Leon the printed pages, dense with abstractions and biblical quotations, he murmured a wooden thank-you without looking at her, already scanning his words.

Rather than sticking to love and brotherhood and the primacy of conscience, Father Leon went right for the hot-button issues, criticizing the permissiveness of American society. "Tolerance of sin is not a Christian virtue, and homosexuality is a sin, full stop," Father Leon had told the congregation during an early weekday Mass. "Even in this house of God, I can smell the stink of Satan. He has found purchase in the hearts of some gathered here today." Crystal pictured him scowling down from the pulpit in his cassock, looking like an unpleasant child forced to play dress-up.

There had been very few people present, but one of them was the president of the Altar Society, whose fourteen-year-old grandson was gay. She'd stormed into the office in a rage. "The stink of Satan? Shame on him," she told Father Paul. "God forgive me, but that man doesn't belong here."

"He's young, he's full of ideas. He's getting his sea legs," Father Paul had said, looking fretful. "We're lucky to have him, with so few young men entering the priesthood."

Father Paul had begun to show signs of tension: the

oversleeping, for one. He also seemed to have amped up his benevolence, as if to compensate for Father Leon's coldness. While Father Leon stayed shut away in his study, Father Paul always seemed to be lying in wait for Crystal when she came to clean, ready with a smile or a kind word. He was lonely, maybe, Crystal thought, or maybe, with Father Leon chipping in, he just had less to do. Over and over he offered her help, over and over he brought up Reconciliation, as if he had an urgent personal stake in her salvation.

So, after months of putting it off, she'd gone to confession. But there, in the dark confessional, something had happened: Crystal had actually felt bad about not having been a virgin since she was sixteen, had almost believed that sex wasn't completely ordinary. The sudden sense of her own remorse had made her words waver, and she was overcome by the vastness of her insult to God. She had believed truly, as she never had before, that Father Paul—this man whose dishes she washed and laundry she folded, who left drops of urine on the toilet seat—could deliver her apology to God. She'd caught her breath and felt tears burn her eyes, until, from the other side of the screen, Father Paul had dropped into his most soothing voice. "We can hate the sin but love the sinner."

Crystal must have been seeking punishment, humiliation, shame. She must have been trying to hold tight to her guilt or to shock him out of his infuriating tenderness, because what else could explain what came out of her mouth next? "But Father, it wasn't just regular sex. He went in behind, too."

There was a long, terrible silence. Beyond the confessional, the empty church breathed and creaked. Outside, a motorcycle roared past. Crystal gripped one hand with the other. Finally, she heard the unsticking of lips and Father

Paul said, "Consider this a new chance, and ask God to help you be the mother your babies deserve."

Confession was confidential, of course, and Father Paul gave no sign that he knew who had been on the other side of the screen—and who knows, maybe he didn't, though he'd have to be a fool not to—but Crystal couldn't stand to be around him for weeks afterward. She felt ambushed and stupid. In the office, she kept her head behind the computer monitor when he passed through. Most afternoons Father Paul had appointments, so she cleaned the rectory when he was out.

Really it was a miracle that she'd managed to avoid him for as long as she had. But on Friday, as Crystal was putting the rags and detergents under the sink, Father Paul had come into the freshly mopped kitchen. He'd leaned against the counter and watched her. "You must miss the father," he'd said, and Crystal had had to sink back on her heels and nod politely.

Father Paul furrowed his brow, and the creases went all the way up his bald red head. "Even if it wasn't the right partnership, it must pain you to be embarking on this alone. But we're here for you." His voice was insistent. "The parish will stand by you and your children."

Father Paul paused. He seemed to be thinking something over, and, with a sense of vertigo, Crystal imagined him imagining her in the throes of all sorts of mortifying, sweaty exertions.

Then he crossed the damp linoleum—leaving dull footprints—and dug in his pocket. He presented her with a laminated prayer card of the Santo Niño de Atocha. "I've been wanting to give you this."

Crystal turned the card in her hand, flushing. The Santo

Niño: Christ Child with long dress and pilgrim's staff, dark curls tucked under wide-brimmed hat, walking under the stars across mesas and winding among piñon. He walked so far and so long, searching for miracles to perform, that he wore the soles of his shoes to nothing. In the chapel in Chimayo devoted to him, along with prayers and petitions and milagros, people left him children's shoes—knit booties and beaded moccasins and sneakers and patent-leather Mary Janes scuffed at the toe.

"Thanks," she mumbled.

Father Paul smiled with relief. He waved her away, pleased with himself. "You should pray with your babies. They can hear you, you know." He stood smiling at her for another torturously long moment, then left.

Crystal gripped the card, enraged. Who was Father Paul to tell her that her life might be saved by a child? What could he possibly know about being trapped forever by your own stupid biology? Or about the defeat of moving home, where every night your mother was on the living room couch, suit skirt unzipped, watching a game show and eating microwaved hash browns slathered in red chile, her smelly panty-hosed feet on the coffee table?

Heartsick, Crystal thought of her old apartment, quiet and hers alone. Maybe she'd never wanted escape, college, a future, she thought bitterly. Maybe some part of her had been seeking a comforting narrowing of possibilities, an excuse to give up on her life. If this was all life was—working in the office of a small Santa Fe parish, living at home with her mother and twin babies—then it was at least manageable.

She had thrown the prayer card out, right there in the kitchen trash. She had slammed the back door, leaving the little Santo Niño with his girlish misty eyes gazing up, daring Father Paul to find him.

NOW, AS CRYSTAL CROSSED the parking lot toward the rectory, she hoped that he hadn't. She'd been bratty, throwing out his gift. Because what would she have preferred? To be scolded? To be made to sit facing the congregation each Sunday during Mass, the way pregnant girls were punished in the old days?

The wind was blowing, and leaves and dust skittered across the blacktop. It was late fall now, chilly, but Crystal was sweating through her shirt. Pregnancy had made her clammy and zitty and fat.

She flapped her arms, willing the dark spots to dry, and pushed open the back door of the rectory. She was greeted by the familiar hush and the smell of old cooking. On the stove were the gray remains of a pan-fried steak; on the counter, a sticky ice cream carton. The sink was full of dishes—couldn't they just put them in the dishwasher?

"Father Paul?" she called. He wasn't in his study. She started down the dim carpeted hall, lightening her step out of habit as she passed Father Leon's closed study door. No matter the hour, the rectory, with its small windows and sheer drapes, always felt muted with late-afternoon light.

"Father Paul?" she called again, as much to announce herself as to find him. She hoped he wasn't still asleep. What if she had to step into his bedroom, shake him awake? She recoiled at the thought of touching his bony shoulder through his pajamas.

But, thank God, the bedroom was empty, the bed with

its incongruous floral spread made in Father Paul's usual hasty way. It was a weird room, she often thought. Maybe it was a result of the vow of poverty, or the sign of a sparse personality, but there were few personal effects: a kachina, a bottle of Jergens lotion, some change, and a couple of bent collars. No boxes of letters or journals or bedside drawers to snoop through—though she'd looked, once, a little. The only trace of the individual who'd slept here for decades was a photograph: Father Paul as a happy young priest standing beside a beaming woman who must be his mother, a woman who, with her high cheekbones and heavy black eyebrows, might have been a distant relative of Crystal herself.

Maybe Father Paul had dropped dead, Crystal thought with a thrill of fear. At the end of the shadowy hall, the bathroom door was open, the pink tile glowing, and she approached with reluctance. "Father Paul?" Empty.

For a long moment she stood outside Father Leon's study. For the first time Crystal wondered how it was for Father Paul, having to mediate between Father Leon and everyone else, how it was for each of them, living here so intimately with a complete stranger.

Finally, she tapped and opened the door. Father Leon looked up from his desk and frowned at her from behind his giant, smoky plastic-rimmed glasses. Barely thirty and already so stern. You wouldn't catch Father Leon admitting mistakes to the congregation. She couldn't begin to guess what went on in his mind.

"Is this important, miss? I am in the midst of doing my work."

"Sorry to bother you," Crystal said. "But have you seen Father Paul? His appointment is waiting."

"I have not seen Father Lujan this morning."

Father Leon would have made a much more sinister dream villain, with his thick accent and his formal English. Though this was probably racist. Crystal shifted in the doorway. "You have no idea where he is? Would you meet with the couple, then?"

Father Leon closed his eyes with forbearance.

"Sorry. Collette told me to ask."

Father Leon regarded her coldly. He paused with his palms on his book, then stood. "I will go."

"Thank you *so* much, Father Leon," she said, her voice bright and emphatic and teetering just this side of sarcasm.

He walked past without looking at her.

In the kitchen, Crystal rinsed the dishes and loaded them into the dishwasher. She didn't care if she was racist or not, Father Leon was a jerk. Crystal couldn't help smiling at the thought of him baffling the couple with his accent, advising them with nervous grimness about natural family planning.

Crystal wiped the counters and rinsed the sponge, which was already slick and smelly, even though she'd just put out a new one. When she shut off the faucet, she heard Father Paul calling from somewhere in the house.

"Crystal?"

She looked in the living room—there was the couch from her dream—and down the hall. Father Paul poked his head out his bedroom door, then withdrew it.

Crystal dried her hands on a dish towel as she retraced her steps.

"Jeez, Father Paul. Where've you been hiding? I looked everywhere for you."

He was in his usual black pants and shirt and collar, but barefoot, standing in the middle of his room.

Crystal hesitated in the doorway; she'd never been in the bedroom when he was there. "Are you okay, Father Paul?"

"He's gone, right?"

"Father Leon? He's down at the office. Meeting with your eight o'clock. Did you forget about them?"

"Come in, please."

"Okay," Crystal said warily. The card. Had he found the card? She scanned the room again—top of the bureau, bedside table—but it wasn't there. Could he tell that she didn't want to go near him?

She stepped unwillingly across the threshold, but Father Paul drew her by the wrist to the closet door. "I need you to throw something away for me." His voice was low. He pointed to a perfectly good rolling carry-on suitcase standing upright under the neat row of black shirts and pants.

"Throw that away? But why?" She hoped it wasn't infested with bedbugs or fleas.

He cleared his throat, seeming to reach for some authority. "Just put it in the dumpster, Crystal." He extended the handle and pushed the suitcase at her. Inside, something clinked softly.

"What's in there, Father Paul? I can't just—" What crime was she being asked to cover up?

"Don't look inside," he said, but he made no move to stop her when she lowered herself with difficulty and drew the zipper.

The suitcase was filled with empty vodka bottles. Nearly all were glass minis, but there were also several cheap plastic fifths. Taaka, Empire, Neva.

"Father Paul," Crystal said carefully, standing. "You've been clean twenty-eight years."

He inclined his head with exaggerated patience. "Yes, Crystal. That is why I need you to get rid of this."

She sniffed. She'd never smelled liquor on him, but you never really got that close to a priest, did you? "Have you been drinking this morning?" she asked, but Father Paul just gave her a withering look.

"Do you need me to get Collette? Let me get Collette." Collette would know what to do. She'd snort and scoff and put Father Paul right.

"No! Listen to me. I can't trust anyone else. You know why he's here, don't you? To force me out."

"Father Leon? That's silly. Father Leon could never replace you." She tried to envision the young priest plotting in his study and laughed a little. "Father Paul, honestly, no one even likes him. You *are* the parish."

Father Paul took off his glasses and rubbed first one lens then the other on his shirt. Without the glasses, his eyes looked small and red, the skin around them wrinkled, shiny, thin. He pinched a lens between his thumb and forefinger. "Let me explain something to you, Crystal. When the bishop makes these assignments, he makes them for a reason. That man"—he jutted his chin toward the door—"the Church in Nigeria, in Africa in general, it's very . . . traditional. The fact is, they think I'm weak, and they've sent him to ruin me."

"That can't be." Crystal supposed what he said was plausible. *The Da Vinci Code*, the sex-abuse scandals: everyone knew the Church could be ruthless. "No one wants to hurt you, Father Paul," she said without conviction.

He replaced the glasses over his closed eyes and seemed

to come to a decision. "The fact is, I don't even know that *I'm* the one drinking. I'm telling you, that man is like a cat, playing his mind games."

"What?"

"I've tried locking the door, but he gets in. I wake up and the bottles are there, and I can feel it in my system. I know he's been here."

"Come on, Father Paul," Crystal said sharply. What was he saying—that Father Leon was creeping into his bedroom at night, plying him with liquor? Or that Father Leon was deploying some dark sorcery?

"You don't believe me. Fine."

Could he possibly believe himself? No one could sleep through that. And however odd and standoffish Father Leon might be, she didn't think he was malicious. Or stupid enough to force liquor down his superior's throat after a few weeks on the job. Which meant that Father Paul was either lying or out of his mind. But she could think of no reason for him to lie; he could easily throw the bottles away in the dead of night. Why seek her out and show her the bottles unless he truly believed he was in danger? This was crazy—and cruel, too, Crystal thought with a rush of outrage, scapegoating a friendless, homesick man. Moments ago, sitting behind his big desk, Father Leon had just looked young and alone. No wonder he hid out in his study.

She thought of Collette's grim warning that alcoholics never recovered. Had Father Paul spent the past twenty-eight years craving self-destruction, pulling back at the last minute each time? Maybe with Father Leon here to share duties, he'd let himself go—just an occasional sip at first, and then everything slid out from under him, leaving him to retreat into this insane story, paranoid and ashamed with his stash of empties.

Crystal flushed with irritation. Why couldn't Father Paul just admit that he'd fallen off the wagon? Why this elaborate ruse? All that hoopla over being late, as if his minor sins needed so much more forgiveness than Crystal's major ones, as if Crystal were expected to screw up, whereas it was a big fucking deal when he did. He couldn't help proving to her just how bad she was, lording it over her, shoving it in her face. It wasn't enough that she'd had to humiliate herself in confession? She had to humor him, too? "I'm going to get Collette," she said.

"No! You can't leave." His voice dropped again. Father Paul reached for her arm, but she dodged his touch. "You have to help me. I've helped you."

Crystal stepped back, looked around the room. "Okay. Fine. I'll throw away your suitcase."

Gladness lit through her at the prospect of escape. She'd walk briskly across the carpet, rolling the suitcase behind her, like a businesswoman at the airport. Down the back steps, and then she'd be outside in the cool day, free from the oppressive hush of the rectory, free from Father Paul and whatever demons had caught hold of him. "It'll be okay," she promised. The cheer in her voice was genuine. "Maybe get a bite to eat, splash some water on your face."

He looked her up and down, his mouth tense. Some new emotion had shifted his expression—dissatisfaction that he hadn't convinced her of Father Leon's treachery, perhaps, or disappointment at her eagerness to leave.

"Why do you keep avoiding me, after all I've done?" Now he was looking not at her but at the sun-faded framed poster above her shoulder: the Pietà, a souvenir from someone's long-ago trip to St. Peter's Basilica. "You know," he said calmly, "Father Leon doesn't like you."

"I know," she said, though she hadn't known, not exactly.

"He said we should let you go. He didn't want you sitting in the front office." Father Paul straightened now, oddly pleased.

Earlier, then, when Father Leon had glared at her from behind his desk, he hadn't been merely irritated at the interruption; she saw now that he'd been horrified by her messy fecundity. No real surprise, but, still, Crystal had let herself believe that her body didn't matter. She'd let herself believe that it was irrelevant to her work, that she was safe here and forgiven.

The real surprise, though, was that Father Paul wanted to hurt her. Courteous, heedful, absurd Father Paul. Father Paul, who saw pain in every face and gesture, whether it was there or not, wanted to hurt her, and that was what stung. She'd thought she could disdain Father Paul's kindness, and that it would somehow remain intact: unconditional, holy, and inhuman. Astonishing that she had been capable of such faith.

"Well, who does that man think he is, telling us how to do things? I defended you. I put myself on the line for you." His tone was wheedling. "I gave you the Santo Niño, too. Did you know the Santo Niño was my mother's favorite?" He stuck out his chin, defiant. "Once a week she went to the Santuario in Chimayo. Used to walk there every Good Friday."

"It was nice of you to give me the card," Crystal said, regarding him with loathing. "I appreciated that."

They stood facing each other, and time held steady. All

her speculation, and Crystal didn't know the first thing about this man. Then Father Paul bent suddenly at the waist, gasping like a sprinter.

When he rose, his face was purple. He backed against the wall, pushing against it with his palms as if it might relent and absorb him. "Forgive me. I never should have said any of that." He slid to the floor. His black pants tugged up, and his head drooped to his knees.

"I forgive you." Her voice was cold.

"Forgiveness," Father Paul said, as though the word disgusted him. "Forgiveness is a drug, too. Believe me. You can forgive and forgive until you're high on it and you can't stop. It'll numb you as much as any of that stuff." He extended his foot and kicked the suitcase, which tipped, spilling bottles onto the carpet.

Crystal had the drowning sense that she'd lost track of what they were talking about.

"I know you don't like me," Father Paul said, looking up at her.

And what could Crystal say? *Don't be silly. Of course I do.* And then there she'd be, lying to a priest.

She should leave, go back to the office and pretend that none of this had happened. Instead, she crossed the room and sat beside him.

"Please just hold me?" He looked at her as if asking permission, and when she neither gave nor withheld it, he leaned into her and rested his head on her shoulder.

She might have expected to be filled with a deep, sexual revulsion, but she wasn't. She didn't touch him, but she didn't push him away, either. Instead, Crystal placed her head against the wall and waited.

Inside her, the babies stirred. She remembered the weekend and the icy horror that had swamped her when she realized how she'd put them at risk. She remembered the ultrasound stills, how she'd studied them, straining to connect the images to children, to her children, children who would come to shape her life. "Have you picked names?" the guy had asked Saturday night. She'd pretended to be asleep so that she wouldn't have to lie. Where were her instincts? Where was the biological imperative to keep them safe? There must be some blockage, some deep damage that left her so cold.

Crystal saw herself standing on that ratty street at dawn, waiting for the cab to take her away from her mistake. But instead of the cab it was the Santo Niño who would find her. The soles of his shoes would be worn away, his little toes poking through the leather. He would take Crystal's hand in his pudgy one and lead her home. It was a lovely notion, and Crystal almost allowed herself to sink into it.

But no. Crystal saw that she had misunderstood. In giving her the Santo Niño, Father Paul hadn't meant that He would save *her*. And he hadn't meant that the twins would save her, either. Even Father Paul, with all his hope, knew better. Instead, he'd been offering the prayer that the Santo Niño might save those babies from whatever Crystal was bound to do to them.

Father Paul's head was heavy, and she could smell his scalp: a warm, sour smell. For a moment in confession, she'd believed that he could absolve her. And, even now that he was diminished and trembling and possibly insane, part of her still believed.

"I don't even talk to them," Crystal said.

Father Paul took a deep, shuddering breath, like a child calming himself after a long cry.

The sun filtered through the lace curtains above their heads. The window's reflection was a mottled square of light on the glass of the framed poster, obscuring the image.

Crystal saw that who she was didn't matter to Father Paul, that in his mind she'd turned into something else completely. Mary Magdalene, maybe: the whore who instead of washing His feet Cloroxed the bathroom. Or the Virgin up there on the wall, holding her dead adult son across her lap. Father Paul's own mother, even. And, for reasons she didn't understand, Crystal didn't resent this. Maybe later she would; maybe in a day, or in an hour, she'd feel compromised and used, and would hate Father Paul for it; but right now it seemed so easy to sit with him. The relief was astonishing, that Crystal could be the kind of person who might meet another person's need.

She watched the square of light in the glass. She breathed, and Father Paul breathed, and she felt the babies shift, navigating the tight space inside her.

And then, on the other side of the rectory, the back door opened and slammed shut. Father Leon's steps crossed the kitchen linoleum. On his way to his study, he would pass Father Paul's open door. He would see the suitcase, the strewn bottles, the two of them nearly embracing on the bedroom floor.

Father Leon would look from one to the other, his expression shading from perplexed to angry, but his gaze would rest on Crystal, because he would understand that she was guilty of something that she couldn't deny or put into words.

Crystal considered pulling away. There was still time. She might still hide the evidence, meet Father Leon casually in the hall, dish towel in hand. Beside her, she felt Father Paul tense and push his face into her shoulder.

"You're fine," Crystal said. She placed her hand over Father Paul's, but she was picturing her babies. Sheer skin, warm tangled limbs, tiny blue beating hearts. "You're fine."

CANUTE COMMANDS
THE TIDES

✦

T HE NOYES'S NEW HOUSE WAS ON A REMOTE HILL NORTHEAST
of Santa Fe surrounded by piñon and chamisa. The first time
they approached, in the real estate agent's Volvo, Margaret
had clutched the armrest. She'd been sure even then that
this was it. As Harold, up front, kept pace with the agent's
steady commentary, Margaret gazed out the window and
collected in her mind the scenes she would paint: an abandoned blank-eyed adobe near the highway exit, a line of
leaning mailboxes foregrounding a purple mesa, two dirty
children playing in an old blue truck on blocks. When they
finally arrived at the base of the long dirt driveway leading up through squat, dense piñon, Margaret found herself
holding her breath. "You'll want a four-wheel drive," the
agent had advised. From here, it was point-seven miles on
the odometer every time. Even now, it gave Margaret pleasure to note it when she returned home.

From the high, wide windows of her studio, Margaret could see for miles: the late summer storms were coming, black clouds packing themselves firmer as they moved across the sky, distant shafts of sunlight breaking through and lighting the pink earth below. This house, with its antique double doors, soft adobe lines, and windows all around, was their retirement home, but Margaret didn't feel old. She was still slim and upright (except for a bony bump at the back of her neck, which she did her best to hide with scarves), she walked daily, and had never once dyed her hair—had, in fact, been pleased when it faded from a rather nondescript blond to shining silver. And she felt more creatively vibrant than she had in years, full of ideas, ready to buckle down.

The way Harold told it, laughing agreeably with their friends, was that out of the blue Margaret had announced that they were moving to New Mexico. "She wouldn't take no for an answer!" Harold was still back in his office in Fairfield, surrounded by legal briefs. Margaret had known he was reluctant to retire and couldn't move right in the middle of a big case, and though she'd made a show of disappointment, she was secretly glad she'd be alone. She insisted she had to leave as soon as possible to get them settled.

Her sister-in-law had offered to accompany her, but Margaret had wanted to drive across the country alone with her dog, Daisy. By the time she arrived, the movers had already unloaded the furniture and boxes and more or less arranged them in rooms according to the diagram Margaret had supplied. Walking through the empty rooms, Daisy close at her heels, Margaret had felt on her bare feet the warm afternoon sunlight and the cool terra-cotta tile, and she thought of their first house in Guilford forty years ago, the furniture from the old apartment spread thinly through the rooms, the bare wood floors, all of it waiting, still and quiet, for the lively clatter of babies.

She spent the first few days seeing the sights. She drove to Tesuque, visited artists' studios and glass foundries, had brunch at the Market. In Santa Fe, she walked the Plaza and dipped in and out of galleries on Canyon Road. One night she went to the Opera—*Rigoletto*—though she was exhausted and left at intermission.

On the way home, Margaret stopped at the convenience store five miles down the highway with the idea of asking about anyone in town who might be available for house-work and to help her settle in. Margaret thought of it as "town," but there was no town, not really. Just the convenience store off the exit and a trailer with a sign over the door that said BEAUTY HAIR NAILS.

At the counter, Margaret wrote her name and number, and was about to jot her address, too, when she thought better of it. The heavy Hispanic woman at the register sat on her stool and watched impassively. "If you think of anyone, have her call me. We can meet, see how we like each other." Margaret thought *interview* sounded pushy, though of course that's what it would be.

A Carmen Baca phoned and arrived at the arranged time with a pink plastic tub of rags and cleaning solutions, apparently thinking she'd already been hired. Legs trembling, Daisy barked at Carmen Baca, who paused uncertainly in the door and held her cleaning supplies high.

Margaret scooped up the dog. "Don't mind Daisy. She thinks she's a guard dog, but she's harmless."

Carmen wore pale jeans and a teal t-shirt snug across her breasts and belly: GOLDEN MESA CASINO: WHERE MORE WINNERS WIN MORE! "I don't know, but dogs have always made me nervous." When the woman smiled, her round face creased good-naturedly. "But this one's cute." With one finger she gingerly patted Daisy behind an ear, pulling her hand back quickly when the dog licked her. "It's a puppy?"

"No," said Margaret, in the pleased, slightly regretful tone she used when people asked this. "She's eight, a Yorkie. Come sit down!" Margaret gestured to the table in the raised dining area, where she'd set out cups pulled directly from a moving carton and a plate of almond butter cookies. "Tea? Coffee? I just brewed a fresh pot."

Carmen placed the tub next to her chair and crossed her white sneakers primly. "My, my," she said, nodding at the cookies.

Margaret wondered if this woman was making fun of her, but Carmen just smiled blandly.

She was in her early forties, no more than five feet tall, hair pulled into a black ponytail that exposed sideburns and a swath of coarse hair growing down the back of her neck. But what Margaret couldn't stop looking at was the scar: a pink ragged line across Carmen's brown throat, raised and stretching at least two inches, nearly to her ear.

Carmen surveyed the sunken great room, furniture still wrapped in plastic, wide foyer, the gleaming steel kitchen. "Pretty fancy," she said.

"It's bigger than we needed," Margaret apologized, "but we couldn't pass it up. We fell in love with the place. I've never seen anything like this light." She thought of some man—boyfriend, husband, stranger—holding Carmen against his chest, his mouth in her thick hair, pressing the blade of the knife against her throat. Margaret circled her own warm neck with her hand.

Carmen twisted in her chair (the scar stretching taut and shiny), nodded at the boxes stacked along the walls. "You got some project here."

"I'll say. That's why I need the help. Harold, my husband, is still in Connecticut. He planned to cut down, work a few weeks at a time back East and spend the rest of the year in New Mexico, but a big case came up." She was talking too much—because of the scar, she was sure. It made her eyes water. Margaret tried to force her thoughts elsewhere, looked hard at Carmen's hands as they spooned sugar into a mug. She counted the etched gold rings tight on the fingers: six. "So you grew up around here?"

"Yep. Live in the same house my dad built." Carmen selected a cookie, pinky turned out, and nibbled as she explained that she lived next door to her diabetic mother. "She's stubborn as heck. Won't let anyone help with the shots, but wants you to stand in the bathroom watching."

Margaret was surprised to learn Carmen had a twenty-five-year-old son and a six-year-old granddaughter, whom Carmen watched in the afternoons. "She lives with her mom, Ruben's old girlfriend. I wanted them to get married, but"—heavy sigh—"what can we do?"

"I'd never have guessed you had a granddaughter. You look so young."

Carmen hooted. "I wish!" She sighed again. "Well, Ruben's not perfect, God knows, but he's my baby."

Margaret was wondering how she'd describe Carmen's accent to Harold. "I'm planning to learn Spanish. Maybe you could tutor me." She said it without thinking, then faltered.

"I don't speak Spanish. Not good, anyways." Carmen shook her head, and for a moment the scar disappeared in the crease of her neck.

Suddenly, Margaret was afraid Carmen might not agree to work here. She was about to explain that she'd only assumed because of the accent when Carmen looked up, grinned. "The only words I know are cusses."

That smile—the white, even teeth—Margaret could have hugged her for that.

Carmen stood, wandered to the kitchen, aimlessly opened an empty cupboard. "I think this will work good."

MARGARET TOLD HAROLD about Carmen that night on the phone while she chopped mushrooms for her salad. "She's wonderful, Harold. Great sense of humor. And a saint, takes care of everyone. She'll come in the mornings and leave in time to collect her granddaughter from school. It's the perfect setup—" Then she added: "At least for now. When you get here we can reconfigure."

"Good, Mags. I wish I *were* there. This case is rough. One useless deposition after another." He talked about work for a while, and Margaret let her mind wander because she could tell he was happy. Carmen had clearly had a difficult life, but she was cheerful, open. The blade of the knife slid smoothly through the pale flesh of the mushroom, and Margaret thought once again of Carmen's scar. She pictured the knife, or the accident—it *might* have been an accident—a piece of glass from a car's windshield, a childhood collision with a sliding door. Whatever it was, there would have been blood everywhere. Her fingers felt weak.

She was on the point of telling him about the scar when Harold's voice trailed away. He cleared his throat. "You're sure everything's okay, Margaret?" he asked. "With us?" His voice was husky, pained, and all at once the harmony drained from the conversation.

Lately, Harold had been oddly intuitive as he'd never been before. Just three weeks ago, as she was packing the kitchen, setting aside duplicate dishes for Harold to use in his new condo, he'd stood in the doorway watching her. His thin wrists seemed gray, exposed by the rolled sleeves of his Oxford. "Are you leaving me?"

"Of course not," Margaret had said, looking at him steadily from the mess of newspapers and dinner plates. He'd searched her face a moment, then relaxed, reassured.

And she'd meant it. In those months leading up to the move, Margaret had felt tremendous tenderness for Harold. She needed to keep him safe as much as she needed to be apart from him.

Now she said: "Of course everything's okay. I forget how late it is there with the time difference. I'll let you go, sweetie."

From the living room, Daisy whined, in response, maybe, to the wail of a coyote too far for Margaret to hear. Daisy wasn't used to the new house yet. She peered around corners, clung to the walls, eyeing the kitchen or bedroom before scrambling wildly across the open spaces, nails clacking on the tile.

Margaret lifted Daisy and held the dog's warm, quivering body against her chest. She pressed her forehead against the cold window, peering past her reflection into the darkness beyond. You had to be careful with little dogs way out here, the real estate agent had said. They could be carried off by coyotes or bobcats or, more rarely, mountain lions. Even a hawk might swoop down and lift little Daisy into the air, tearing her silky gray fur with razor talons.

MARGARET HAD HAD OCCASIONAL gallery shows in Rockland, Maine, near where they spent their summers, and she periodically illustrated text-heavy children's books about historical events. While the books never sold very well, two had won obscure awards for historical accuracy; and over the years she'd sold a number of paintings—fourteen—of abandoned farmhouses and docks and lobster boats, children crouched at the water's edge. It wasn't much, perhaps, but many artists did their best work in their later years, and Margaret hoped—with all her heart she hoped—that this would be true of herself.

Her current project, *Canute Commands the Tides*, was promising, completely different from anything she'd done before—more personal, more urgent. It was based on the legend of Canute, the Danish king of England, old fool, who, claiming he could stop the tides, ordered his throne carried to the waterline, where, predictably, it was swamped by waves. It seemed to Margaret there was something marvelous about Canute's determination. Instead of submitting to the tide of life, letting old age drag him away and under, Canute had railed against it.

She'd started *Canute Commands the Tides* two years ago,

after their daughter Charlotte relocated to Johannesburg. Margaret hadn't even known they'd been considering a move until Charlotte and her husband announced they'd be packing up the girls and going clear across the ocean.

What had really shocked Margaret, though, was the stunning, paralyzing sense of abandonment she'd felt. When Harold was at work and Margaret had the house to herself, it seemed she couldn't stop crying, and when she wasn't crying, she wandered from room to room, feeling utterly without purpose. "I don't think it's nice," she told Charlotte coldly, long-distance, hating herself. "We're not young, you know. We need our granddaughters."

The real problem, she realized, when she began to get hold of herself, was that all her life, she'd never really *chosen*, just allowed the currents to pull her this way and that. Even her art—especially her art—she'd just let happen to her. She'd never truly *decided*, thrown herself into it head-long, made it matter.

Canute himself was not in any of Margaret's paintings: just his throne and the lapping white-tipped waves. In her first attempt, the throne was gilt-edged and red velvet, sinking in the sand, upholstery sodden. But the year was so early, 1015. She pictured what she knew of those feudal lords. Brutal battles fought with clubs and spears and seaxes. Thanes. Thralls. Feasting kings distributing the spoils of war among subjects in heavy-beamed mead halls. The next version of the throne was a plank-backed wood armchair, high and hard. In her next attempt, she downgraded Canute again, giving him one of the yellow-spindled kitchen chairs that had been in her childhood home in Marblehead. Still, the painting wasn't right.

Now, in her new home, Margaret sliced the packing boards from her canvases and laid the paintings side by side on the floor, discouraged by the blank backgrounds, the crooked sketched lines, the paint that had been worked and reworked into mud. Daisy nosed the corner of one, and Margaret nudged her away with a toe, still studying her attempts.

Margaret rubbed her face with anxious hands, and the familiar and nauseating cocktail of emotions surged: guilt, impatience, dread, ambition. She must get herself organized: set up the studio, begin a strict schedule. She would tackle Canute; she would move forward.

THE NEXT SEVERAL DAYS were spent unpacking. At Carmen's insistence, they dealt with the house room by room, beginning with the studio. "Lord," said Carmen, hands on hips, as she stood in the doorway. "Looks like you had pigs rooting around in here." Margaret watched with admiration as Carmen's quick hands sorted her materials into piles, filled toolboxes and coffee cans and bookshelves, made it all manageable so that after only one morning the studio was ready.

"This is what I'm working on," Margaret confided, turning a canvas that was facing the wall, the painting of the kitchen chair.

Carmen, crouched by the bookshelf, looked over her shoulder briefly. "What's that chair doing on the beach?"

"It's based on a myth—"

"It's a pretty picture. Reminds me of when me and my sister went to San Diego, oh, ten, twelve years ago. I love the beach." Sigh. "What would I give."

—

Margaret had been uneasy about getting rid of things from the old house when they'd moved, so she hadn't, the result being that the more she and Carmen unpacked, the more claustrophobic she felt. The cornflower striped couch, the one she'd loved and which had looked so elegant and Colonial in Connecticut looked terrible here: fussy and wrong. So many of their things were like that.

"You must miss your husband," said Carmen as she unwrapped the stemware.

"Of course it's hard, but he has work there and I have my work here." It wasn't good for men to be on their own, Margaret knew that. They suffered without their wives, died earlier. In those same studies she'd read that married women were unhappier than those who lived alone.

Carmen looked at her, head tilted, questioning.

Her fury, this last year, had been as debilitating as her depression, and it was directed squarely at Harold—and why? Because he'd married her? Because they'd had a lovely girl together and their lives had been blessed, and he'd had a purpose while Margaret had drifted through it all? Margaret couldn't articulate her fury, and Harold wouldn't have known what to do with it even if she could.

Instead, night after night Margaret initiated in bed, and usually Harold responded, laughing, joking about her new insatiability. She demanded that he fuck her—said those words, though she never had before—and he did, his face serious and intent above her. She came in silent, anguished rage, and each time after, she cried—another thing she'd never done. Poor Harold was solicitous and baffled. He stroked her hair and asked what was wrong; had he been too rough, had he hurt her?

Carmen had moved on to the wedding china, wiping each piece with a dishcloth. "I have a set like this," she said, holding up a plate. "It was a door prize at the Golden Mesa."

"Oh," said Margaret, deeply embarrassed for Carmen. She gassed up at the casinos; gas was cheaper there, and the restrooms always clean. Once, on an impulse, she'd pushed through the glass door that separated the convenience store from the casino itself. Inside it was dark, air thick with cigarette smoke, walls lined with mirrors reflecting the rows and rows of old people sitting before the blinking slots. Jangling manic sounds, frenetic lights, and, suspended from the ceiling, giant pots painted in the black and white geometrics of the Anasazi. Margaret had felt profoundly depressed, too depressed even to flee, until a skinny red-eyed man offered to buy her a drink. She'd shaken her head mutely and turned to go, grateful and disoriented when she stepped into the bright sunlight. It was all so tasteless, she'd told Harold later on the phone, such a misguided cheapening of culture.

"It seems like the casinos could cause a lot of social problems on the reservations," Margaret ventured.

"Oh, I know," said Carmen, tucking a strand of hair into her ponytail. "They're getting so rich." Sigh. "Oh, well. The slots relax me." Carmen stood, pressing herself up on her thighs, then carried the stack of plates to the kitchen.

Margaret smiled brightly and sliced the packing tape on another box.

Why had she never noticed how much fabric she'd been surrounded by in her old life? The plush towels, the brocade and rugs, all the throw pillows and merino afghans, all meant to swaddle and muffle. And her clothes—heels, tailored jackets, stiff leather handbags—boxes and boxes of the stuff.

Carmen held a silk charmeuse blouse by the neck, displaying the label. "Ooh, Calvin Klein. Fancy lady." Daisy nosed Carmen, who rolled her over with a palm and rubbed the soft pink belly.

"Take it." Margaret examined then tossed aside a herringbone skirt. "I can't believe I wore all this."

"Are you sure?" Carmen asked about each item as she folded it neatly and set it behind her.

"God, yes! Take it all." There was no way Carmen would fit into most of the clothes, but perhaps she would make them over.

Each day when Carmen left, she swung full garbage bags into the trunk of her dented Chrysler LeBaron, and each day Margaret felt lighter. It pleased Margaret to think of Carmen using her things. It must have felt like a windfall for her. Most of Margaret's belongings weren't cheap, were probably nicer than the things Carmen bought for herself. And perhaps she sold some of it, though Margaret didn't care for that thought nearly as much.

In the end, Margaret kept a few of the ornate mahogany bureaus and side tables—family pieces—and the dining room set. Harold's brown leather chair and about half the books. In the end, it was mostly her things she got rid of. All she wanted now were clean surfaces and straight lines, mental and creative space.

She packed Charlotte's old drawings and school papers, ceramic frogs and elephants, spent a fortune to mail the box all the way to Johannesburg. Just last year, she'd sooner have died than part with these wobbly self-portraits and plaster handprints. Standing in line at the post office now, though, it felt essential to shed the weight of them. Charlotte would be wounded, but she was grown now, and Margaret was not, after all, an archive.

CARMEN'S TECHNIQUES WERE pleasingly old-fashioned: she cleaned with scalding water, bleach, white vinegar, wiped the windows with newspaper, scrubbed the kitchen floor with rags on her hands and knees. "Mops don't do nothing," she declared. "They just move the dirt around."

She watched television while she worked. First the news programs, then the morning game shows. Soaps, talk shows. They worked their way through the day. Margaret found herself looking forward to some of the programs, talking about the personalities as though they were common acquaintances. "Bob Barker must be a million years old."

"Oh," said Carmen knowingly, "he's had work. Just look at that neck."

Of course, Margaret thought afterward, these television personalities *were* the only common acquaintances she and Carmen had.

If Margaret went for a walk, when she returned, the channel was often switched to a Spanish station, where women with bright makeup and clothes too sparkly and tight wept and ranted at surly, hard-jawed men. "Sorry," Carmen would say and change it back to one of the English networks.

"No, no," Margaret protested, but Carmen waved her away.

"It's more fun if we can talk about it," she said.

And talk Carmen did. Instead of painting, Margaret spent the mornings with her, sometimes paying bills, sometimes working alongside, sometimes just watching. Carmen's own grandmother had been a traditional healer, a *curandera*.

"Oh, she was *mean*. The other kids were scared of her because she always wore black dresses down to here, and, my God, did she complain. She used to tell us stories to make us behave, about how La Llorona was going to go drown us in the river." Carmen laughed. "Me and my brother ran away from her when she was watching us one night. We ran to our cousins' and slept on their porch. All night on the porch, up against each other like puppies. Were we *spanked* when they found us!" She laughed and wiped her forehead with her arm, holding the wet rubber gloves over the sink so the water wouldn't drip down her sleeves.

Sometimes during the soap operas, if a character was particularly charming and incorrigible, Carmen mentioned her troubles with her son. It seemed she supported him entirely. "Ruben tries, poor baby, but those supervisors. You know how people can be when they get power, and if they treat him so terrible, of course he's going to get mad. He's doing good now, though, got himself a new job, driving equipment to the road crews up there in Raton and all over." Carmen snapped a towel, folded it exactly without even looking. "He tells me in the break room they got a sign that says DRINK ON THE JOB AND KISS THE JOB GOODBYE. My daughter, she says if he's good for six months, really serious, she'll help him pay for long-term therapy."

Carmen's daughter Vivian was a high school teacher. She'd married well and lived in Albuquerque in a house with two sinks in the kitchen and three and a half baths. Every month or so Carmen visited, and her daughter took her to dinner and various touring performances. "Oh, the play was beautiful," Carmen told Margaret after *Lord of the Dance.* "You should have seen the clothes."

"Has he tried rehab before?" Margaret fingered the laundry piled between them on the couch. She wished she could have been the one to offer to pay for Ruben's therapy. These sorts of thoughts had begun to occur to her— that she'd like to give Carmen something, do something to make her life easier.

"The state paid for an eight-day detox just last year after his DUIs. And some therapist sessions. I just pray to God this time he'll get better."

"It can be hard," Margaret said, "but sometimes the best way to help someone like Ruben is to cut him off. Let him know that you trust he can pull it together on his own."

"I know, I know." Carmen sighed. "That's what Vivian tells me, but he's my baby, you know. And the law sure don't make it easy for him—like last year, they take away his license and still they make him show up once a week to meetings. Plus he has work. Well, how's he supposed to get there if he can't drive?"

"Ah," said Margaret.

"You got to help your kids until you can't. Besides, there's Autumn to think about. She can't do without, just to teach Ruben a lesson. Maybe he won't make good of himself, but at least I can try. Autumn's mom never gave him the emotional support he needs, and now she's talking about trying to take his custody. It's terrible. Nothing's ever come easy for him, not one thing."

Carmen put the stacked towels in the basket. "You know, Ruben's real good at fixing stuff." She glanced around the room, as though looking for items that needed fixing. "You give him an engine, and he can figure out what's wrong with it in no time. He retiled my whole bathroom. Anything you need done."

"I'll keep that in mind," said Margaret, and wondered if there were some outdoor jobs she could give the boy. Maybe it would encourage him to stay on the right path. She imagined getting to know the family, being invited to their big parties, then caught herself and blushed. "I'll keep it in mind."

That afternoon, as she was leaving, Carmen said, "Honey, you don't need me every day. You don't make near enough mess."

"Yes, I do." Margaret was surprised by the insistence in her voice. "There's so much that needs to be done. The windows. And the linens need to be rewashed. The van must have been stuffy."

IN THE AFTERNOONS, after Carmen left, Margaret found herself taking frequent stock of the kitchen cupboards, looking for a reason to drive into town and away from her studio, a mission for the day that was both achievable and time-consuming, anything to keep from having to be alone with her painting. There was so much to do, but Margaret didn't know what, and she couldn't sit still long enough to let it come. So instead, she organized her supplies, cleaned her brushes, made lists of colors she needed.

One afternoon, on one of these errands, she drove with Daisy to Santa Fe, bought lunch downtown and ate it on a bench on the Plaza. As the shadows of leaves shifted around her, she watched the faces of the other women. Perhaps she would meet someone—for some reason the black and white photographs of Georgia O'Keefe always rose in her mind—with whom she could talk about her art. But they all seemed to be tourists. She wished there weren't so many people, wished the Five & Dime didn't just sell disposable cameras and plastic chile ristras and cheap postcards and souvenir scorpion magnets. She would have liked it all to be a little more real, and felt a pang of regret for not having moved out here twenty, thirty years ago.

Two elegantly dressed women her age walked toward her with shopping bags in their hands. They didn't gaze in shop windows or photograph the Native Americans under the portico of the Palace of the Governors. They walked like they belonged here. One wore a silver squash blossom necklace over a black silk shift.

As they approached, Daisy spied a hot dog wrapper in the path. She strained on her leash, whining.

The squash-blossom woman smiled as she passed. "A beauty! I have two Yorkies of my own."

Margaret tugged Daisy back sharply, irritated. These women were the kind of people Carmen would despise, the kind of people Margaret might be mistaken for.

—

WHEN SHE DID FORCE herself to pour out linseed oil and squeeze paint onto the palette, Margaret took a great deal of time over the preparations, and for every dab of paint on the canvas, she stepped back and considered. The perspective was off on one of the chair legs, the waves looked sculpted in plasticine, there wasn't nearly enough contrast. It was so hard to get into her work; she pushed tiny bits of paint across the edge of the canvas, avoiding, avoiding, avoiding. After only twenty or thirty minutes, she wanted to stamp her foot and whine like Charlotte had when she was four and frustrated over her shoelaces: *It's too hard.*

Early one morning, however—Sunday, Carmen wouldn't be in today—Margaret awoke thinking of the sandstone formations along the highway to Santa Fe and decided she'd integrate them into her piece. After all, this place had changed her, and *Canute Commands the Tides* should reflect that. Old Canute would not be on the Maine coast, but on a mythical desert-like beach that had never existed, a beach ringed with cliffs and red sandstone balanced like meringue.

Without brushing her teeth or putting in her contacts, Margaret ran to her studio in her nightgown, exhilarated. She stepped out on the cold patio in bare feet to scoop sand, which she drizzled through her fingers onto the palette. Oranges and reds and browns, paint mounded thick. All morning she worked, chilly, yet sweating along her sides and at the back of her neck. Under her feet, sand gritted.

When she stepped back, the euphoria was lost. It's true

her cliffs resembled Camel Rock and the others, but the whole effect was self-consciously mystical, like an image on a new-agey Taroh card. And this kind of textured painting had already been done, and done better.

How to capture it? How to convey what the story meant to her, what Canute meant? Margaret looked with despair at all her attempts, lined up around the studio. It wasn't fair. She tried and she tried, but this rot could be hanging in any motel, except with a yellow kitchen chair dropped in. And now the metaphor was becoming tangled in Margaret's mind. Was the story about admirable gumption, Canute's resolve to determine his destiny in the face of mighty, indifferent reality? Or about his foolish, maniacal arrogance? Some sources, insisting on his wisdom, said Canute had actually ordered his throne carried to the sea to prove to his admiring courtiers the absurdity of arguing against God and nature. Perhaps *this* is what her subject should actually be: gracious yielding to the forces that had shaped her life. Or maybe the whole thing was just a joke and the story was about nothing more than plain old defeat.

Angrily, Margaret flung her brush at the canvas. It flipped to the ground, splattering the tile. She dropped to her knees, swiped the floor with her rag of turpentine, but the oil spread across the clay.

IT HAD NEVER OCCURRED to Margaret that she might forget what the ocean looked like. She thought she would always see the water clearly in her mind's eye, having always lived so near it. But now it eluded her. She found herself painting not water, but likenesses of water she had painted before, imitations of other artists' renditions of water. One night she filled the stainless-steel kitchen sink and tried to make currents in it with her hands, watched the kitchen light waver against the sides.

Outside, only darkness. Margaret leaned over the sink, closer to the window, trying to see past her reflection. Perhaps she should set the chair *here*, among the round hills and piñon woodland. The subject caught her, and for a moment she was pleased with the novelty of her idea, the unlikely twist.

But here there was nothing to threaten the chair, just time and sun and occasional rains. Here mud structures took hundreds of years to wash away. Even the bodies of rabbits and coyotes killed on the highway didn't rot and rejoin the earth, but shrank and stiffened. Here the problem wasn't that nothing lasted, but that nothing disappeared.

FOR THREE WEEKS Carmen was on time and never missed a day. Then one day she didn't show. Margaret called her house and left a message. She vacillated between irritation—she'd come to depend on Carmen's presence—and guilt over her irritation. Maybe something had happened to the diabetic mother.

It was noon before Carmen arrived with her granddaughter Autumn in tow. "Sorry," she said at the door. "No school today. I hope you don't mind." She turned to the girl. "You be good and don't go touch nothing." Autumn, wearing lavender platform flip-flops, jeans, and a pink halter-top, stood close to her grandmother. Her hair was pulled back so tightly it tugged the corners of her eyes, and the curls of her ponytail were stiff with gel.

"What a day," said Carmen. "Ruben's got my car. His truck's in the shop, and he has to go down to Albuquerque. But he'll be back in time to get us." She was already rummaging under the kitchen sink, pulling out bleach and sponges. "I got Autumn's lunch here—" she gestured at a bag of Taco Bell on the counter. "She brought her Barbies, and she'll be happy watching TV."

"Do you like art?" Margaret asked the girl. "Let's see if we can't get you some pastels and good paper. Come with me."

Autumn didn't follow, just stood with her backpack on her skinny shoulders. She still hadn't budged when Margaret returned, arms full of supplies.

"We'll set you up at the table."

As though she'd been waiting for permission to move, Autumn walked slowly around the living room, touching each picture frame lightly with one finger. "These are your grandkids?"

"They are. Nine and eleven."

Autumn bit her lip. "Are they sisters?" Her teeth were small and sharp and slightly bluish, the color of skim milk.

Margaret nodded. "They live far away now. In South Africa, which is a country in the continent of Africa."

Autumn examined another picture from years ago: Margaret and Charlotte in the kitchen, flour-covered, smiling up from their work of tracing maple leaves into piecrust.

"That's my daughter, Charlotte. She's an only child."

"Like me," said Autumn.

Autumn spent the morning drawing page after page,

frowning earnestly at her work. Margaret showed her how the pastels could be blended; soon Autumn's fingertips were thick with green-brown waxy smears.

Carmen spread newspapers and brought out the tub of silver polish and rags, then settled at the table next to the child with Margaret's grandmother's tea service, which hadn't been touched in years. "Look at that. She's gone and used up all your colors."

"That's what they're for." Margaret wanted to give this child things, lifelike stuffed animals and educational toys. She wished Autumn were her grandchild. Her own were so assertive and articulate now, so at home in the world, absorbing it all—their private school, safaris, school vacations in Thailand and Indonesia—without a flicker of self-doubt. With Autumn she could make a difference.

It was relaxing to watch the child work. Autumn tilted her head, considered, then bent back over the page. Her shoulder and whole arm moved with her hand. Soon the table was strewn with lush green landscapes that had nothing to do with New Mexico.

"Autumn is lovely," Margaret told Carmen.

Carmen nodded, scouring the sugar bowl with her rag. "She's my blessing." At the sound of her grandmother's voice, Autumn stood and put her hand on her grandmother's knee, looked up at Margaret gravely. The child's expression struck Margaret as one less of affection than allegiance.

Margaret felt a sudden jealousy. She remembered holding Charlotte when she was tiny and asleep, that trusting limp weight against her chest, how she'd bend her neck over Charlotte's, bury her face in the warm skin, wanting so much to merge with her again.

BY SIX O'CLOCK, Ruben still hadn't arrived. Carmen tried calling. "He must not got his cell with him."

"No problem, I can drive you."

"I'm sure he'll be here," Carmen said doubtfully. "I hope he's okay."

Autumn rolled her eyes. "Daddy always forgets."

"I know—you and Autumn could stay here tonight! If you want. I have extra toothbrushes, anything you could need. We'll have a girls' night, eat pizza, do masks. Autumn, I can set up a real canvas for you in the studio." Margaret's pulse throbbed in her neck, and she could feel her head warming. With Autumn here, the day already had a holiday feel to it. They'd stay up late, drinking wine and laughing. She looked at Carmen. "If you want."

Carmen shook her head. "We couldn't." Her voice was uneasy.

Autumn pulled on her grandmother's shirt. "Yes! Yes!"

"It's just one night. At least have dinner. If you change your mind I can drive you guys home before bed."

While Margaret cooked, they listened to Autumn's CD on the stereo—pop music sung by some blond girl in a tube top—and the three of them danced around the house. In the studio, Margaret had set up a new canvas and adjusted the easel so it was Autumn's height. Soon Carmen seemed to relax. They stood around talking and laughing, drinking wine, while Autumn squeezed the bright acrylics onto a fresh palette—too much, but Margaret didn't stop her.

After dinner, Carmen dug through her purse for a bottle of pink nail polish. She propped her feet on the coffee table and buffed and painted her toenails. "Here," she said, waving the bottle at Margaret. "I'll do you."

Margaret sipped her wine and shook her head. "No. My toes look terrible. I'd hate for anyone to touch them." She thought of her feet, long and pale, the skin thin and dry. An old woman's feet.

"You're sure? I used to do hair and nails professionally."

Margaret hesitated, nearly changed her mind. Autumn was stretched on the carpet with Margaret's oversized sketchpad, drawing intricate lines with a pencil.

"If you wanted, you could do something with my hair," Margaret said shyly.

Carmen nodded. "Sit."

Autumn glanced up. "She's really good."

Margaret sat on the floor between Carmen's knees, and Carmen began to rake her fingers across her scalp. Autumn's pencil scratched. After a moment Margaret allowed herself to relax against the couch, her whole body warm and electric with Carmen's touch. She was drunker than she thought.

"You've got good curl. I used to love giving permanents."

She remembered her friends at Mount Holyoke, winding each other's hair in curlers at night, the smuggled bottles of rum they mixed with pineapple juice from large cans and drank out of their coffee mugs. It wasn't the nights they snuck out with boys from Amherst or UMass that she missed; it was the nights they spent in, intending to read, that instead unfolded in wonderful laughter and silliness.

In college Margaret had slept with three boys: two boyfriends, the other the visiting brother of her roommate. Margaret liked sex, liked the intrigue, the playacting, the real passion that invariably caught her by surprise. She also liked the ultimate safety of it, orchestrated and anticipated and reviewed as it was with her friends. It was this intimacy, the intimacy with women, that had really mattered.

Margaret shifted ever so slightly, leaned her shoulder into Carmen's thigh.

"What happened?" Margaret murmured.

"Oh, I got away from it, and six years ago Reina Sanchez opened the salon by the gas station. Anymore, I have a heck of a time getting the energy to do my own hair."

AFTER AUTUMN HAD BEEN put to bed—both Carmen and Margaret had tucked her in—they sat in the living room petting Daisy and watching a late show. It was past eleven when the driveway light flicked on. Margaret went to the window and looked out. She could see Ruben backlit by the glow of the spotlight, a dark, unsmiling face in the driver's seat. He wasn't looking toward the house, but at some point in the distance.

She backed away from the window, suddenly afraid of being seen. When the doorbell rang, she didn't move to answer it.

"Ruben." Carmen sighed and rose to open the door, as if she lived here. Daisy trotted after her.

Up close, Ruben wasn't nearly as tall as Margaret had imagined, just an inch or two taller than she. His facial hair was scraggly and long, his teeth crooked and scummy-looking.

"What's wrong, hijito?" Carmen said.

The remaining sensation of drunkenness washed away and Margaret felt sharp and dry and alert. "Come in," she said politely, even though he was already inside and something was clearly wrong.

Ruben looked over Carmen and Margaret's shoulders, his head darting about in quick stabs. Margaret had imagined him handsome, disarming; she had imagined she might have to brace herself against his charm. Instead, she was repulsed. *This* was the son Carmen spent all her money on? This was the man responsible for half Autumn's genes?

"Where's my daughter?" he said, head jerking. He moved into the living room.

"Hijito," Carmen said again, voice wary. "What's the matter?"

"Where were you? Where have you been?" His voice was whiny.

Daisy began to yap foolishly. Over the noise, Carmen continued to step toward her son. "We've been waiting for you." Her eyes were on something in his hand.

With a horror that flooded her throat and extremities, Margaret realized Ruben was holding a gun. She'd never seen a real handgun before—shockingly solid and metallic.

Margaret had the impulse to run to the child, asleep in the guestroom, and push her deep under the bed. The old childhood memories of hiding from her shouting father. Autumn must have the same instincts.

"Where's my fucking daughter?" He scratched at his neck as though clawing something out of him. "You been talking to that bitch Chelsea? The two of you keeping my daughter from me?"

Margaret drew herself up. "You need to leave my house. You need to go." She extended a hand toward the door, an absurdly formal gesture.

But Ruben didn't hear. He lunged at Carmen, the gun swinging at his side. "You stupid cunt bitch, trying to—" He stopped short without touching her, put his face right into hers. "Where's my *fucking* daughter?"

"I'm not keeping her from you, honey. We've been here, waiting. For you." Carmen's voice was imploring. She didn't shift her eyes from her son's.

Without warning, Ruben lifted the gun, shot it into the ceiling, barely missing a recessed light. The crack stunned Daisy into silence, and they all stood frozen as the gypsum dust rained down. Then Daisy started yapping again.

Margaret tried to think how far out the police would be. Ten minutes. Longer. Maybe a highway patrol would be near. Maybe not. They might have trouble finding the turnoff, navigating the dirt road at night. A lot could happen in that time.

"I'm calling the police."

"Please," cried Carmen. She did not shift her eyes from Ruben's. "Please! He's a good boy. He'll stop."

Margaret looked wildly at the German knives lined up in the block on the kitchen counter. She remembered something she'd heard about knives being no good for self-defense because they can so easily be turned against you. She lifted her hands, looked at them: so thin, veins showing blue through her skin, the wedding band heavy and loose.

Ruben's voice rose. "You better listen to me. Listen to me, listen to me. You never listen to me." He moaned as he spoke, as if in physical pain.

"I'm listening, Ruben. I'm listening. Tell me what you have to say, and I'm listening."

"Don't you fucking tell me what to do!"

He was shaking, jumping, scratching at his neck, so there were red lines running down it. Margaret wondered if the skin might break. Margaret wondered if this was meth, if this was drunkenness, if it was a combination of the two.

Margaret imagined the scene from outside, where she wanted to be: the house all lit up like a silent stage, the terrible drama going on inside. But the house couldn't be seen from the road. And any shout would sound like the wail of a coyote.

The car keys were on the counter in the kitchen. With her purse and her cell phone. Could she grab Autumn, grab the keys? It would take too long. There were too many open spaces in this house. It was all exposure and space. These were surfaces you could crack your head on.

Daisy's bark hammered off the high ceilings, incessant. Margaret longed to run to her, clamp her mouth shut, longed for her to shut up so she could think. "I'll give you money," Margaret cried, hands shaking. She swung her arm wildly. "Take whatever you want, just leave us . . ."

Ruben turned fast, and Margaret shrank against the wall. "Fuck you," he said, the words cutting. "I don't want your money, rich cunt. *Fuck you.*"

Give this maniac Carmen, give him Autumn. Negotiate. You can have them all, she shouted in her head. Just leave, just leave.

"Calm down, hijito. Calm down."

He turned back to his mother. "Don't you fucking get near me! You want to keep me sucking at your fat tits." Sinking to a crouch, Ruben buried his head in his arms, weeping. The gun hung loosely from his hand. Carmen knelt beside him and touched his shoulder gently.

Margaret's courage returned. In a loud voice, so that she could be heard over Daisy's panicked barking, she declared, "Get out now. I will not allow you to terrorize us."

Carmen whipped around, eyes savage. Her voice was quiet, cruel. "You leave him alone."

Whatever this was, they all understood it. Even Autumn. The terror and fury and love and whatever else was mixed up in it was theirs alone, and it was Margaret's own stupid fault it was taking place in her house. She wanted them out, all of them, the little girl, too. She didn't care what happened to them—they could tear each other limb from limb for all she cared—she just wanted them away from her. She wanted it all gone: the sun finding its way in, the dust sifting under the doors. Rattlesnakes. Coyotes and scorpions. God knows what else. Everything wailing, crying, howling.

Daisy barked, sharp, relentless.

Ruben rose in a sudden roar, grabbed the dog in his thick hands. *"Shut the fuck up!"*

Daisy squealed when he threw her across the great room. Her body hit the window with a thud, dropped to the ground in a gray heap. The thick pane didn't break.

When she stood, her black eyes were open, glassy, and she breathed in quick shallow breaths.

There was blood, just a little, in the fur at her ear. Daisy made her way unevenly toward Margaret, tags jingling, then stopped and tipped her head as if perplexed.

Margaret made her move: swept Daisy into her arms, ran across the tile to the heavy door, pushed it open, and burst into the cold night. Point-seven miles to the road. Her feet tore on the stones of the driveway as she ran.

After a time, she realized she was sobbing. She stopped and looked up the hill at the lit house, clutching the dog's little body to her chest, her breath ripping through her. The scent of piñon was sharp and acrid in the cold air.

Above, the bright window hung against the darkness like a canvas on a gallery wall, framing Carmen and her son. They were motionless, as minutely wrought as figures in a medieval miniature. His face was buried in her lap, and she bent over him, so close their heads were nearly touching, the two of them as destructive and unstoppable as any force of nature.

THE MANZANOS

★

My NAME IS MY GRANDMOTHER'S: OFELIA ALMA ZAMORA. I am eleven years old and too young to die, but I am dying nonetheless. I have been dying since the day my mother went away. I've been to doctors—to the clinic in Estancia, and all the way to Albuquerque—but they take my temperature, knead my stomach, check my throat, and tell my grandfather the same thing: perhaps it is a minor infection or virus, one of the usual brief illnesses of childhood, and they see nothing seriously wrong. They don't know about the ojo, the evil eye.

There is no one left in this town who can cure me, so for now I sit at the edge of the yard, my feet in the road, turning a piece of broken asphalt in my hands, in case a stranger passes. Are you a healer? I'll ask her. I think of how it will be when I find her, how when she lays her hands on my head I'll close my eyes and feel the blessing pass through me like fire.

I imagine this, knowing I can't be cured, knowing I couldn't bear to be.

I'M WAITING FOR MY GRANDFATHER, relieved because today, finally, he has gotten up and dressed for the city: plaid shirt buttoned all the way up his thin tortoise neck, bolo tie with the silver dollar set in a ring of turquoise. Face scrubbed, white hair combed in lines over the brown crown of his head. He's in the house rinsing our coffee cups and wiping toast crumbs from the oilcloth.

I am ready, too, wearing my blue dress (though the sleeves no longer cover my wrists), white tights (dingy and loose at the knees), and my sneakers. In my pocket is the address for the VA clinic, which I have copied from some papers in my grandfather's desk. This morning my grandfather braided my hair and fastened the ends with rubber bands from the newspaper. Because I'm tall, I sat at the kitchen chair, and he leaned over me, his trembling fingers slowly working the braid into shape. When I was younger, he would tease me as he combed out the knots, pretend to find things in the tangled mass. "A jackrabbit!" he'd cry. "My pliers!" I'd laugh as the yank of the comb brought tears to my eyes.

Behind me, the porch sags under the weight of the refrigerator and the gyrating washing machine on legs that my grandparents bought during a good year in the fifties. There are places we cannot step, because the boards are gray and fragile with rot. "I'll fix the porch," my grandfather says. "One day I'll find the time and shore it up." But the truth is that for years he has been unable to do jobs that he once did without even thinking.

Every day for a week I have dressed for Albuquerque, and every day he has shivered and shaken his head. "Not today, mi hijita. Perhaps the weather will be better tomorrow."

He spent those mornings in his pajamas, blanket pulled tight around him. It's late spring, the sky above the swaying cottonwoods so blue it has a texture, but he wore his wool cap, sweating. He would not let me go to the neighbors or the priest.

But today he is up and dressed, preparing for our monthly trip to Albuquerque. We will shop for what we need, and we will have lunch in a restaurant, and my grandfather will see the doctor, though he doesn't know this yet.

I touch the slip of paper in my pocket. I catalogue every detail of my grandfather as he is now, as if by leaving nothing out I can keep him safe. I catalogue the smooth, pink mole on his neck, the brown spots like smudged fingerprints on his temples. His eyebrows, gray and wiry and curled. Often a drop of clear fluid hangs from the end of his nose. My grandfather's nose is large now, almost a beak, but it wasn't always that way. In my cigar box, I have a picture of him as a slight, handsome soldier in the army, his features delicate: serious mouth, light eyes, black lashes.

THERE ARE A FEW families still in our town—mostly old people, no other children—and those of us who are left are used to the high weeds, the crumbling houses of neighbors, the plaster that falls like puzzle pieces. The exposed mud bricks dissolve a little more each time it rains.

Across the road from where I sit is the dance hall that belonged to dead Uncle Fidel. It hasn't been a dance hall since long before I was born—hasn't been anything but empty and overgrown with branches—but there is still the green silhouette of a bottle painted on the cracked wooden door. When he was young, my grandfather tells me, there were bailes every Saturday night, and, if he'd had a drink and his shyness left him, he would dance until he was breathless and sweaty, twirling the girls, clapping and stomping with the rest of the town through cuadrillas and polcas. In those days they sprinkled water on the ground to keep the dust down, and dirt clotted on the black toes of his shoes.

At night I imagine I can hear the accordions and fiddles and guitars across the street, but it takes effort, and soon I am weary and overcome with the sense that I have arrived too late. I long for that other Cuipas, for the families and the river. I want to have known my grandfather as he was then, to have been with him all those long years.

THE SUN STRETCHES ALONG the road and warms my legs in my tights. If I turn my face to its heat, I must close my eyes, and in the drowsy redness behind my eyelids I remember what makes me uneasy. Last night I lay stiff in my bed— which I used to share with my mother, which I imagine still smells of her—kept awake not by the ojo, but by a sound I'd never heard before. Instead of my grandfather's steady sleeping breath from across the kitchen and through the open door of his bedroom, I could hear a rattling, chattering gurgle. The sound, so much like an animal—but an animal I have never heard and cannot picture—kept me tense and afraid until dawn, when my grandfather stirred, his bed creaked, and his slow footsteps assured me that he was okay.

SOME DAYS I GO to school, some days I don't; like a fever, the ojo comes and goes. I try not to bother my grandfather with it. When I am well enough, I ride the bus into Estancia, listen to what they tell me. I buy my lunch in the cafeteria and sit with the younger children, who don't ask questions when I am silent.

My grades aren't good. I struggle to form letters on the page. Three times a week I'm called from the classroom by the resource teacher, a young woman—as young, perhaps, as my mother—whose skirt swishes against her hose when she walks. She and I sit together under a fluorescent light in a room that was intended to be a closet. She shows me flashcards, asks me to write sentences, tries to make me explain what I am thinking. I tilt my head. When she tires of waiting, she'll pat my hand and sigh and give me a chocolate wrapped in red foil. I learned this during my time at school: they want to replace the past with their rhymes and procedures, their *i before e* and *carry the one.*

When I was in kindergarten, I used to beg my grandfather to move us to Estancia, because it is a town with a store and a school and a senior center, where he and I can have lunch for a dollar, dessert included. Now I understand what he has never told me, that we must watch over Cuipas until it shrinks to nothing, until the houses are mud once more, and dead Uncle Fidel's bar collapses to splinters.

SOMETIMES, WHEN MY GRANDFATHER is well and I skip school, we walk together, and he tells me again the history of this place: the original land grant, thirty thousand acres given years ago to my grandfather's great-great-great-grandfather, parceled smaller and smaller through the generations, until our piece, my grandfather's and mine, which he put in my name on my seventh birthday, became twenty-five acres, and not the best twenty-five, but grassland. I wish it were in the mountains, with a spring and tall, fragrant piñon. I would walk there in the fall and gather the dropped nuts, roast them to eat through the winter, sell the surplus in bags along the road. But my land is good only for cattle, which I do not have.

"When I was a boy," my grandfather said last time, as we stepped across the dry riverbed, "the water ran all the time. My cousins and me, we used to catch tadpoles and crayfish in jars."

"Where did the water go?" I asked.

My grandfather squinted as if trying to remember. "Perhaps it was diverted into the bean fields. Perhaps it rains less now. Perhaps it all happened when I was at war."

My grandfather has told me that Cuipas was one place before he left and another when he returned. Though he was in the Army for two years, the war had already ended, so he lived in Rome, an eighteen-month vacation, he said, on the government's dime. Each day he swam in Mussolini's pool. It was the first and best pool he'd ever seen, huge, lined with marble smooth under his feet. My grandfather was strong, glistening, brown muscle in blue water.

He almost married a girl there. Silvia Donati. As we walked along a furrow in the bean field—the plants no higher than my calf, leaves broad and soft and heart-shaped—I asked him to tell me about her again.

She had buckteeth, my grandfather said, and the palest, rosiest skin he had ever seen, and black-black hair. She lived with her mother above their hat shop, and she made ladies' hats.

Each afternoon after his swim—back in his uniform, wet hair combed—my grandfather sat across from her at the table by the open window, waiting as she finished her work. He listened to the sharp scissors pressing through wool felt and to voices in the street below, watched her pale hands as she steamed and formed the pieces on faceless wooden heads. When my grandfather left Italy, she gave him a hat for his mother in Cuipas: gray with pink velvet roses. For years my great-grandmother and Silvia Donati wrote each other, one in Spanish, the other in Italian, until my great-grandmother died. I often wonder if Silvia Donati heard about my grandfather's marriage, or my mother's birth, or my grandmother's death in one of those letters. I wonder if she heard about me, if she knows that these days we live alone.

She would be an old woman now. I like to think she does not dye her hair. I like to think she has kept a trim figure and pink cheeks, perhaps remained a virgin for my grandfather. (This is important, I know, from the romance novels my mother left behind.) I imagine they marry, raise me in Italy beside the sea. They hold hands and walk along the beach, and I trail behind, all of us wearing hats that were fashionable once.

MY GRANDFATHER'S UNIFORM is folded in the cedar chest in the crowded back bedroom where I sleep, and which I once shared with my mother. This is my grandmother's wedding veil (netting torn), my grandfather's garrison cap. I don't know what became of my great-grandmother's gray hat, whether she wore it until it lost its shape and color, or it was trampled by a horse, or a gust of wind caught it and flung it across fields and mesas. Perhaps she left it on a bus in Albuquerque. Perhaps she gave it away.

There are some papers here, too, records of business long since concluded. And here, the baptismal gowns of lost children, like limp little ghosts.

WHEN THE RIVER DOES RUN, after the late-summer storms, I sometimes pull on a pair of my mother's old shorts and wade in the muddy water, thinking of Mussolini's pool. I cup the water in my hands and fling it in a sparkling arc around my head.

If the old women see me walking home, calves muddy, shorts wet, they will shake their heads at my bare legs and call me a cabrasita. Bad little goat. But they don't blame me too much for my wild ways; they tell each other I am not at fault for being raised by a man alone. They don't know that I am at fault.

OUR TOWN IS SURROUNDED by grass. Yellow grass on land that shifts and dips like waves. Distance is difficult to judge; the grass is deceptive. The Manzanos rise just beyond our town. I have tried to walk to the mountains, where a man lived for weeks after killing his father-in-law with an iron poker. My grandfather's father was part of the posse that searched for him. My grandfather has taken me in the car, pointed to the distant spot among the juniper and piñon where they found the murderer's camp: fire burned down, dusty bedroll. They never found him, though; I imagine him running from their excited voices and the clomp of hooves in dry soil.

Once when I was seven, I played a game that I was the murderer and would be safe when I reached the mountains. The mountains loomed, and I ran through the tall grass and into the sun, burrs catching on my socks and pants. When my breath burned my throat and I could no longer run, I walked, my pursuers getting closer, and fear and guilt clogged my heart. At a barbed fence I parted the wires and slid through, snaring my shirt above my shoulder blade. Long-horned cattle, black and white and mottled, backed away from me, the calves close to their mothers. Two rattlesnakes slithered from my footsteps, sounded a warning. Even the breeze knew what I'd done. When the sun sank behind the Manzanos, Cuipas was small behind me under a depthless violet sky, and the mountains were no closer.

—

Here are the places I've seen my mother: crossing the field behind the courthouse, hair loose and tangled in the winter wind; through the front window of a bank, filling out a deposit slip; in the school library, glimpsed through the stacks. When I see my mother, it is always from afar or from behind or through glass. Each time my heart flips like a fish in my chest, and each time she is someone else.

My mother left us seven years ago to live in Albuquerque. Perhaps she is there still; perhaps she has moved on to other places: Los Angeles or Chicago or England. She would choose someplace big, I'm sure. She was too young, my grandfather tells me. Never could take responsibility.

My grandfather knows the stories of every grave in the dirt churchyard: This is a great-aunt, this a cousin, this a whole family killed by the Spanish flu. The murdered man is here, here a woman who hung herself from a viga in her kitchen after her third stillborn child, but they buried her in sacred ground nonetheless. *Profirio Narciso, Nacio Valentin. Maria Candelarita. Maria Ascension.* And this here, beside the plaster statue of the Blessed Mother, is my name: my grandmother, whom I never met. When my mother was thirteen, my grandmother left for Santa Fe, where she found work in the post office. My grandfather went after her several times, but each time she refused to return. She came home only to be buried—a heart attack.

Once I asked my grandfather why she left, but he shook his head.

Some of the graves have iron fences around them, with little gates as though for children. Some are decorated with plastic flowers, petals bleached from the sun. I imagine I know which spot will be mine in the churchyard: pressed between my grandfather and the boy whose neck was snapped so many years ago when he was thrown from a horse. Once we are gone, the memory of my mother will be extinguished as well. I wish I could reorder the graves in the yard, straighten the slanting stones, arrange them by date or name.

I CAN FEEL THE OJO in my bones, which ache in the morning and at night, and in my skin, which is prickly and electric. Growing pains, the doctor at the clinic tells me. Still, I must put my affairs in order. First, there is the problem of the land. When I'm gone it will go to the distant offspring of a cousin of my grandfather's. My grandfather doesn't know I know this, doesn't know I won't have children of my own.

I have toys and books that must be disposed of, too. A collection of stones.

THE OLD WOMEN SAY the ojo is caused by a covetous glance, by looking overlong. The man who gave it did not admire me, however, and looked for only a moment. The one thing of mine he desired, he took.

These are the symptoms: At night heaviness crouches on my chest and I wake gasping for air. Occasionally my eyes blur for no reason and Cuipas slants and washes away.

At my worst, I shiver and burn, and my grandfather wraps my feet in cold rags.

My memories of my mother are insubstantial. I see her lying on her back on the living room floor, a beauty magazine held above her head as she reads, limp pages rustling. Holding me in the yard at night, bare feet, my hand gripping the flannel nightgown at her breast as I follow with my eyes her pointed finger to the moon. A dish of yogurt cracked on the board floors of the kitchen, my mother crying. I do not know if my grandfather remembers these moments, but he must remember others: my mother as a laughing toddler, perhaps, my mother at her first communion, my mother too young and pregnant with me. Possibly he remembers the sound of her voice.

Once a month we drive west to Albuquerque, once a week we drive east to Estancia. In Estancia we buy groceries and the newspaper. At home my grandfather prepares our favorite lunch: cheese and mustard sandwiches and a glass of milk. We wash our dishes, and then it is time for the paper. We turn to the back, to the comics, but we don't read them. Very carefully my grandfather tears out the puzzles, the spot-the-differences for me, the word search for him.

We sit, working with our pencils.

"These are good for my eyes," he tells me. "They keep my mind sharp."

His favorites are the ones that match English and Spanish words. Sometimes my grandfather disagrees with the paper's translation. "*Moths* are *palomitas*," he tells me, "not *polillas,"* and I look up, try to remember. When I finish my puzzle, I stand beside my grandfather's chair and point out words he's missed.

At night, if I can't sleep, I creep to the kitchen and take the paper from the crate by the woodstove. I spread it on the bedclothes. Somewhere north of here they are building a new casino. They are angry about the economy. In a country far away something has changed. I lie back on my pillow and try to imagine living in the world where these things matter. In the morning, when my grandfather wakes me for my oatmeal, he gathers the paper and replaces it beside the stove.

Sometimes my grandfather remembers church, and if it is Sunday, he shakes me awake and braids my hair, and we walk to the chapel. We sit in the pews with our neighbors and try to listen. The priest talks about the soul, as beside me my grandfather's chin sinks to his chest. The soul is a ball of light or a jewel that must be treasured, given to Jesus.

"Christ calls for our souls though we are foul in body," says the priest.

Jesus looks down on us from the cross, mournful and distant and preoccupied with his own story.

I feel my soul inside me, made of thin, pale paper, fragile as a Japanese lantern, resting above my heart. I move with care and take shallow breaths so as not to crush it.

Christ's frozen eyes gaze at the ground. He declines to see my sleeping grandfather; He declines to see what He has abandoned. Rage rises in my chest, threatening to crumple my soul. Christ has no time for Cuipas, no time for my grandfather.

"Peace be with you," the priest says, and my grandfather wakes, squeezes my hand.

I HAVE NEVER SEEN a Japanese lantern, only read about them in my mother's novels. Used chiefly at night parties, they sway from strings above wide lawns, while music plays and women in backless gowns sip champagne.

MY GRANDFATHER OWNS nine vehicles, several of which run, though none are insured. When we go to Albuquerque, he lets me choose the car. Usually, I pick the old blue truck or the heavy brown ancient Mercedes with the rat's nest in the heating vent, which a man up north gave my grand-father as payment for a stone fireplace in his guesthouse. These are cars my mother will recognize.

Together my grandfather and I walk behind the house, where the vehicles sit, some with cracked tires, some parked on blocks. I hear him breathe beside me, even and smooth, familiar.

Today I pick the Mercedes.

In the car, we roll down the stiff windows and trail our hands in the air outside. Along the road the yellow grass sifts the wind.

When my grandfather begins to talk, it isn't about the past but about a future in the world outside Cuipas.

"You must not be shy," he tells me.

"You must be happy and laugh."

"You must talk to strangers."

I nod and tell him, "I will, I'll try," and panic rises in me.

"This is no place for a young person," my grandfather says. I know he thinks of a day—a day that will never exist but that is as real to him as if it already did—when I will shoulder a bag and climb up and over the Manzanos without turning back. He says again, "This is no place for a child."

I want to make him take it back. Instead, I pull the slip of paper from my pocket. "I want to stop here," I say firmly. "I need to stop at this clinic."

He takes the slip from my hand and frowns at it. I nearly grab the wheel, but his one hand is steady and the road is straight. He lifts his foot from the pedal and the car loses power. He turns to look at me for a moment, then turns back to the road. He folds the slip of paper, tucks it into his breast pocket, and gives the car gas.

"So can we? Can we stop?"

"No," he says, in a voice he rarely uses with me, a voice that is harsh and foreign and final. The ojo stirs and my vision smears. I think of my mother. I'll never leave my grandfather, but it isn't even my loyalty he wants.

The road twists and curves and begins to rise. When we are in the Manzanos, I swallow the stone in my throat, look out over the piñon, imagine the murderer in these mountains, alone with the knowledge of his crime.

IN THE CITY, the bright billboards flash along the highway, and white sun glints off the windows of the tall hospitals and hotels. As the fast cars pass, I look for my mother. I don't think she will be in the driver's seat of one of the fancy cars, but I watch the faces anyway. Her hair could be different by now. Other things might be different for her, too, I know, because in the world people's fortunes rise and fall.

If I find her, I think, then my grandfather will see the doctor. He will see the doctor and he will be cured and together we will bring my mother home.

I wonder if he is looking as well. He gives no indication, keeps both hands on the steering wheel. It's harder for him to drive now, and the traffic makes him nervous.

"Look, hijita," he tells me before we shift lanes. His voice is familiar again. "Am I clear?" And I crane my neck, watch the cars coming at us, tell him yes.

At the Kmart we load our cart with things we will need for the next month: tubes of toothpaste, large packages of paper towels, corn flakes, sometimes new sneakers for me, undershirts for him. My grandfather buys me toys also, plastic dolls, characters from films and television shows I have never seen. He will ask me to open the toys in the car, and I will scatter the bright plastic packaging on the floorboard. As he drops the toys into the cart, I smile and exclaim, though I'm too old for them and wish he would save our money. At home I will line them up on the windowsill in my room, leave a few scattered on the floor, so my grandfather, walking by, will think I have been playing.

When we've found all the things we need, we continue to push the cart down aisles under fluorescent lights. We are both a little dazed by the colors of this place, the bustle, both unwilling, it seems, to leave and be alone together. We push the cart, turning our heads left and right.

The woman at the checkout is stout and middle-aged and wears braces on her teeth. She asks what we think should happen to the horses. When we look at her blankly, she asks if we're from here.

"Cuipas," my grandfather says.

The horses, the cashier explains, are wild. They came down from the mountains because they were starving from the drought. They gather along the highway to eat chamisa and grass and the corn tossed to them by concerned citizens.

"I can't believe you don't know," the cashier says. "It's all over the TV. They say the horses are the same ones brought by the Spanish hundreds of years ago."

The cashier scans each item as she talks. She moves too quickly. I'm afraid she will be done before she has told us everything about the horses.

"What will happen to them?" I ask.

"Who knows? People have to fight about it, like everything else. I saw on the news where some people are saying they'll have to be slaughtered because there just isn't enough grass, what with the drought."

My grandfather fingers the bills in his hand, ready to count them out when she gives us the total.

"Some people say the state should feed them until the rains come, some say they should be driven to Colorado or Wyoming." The cashier pauses, tongues her braces. "The one sure thing is no one's going to leave them alone. People will interfere."

When I look toward the doors, I know it's for a reason. It takes a few moments for me to see her. My mother. She pushes a cart, the corner of a box of sugared cereal poking out of a bag. She is as young as I remember, her hair as straight and heavy. She squints up, her gaze brushing over my face.

When I turn to him, I know from the way he holds the bills in his trembling hands that my grandfather has seen her, too.

If it really were her, I would run across the crowded store, throw myself against her. If it were her, I would beat at her chest and belly with my fists. The cashier sighs and says that everything is expensive nowadays. I want so much for this woman to be my mother, and suddenly I fear it, too. If she returns, my grandfather will get better, but he will also remember everything she put him through. If she returns she might leave again, and then he might get worse. But it isn't her, of course, and the woman passes through the automatic doors.

My grandfather is still looking toward the doors. His face is open and longing.

"Grandpa," I say, to draw his attention. "I'm hungry. I want my lunch."

Slowly he turns to me. He blinks, and then his face is shuttered.

IN THE CAR my grandfather asks where I want to eat.

"I want to go home. Let's eat at home. We'll have cheese and mustard sandwiches."

He nods, and we drive in silence until he begins to speak.

"Your mother never forgave me for the way I treated your grandma," he says, looking hard at the road.

"It wasn't her," I tell him. "It was just someone who looked like her."

My grandfather sits upright, close to the steering wheel, his gaze fixed on the horizon. "Once I shook your grandma so hard the skin around her eyes bruised," he says. "Your mother stood against the wall and watched."

"Grandpa, that lady didn't even look like her, not really."

He says, "Your grandma's head went back and forth."

I won't look at him. I won't.

"It took a week for the black to fade, and during those days I stayed away from the house. One night I even slept at a job site. On the weekend I worked on the cars. I changed the fluids in every single one, checked the pressure on every tire, recorded the mileage. I couldn't go into the house where they were."

The ojo begins to flare. I want his story to stop. My skin burns.

"It wasn't her," I say.

He clears his throat. "I never touched your grandma again. I wouldn't have, even if she hadn't left. And I never touched your mother. But that didn't matter, because your mother never forgave me."

I can't stand it, but he keeps going. I hear him even over the hot throbbing in my ears. I think of his voice earlier, that hard, hoarse severity, and think of Ofelia Alma Zamora, my grandmother, being shaken so hard the fragile skin around her eyes bruised. I've never heard this story, but now I understand that I knew it all along. I need him to stop.

"She blamed me for her mother leaving her, and maybe she was right."

—

Usually as we leave the rush and concrete of Albuquerque, the vast beige housing developments, my grandfather and I begin to relax and breathe. Today, though, his terrible story remains packed around us, as thick and suffocating as cotton. I feel it would take great effort for me to move.

As we wind up and over the Manzanos, I thank him for the trip, say I'll be glad to get home. My voice is stiff. He pats my hand, and behind his glasses his eyes are rimmed red with age.

And because of what he has said, I remember the thing I nearly always succeed in forgetting, the thing my grandfather believes I can't remember because I was four: the day I last saw my mother.

She had been gone for three weeks, left without telling us. One day she returned in a truck I'd never seen, driven by a man I'd never seen. She jumped from the passenger seat, and what I remember is being furious, but I ran to her because I couldn't stop myself. When she opened her arms, I backed against the house and yelled at her to go away. She looked at me, lips parted in hurt surprise, and I thought she'd come to me, but instead she walked into the house.

The man in the truck—Anglo, cowboy hat tilted forward—looked straight ahead, tapping his thumbs on the steering wheel.

My grandfather sat silently at the kitchen table, while in the tiny back room she packed. I stood in the doorway, where by turning my head left or right I could see them both, my grandfather sitting still, one palm pressed against the table, and my mother working fast, shoving skirts and blouses into my grandfather's canvas army duffel. Outside in the truck, the man waited.

My mother's back was to me and she cried as she packed. I looked at her with hate that burned her edges, until she browned and curled like a photograph cast into the stove. I looked at her and sliced through her with cuts so fine she hardly knew they were there until pieces of her began to drop away. I looked at her and she began to dry up and shrink from my gaze, until she was as cold and brittle as a marigold in November.

I wish now I had cried and flung myself at her and gripped the hem of her shirt. If I had, she might have stayed. Instead, I trailed her stiffly. Out on the porch she kneeled to hug me, and I remained rigid with hate, and over her shoulder I could see the man watching us. My mother was crying and murmuring in my ear, love or promises, but I couldn't listen. The man's eye caught mine, and that's when the ojo began to spread through me. My mother pulled away, jogged to the street, where she swung her bag into the back. She didn't call to me when they drove away.

For a long time I watched the road that led to the Manzanos, and beyond, to Albuquerque. I watched until the sun dropped so low in the sky that it burned my eyes and I had to turn my head.

I don't remember what I did when I lost sight of the truck, but I imagine I went inside to where my grandfather was sitting in the kitchen. I imagine when he heard my step he looked up and saw me.

—

Now he says, "I told her to go, hijita."

Outside, the landscape blurs.

"I told her she couldn't come home. I didn't think she'd listen to me—when had she ever listened before?—but she did. She left you."

It wasn't the man's gaze at all, I realize now. It was my own eye that was evil, my own look that was covetous and overlong, my own furious, envious gaze that has made me sick. I wanted my mother and she'd gone to him.

We have begun our descent through the Manzanos—Cuipas is a meager cluster of buildings in the distance—when we see them, the wild horses. There are two, pulling at the dry grass. My grandfather slows the Mercedes in the middle of the road. The horses are thin. Ribs visible through dusty coats. The Mercedes thrums, diesel coursing, so he turns off the engine. It shudders and goes silent, and then we hear the wind in the grass, weeds scraping against the asphalt edges of the road, and, I'm sure of it, the sound of their mouths as they eat. One of them raises her head, cocks her ears, listening. The light is silver on her velvet muzzle. I'm certain she is aware of us, will raise the alarm, but she dips her head once more and tears at the grass with yellow teeth. I think about a relative long ago losing his horse, calling her name through the mountains, returning to the fort or mission on foot, perhaps never making it, his name lost to history. A third horse emerges from the piñon, swats at the air with her tail.

If I could time my death, I would time it thus: exactly fifteen seconds after my grandfather. I would like to die in my sleep, but I must be certain I outlive him. I will lay my ear against his thin chest, listen to the silence beneath his humped sternum, and then, when I am sure, it will be my turn. Fifteen seconds is good: any longer and I might feel grief. Any longer and I might raise my head to the world opening up before me, wide and calling.

In a moment my grandfather will pat me again, and his hand will stay there, resting on mine. I'll look down, run a finger along the veins knotted and bruised under his thin brown skin. I wait for his touch. But for now we watch the horses separately, sitting as still as we know how.

A C K N O W L E D G M E N T S

FIRST, MY HEARTFELT GRATITUDE TO MY WONDERFUL EDItor, Jill Bialosky, for her incredible insight and for making this a far better book, and to my amazing agent, Denise Shannon, for being such a generous champion of my work (and for giving me a nudge forward now and again). I still can't believe my good fortune at getting to work with such brilliance. Thank you also to Bill Rusin, Fred Wiemer, Rebecca Schultz, Steve Colca, Angie Shih, Erin Sinesky Lovett, Francine Kass, Don Rifkin, and to all the other people at Norton who helped guide my book into being.

For time, space, and support, without which I'd probably be in some other field entirely, I am eternally grateful to the Stanford Creative Writing Program, the University of Oregon Writing Program, the MacDowell Colony, the Corporation of Yaddo, Bread Loaf, the Sitka Center for Art and Ecology, the James Merrill House, the Elizabeth George Foundation, and the Rona Jaffe Foundation. Thank you for the faith.

I have been blessed with extraordinary teachers who, in the classroom and in the splendid pages of their own books, have challenged me and taught me what a story can do. My deepest gratitude to Tobias Wolff, Elizabeth Tallent, John L'Heureux, and Ehud Havazelet, rigorous and compassionate writers who have pushed me to hold my work and the endeavor to the highest standards. I feel so lucky to have worked closely with them over the years. My thanks also to Adam Johnson, Laurie Lynn Drummond, David Bradley, Peter Ho Davies, and David Wevill, and to the late Charles Terry and Fred Tremallo. For over a decade, Eavan Boland has been a mentor and model for the writer's role in the world: generous and humane, both in her work and in life.

My gratitude to the members of my workshops at Stanford and the University of Oregon. Thank you also to all my colleagues and students at Stanford and the University of Michigan, who make my job such a pleasure.

So many thanks to Willing Davidson, Carol Edgarian, Tom Jenks, Meakin Armstrong, and Emily Nevins, consummate editors who have made some of these stories worthy of placement in the pages of their journals. Thank you also to the editors who selected some of these stories for inclusion in their anthologies: Laura Furman, Seth Horton, Brett Garcia Myhren, Heidi Pitlor, Elizabeth Strout, and James Thomas.

Particular thanks are due to the dear friends and readers who have left their marks on these stories, whose work inspires me, and whose friendship sustains me: C. J. Álvarez, Molly Antopol, Leslie Barnard, Jason Brown, Harriet Clark, Anna Drexler, Jennifer duBois, Sara Keilholtz, Ryan McIlvain, Kärstin Painter, Brittany Perham, Lara Perkins, Justin Perry, Nina Schloesser, Maggie Shipstead, and Justin Torres. The concept of the painting in "Canute Commands the Tides" was inspired by conversations with the brilliant artist Heather Green, and by her gorgeous series *Tide Cycle* in particular. *Tide Cycle* and her other work can be found at heathergreen-art.com. And I am especially grateful to Lydia Conklin, who has been beyond generous with her dazzling critical energies, and whose work and humor and presence bring me such joy.

Finally, mostly, thank you to my family—my parents, Barbra and Jay, my siblings, Gratianne and Emeric, and my grandparents, both Valdez and Quade—for everything, always.

KIRSTIN VALDEZ QUADE HAS RECEIVED A "5 UNDER 35" award from the National Book Foundation in addition to the Rona Jaffe Foundation Writer's Award and the 2013 Narrative Prize. Her work has appeared in *The New Yorker, Narrative, The Best American Short Stories, The O. Henry Prize Stories,* and elsewhere. She was a Wallace Stegner Fellow and a Jones Lecturer at Stanford University and is currently the Nicholas Delbanco Visiting Professor at the University of Michigan.